Link Arms with Toads!

Rhys Hughes

Whether you are a ghost, a robot or just an apeman, you can always link arms with toads!

Chômu Press

Link Arms with Toads!

by Rhys Hughes

Published by Chômu Press, MMXI

Link Arms with Toads! copyright © Rhys Hughes 2010

The right of Rhys Hughes to be identified as Author of this Work has been asserted by him in accordance with the Copyright, Designs and Patents Act 1988.

Published in May 2011 by Chômu Press.
by arrangement with the author.
All rights reserved by the author.

ISBN: 978-1-907681-08-0

First Edition

This book is a work of fiction. Names, characters, places and incidents either are products of the author's imagination or are used fictitiously. Any resemblance to actual events or locales or persons, living or dead, is entirely coincidental.

Design and layout by: Bigeyebrow and Chômu Press
Character illustration by: Torso Vertical

E-mail: info@chomupress.com
Internet: chomupress.com

A showcase of
Romanti-Cynical Stories

Dedicated to!

*The beautiful, wonderful, marvellous,
superlative, incredible, delectable
and incomparable*

Adele Whittle

"Rhys Hughes seems almost the sum of our planet's literature... As well as being drunk on language and wild imagery, he is also sober on the essentials of thought. He has something of Mervyn Peake's glorious invention, something of John Cowper Powys's contemplative, almost disdainful existentialism, a sensuality, a relish, an addiction to the delicious. He's as tricky as his own characters... He toys with convention. He makes the metaphysical political, the personal incredible and the comic hints at subtle pain. Few living fictioneers approach this chef's sardonic confections, certainly not in English."
Michael Moorcock

"Hughes' world is a magical one, and his language is the most magical thing of all."
T.E.D. Klein

"It's a crime that Rhys Hughes is not as widely known as Italo Calvino and other writers of that stature. Brilliantly written and conceived, Hughes' fiction has few parallels anywhere in the world. In some alternate universe with a better sense of justice, his work triumphantly parades across all bestseller lists."
Jeff VanderMeer

Contents

The Troubadours of Perception	1
Number 13½	8
The Taste of the Moon	25
Lunarhampton	46
The Expanding Woman	75
All Shapes Are Cretans	85
The Innumerable Chambers of the Heart	93
Pity the Pendulum	102
333 and a Third	127
The Candid Slyness of Scurrility Forepaws	136
Ye Olde Resignation	153
Castle Cesare	168
The Mirror in the Looking Glass	185
Oh Ho!	190
Loneliness	206
Hell Toupée	212
Inside the Outline	242
Discrepancy	255
Afterword	*263*
Publishing History	
Acknowledgements	
About the Author	

The Troubadours of Perception

Rosa is harsh and meaty, like an old glass of red wine. She wants to play duets in the dusky twilight. Alice is slow and cool, like a watermelon that takes several days to consume. She still has trouble tuning her instrument. Clara and Gabrielle wander the fretboard in the search for a fuller sound. I want to make love to Gabrielle but I am unsure of the fingering.

In the lounge of a pleasant suburban house in Solihull, I dally with Christine. The lamps are turned low, there is a real fire in the hearth. I bless the mirror above the mantelpiece that reflects my profile back at me. The shadow of an emerging beard, the long shiny hair that curls around my shoulders, the glittering of an earring. I have the accent down to perfection, the rascally shrug.

Christine is not really interested in the guitar. She wants to talk. She does not care that my own is strung with silver strings to give a sweeter sound. Her husband is away on a business trip. She suspects that he is losing enthusiasm for the relationship, that he has been bitten by the fleas of new desire. She has a similar itch, a need to be scratched. I tease, I croon, I softly sing. The fleas that tease in the high Pyrenees. O Christine!

Afterwards we sip coffee and I listen to an account of their early life together. It had all been fun then. Or had it? Her doubts are growing, they are beginning to encompass the past. I ask her how she sees her role within the shifting mores of a modern society. In all this time, a single note has she played. But my fees will be the same. I can humour the dabblers, the dilettantes, but I cannot afford to indulge them. It is my way of life.

The bedsheets are chill around Christine's lithe body. Her musky scent reminds me of incense, honeysuckle, the taste of caramel. Candles float in little vases full of water. Her room is tastefully furnished, almost sparse. I trace delicate pathways along her stomach with my tongue. I used to teach the piano. I used to dream of possessing such women as Christine on the stool while our fingers explored their own crescendo. But I have learned from experience. Ivory and ebony keys do not turn locks of hearts; what is required are the chords that bind.

I leave Christine and catch the bus back into town. Dust and leaves swirl before me. I feel self-consciously romantic in my waistcoat, the white shirt whose huge flapping cuffs I must leave unbuttoned, face and hands never too clean. We trundle through streets dim and featureless to those who do not know. I have finally solved the enigma of these suburban boulevards, treeless avenues and bowbacked crescents. The language of the pavements is in my blood, my greasy veins. Behind each pair of William Morris curtains there are shattered fragments of secret lusts, shards of which have lodged in my heart.

Jessica presents a quite different prospect. There is a more subtle understanding between us. Her husband is possibly a little too devoted. It would be difficult for her to betray him without feeling guilt. Her frustration manifests itself in the sly look, the parted lips. She has become an expert in the ways of the flirt. Sometimes I think that I am imagining her responses, so skillfully does she proceed.

She also happens to be a very good player. With the possible exception of Catherine, she is my most talented pupil. It seems that soon there will be little more I can teach her. I will have to depart forever then, with only the taste of a lost chance to remember her by. She sings as she plays, and her voice is surprisingly homespun among the exotic artifacts of her living room, the indigo batiks, the wooden carvings and ethnic throws. Homespun from gold, her hair.

I correct her fingering in one place only and I do this by taking her hand. She wants to know what it is like out there, life on the pavement. Thrilling, dirty, absurd, I tell her. She is not quite enchanted but she is tempted to smile. I have seen her smile, I know that it is radiant, trembling, all that my own smile is not. My own smile is wicked and charming. Wickedly charming.

Jessica is on my mind a great deal of the time. So too Amelia, a direct descendant of the last man to fight a legal duel in England. The victor, I assume; I have never questioned her on this point. So Amelia needs no work, no flash of chipped incisor. She is already mine, became mine right from the beginning, though in one way only. Her bosom heaves. It is very gratifying to learn that she shares my passion for the poet, the only poet. *Le ciel est triste et beau comme un grand reposoir.* We watch the clouds part for long afternoon hours. Over the crumbling brick walls of her semi-detached garden, the clematis hugging tight to its lattice, the morning glory, the sun drowns in its vermilion.

Out again into the dusk. Amelia does not dance. Amelia prefers to languish in a curiously undramatic way. It is Isabella who likes to dance. I play her a valse and a saraband and she is stately, graceful, a little sad among the frosty adjuncts of the kitchen, where she always affects to have her lessons. I guess that only here the neighbours may spy on her. She is cultivating her reputation.

Isabella's husband is a salesman, a surly fellow I once met and liked. But Isabella tells me that his manner is pure guile. He is contented with life, his cynicism is mere sophistication. He is also a devoted Adventist. His chosen method is to knock on doors, following much the same routes as myself, and to ask the occupants whether they would like to talk about God. Usually they say no. He then asks if he can sell them some double-glazing instead.

I watch Isabella stretch upwards, her eyes fixed on some remote point beyond the shelf of spice jars, her bare calves as smooth as a legato. I watch her weave between the oven and the washing machine. Later, when the mood takes her, she will sit on the latter during spin cycle while I watch with hooded eyes. The neighbours will make notes. Her paramour is a parvenu, they will say. A roguish fellow.

With Isabella I play old Spanish airs. With Lydia I tour the oeuvre of Guiraut Riquier, still a neglected composer. Lydia is an exception to one rule of my calling. She does not share the general acceptance of the grime any true romantic must carry on his boots. She insists I remove my footwear on her threshold. Toes wriggle in chilly anticipation. Will I ever bear her over another threshold? Will I ever hear her loosen her restraints with a shriek as piercing as a split harmonic? I am working on Lydia, practice is what it takes. *Chapeaux bas!*

Out on the pavements, weaving their own destiny, there are others like me. They are colleagues, rivals. I see them trailing their worn instruments in the dirt behind them. Our paths frequently cross. Over all the cities of the land, the suburbs, we are engaged in absorbing the fantasies of a million wives. Our travels are netting the happy hamlets, the conurbia of mock-Tudor ideals, the security of the scrubbed, the pools of quiet desperation with their shallow bathers. We are gouging the conduits of a freer life, evolving a whole nervous system down which emotions can flow like honeyed wine.

But it is not all certainty, this game of ours. The control can be lost easily enough. In the park, in winter, I often serenade the trees; an aubade to a false dawn. Hunched, cold, I neither welcome nor mock the sun. My fingers are like the highest twigs themselves, covered in sleet. The power slips between. Sometimes I meet my match, or more than my match. They are out there. No one who takes this profession seriously can be deceived for long. Many of them, innumerable.

I fear them. I fear their strength and their mystery. There is Madeleine, who likes to bounce me on her knee while I play. There is Yvette, who speaks not a word and hides behind widow's weeds though her husband is very much alive, propped up in an old armchair, drooling, facing us as we trill. There is Arabella, who furnishes her house all in black and has set a worm-gnawed Grandfather clock in every room. There is Rebecca, who does not care for my silver strings. There is Melissa, who keeps a collection of love letters in a coffin in her attic. Her house is full of a delicate mist, cobwebs. There is Leonora, who I am at a loss to describe because she stays always behind me, always, no matter how fast I turn.

Helena is the one who disturbs me the most. I would like to break off our arrangement, I would like to depart from her and never return. But there is a hold, a morbid influence that she exerts on me. Her house is full of jars. I ask her what she keeps in them. She taps her nose and winks. Dreams, she replies; the dreams of all her past lovers. She collects the residue from her own generous thighs after she has toyed with them. I have not succumbed. I feel drained with Helena, enervated, sucked dry. It is only a matter of time.

Something else is happening. There have been developments. Hazel, who has been separated from her husband for nearly a year, persuades me to pay him a visit. His house lies on the other side of town. I find that he wants to pay for lessons as well. So I am able to listen to his side of the story. He knows all about my experiments with Hazel. It has reawakened his feelings, anger and deep love. They are reunited because of me. Then they break off contact. Music was the food of love, but now they are full. They are devoted. Who am I to protest?

This is happening to my colleagues and rivals, I hear. Many of them now have more male pupils than female. What can this mean? Will we be forced to work for money alone? Will they all abandon me, one by one? Barbara,

Candida, Deborah, Eulalia, Fiona, Faustina, Gwyneth? What will happen to my soul, my essential nature? Will Rosa no longer want to play duets in the dusky twilight? Will Alice learn to tune her instrument without me? Will Clara and Gabrielle succeed in their quest for a fuller sound?

A crisis meeting is called between all members of our fraternity. We gather in a crumbling café in the metropolis, an establishment that has served our kind for generations. We fill the place to bursting. There are more players in this tarnished age of ours than listeners. There is talk of returning to the piano. But I do not want to lose my hair, my patience. I do not want to have to wear tiny round spectacles. Are there really no alternatives? There is talk of finding a use for men, of somehow fitting them into our worldview. But what use can I find for men? I am lonely, lonely. I am so lonely.

While we argue, debate, cajole, the waiter serves us all supper. We need to fortify ourselves for the tribulations ahead. But we must not be defiled. We are minstrels, the lyric poets of the garden cities. Music alone is the reason for our being, we require no other sustenance. In this particular café our needs are understood. Do not fret. We shall rebuild Carcassonne, we shall. Solemnly, in the sinister light that emanates from the charcoal ovens, we dine on manuscript stew and violin steaks and pick splinters from between our broken teeth.

(1994)

Number 13½

Among the Isles of Scilly, Tresco justifiably holds a high place. Not that any of the members of the archipelago should really be described as high, for at no point do they rise much above 100ft. Yet they are alluring enough to tempt the curio hunter, the seeker of solitude or the college refugee. Tresco in particular has nets enough to snare the incautious tourist – once the private estate of a priory, it retains a cloistered air; a privileged atmosphere that owes partly to its impressive ruins and partly to its absence of budget accommodation.

Travellers to the islands have a choice of braving the stormy seas between Penzance and the largest of the group, St. Mary's, or of taking to the air for the brief flight to the small airport outside Hugh Town. There are few direct flights to Tresco and only one hotel to be found, the Island Hotel – expensive but all that can be desired. It is now run by a Swede, Wilhelm Magnus, who was shipwrecked on one of the beaches during an attempt to sail single-handed around the globe in a coracle. His account of the affair, *Journal of a Scilly Billy*, is a fair specimen of the class of books to which I have not yet alluded.

In the spring of 1997, two mainlanders arrived at this isolated place, in an attempt to assuage a peculiar kind of brain fever. They were both Birmingham men, academics from that greatly regarded bastion of learning, the Moseley

College of Further Education. They were (it is certain) physicists currently engaged on certain researches into the nature of subatomic particles. We shall dignify their experiences by naming them Baring-Gould and Purnell. The former was much interested in the behaviour of photons; the latter detested photons and had time only for neutrinos. Yet they contrived somehow to remain good friends, even taking with good grace the insults each hurled on the other's favourite elements, hydrogen and argon respectively.

One thing they did share and that was a fear of flying. Thus it was that on April 13th they braved the stormy seas beyond Land's End in a leaky ferry, the *Mezzotint*, whose Italian Captain, Giovanni Paoli, had left his heart in England as a small boy. Baring-Gould sought relief from the buffeting waves on the highest deck; Purnell was of a like stomach. Together they turned green and clutched to the rails for dear life. Captain Paoli solemnly announced over the tannoy that he had never witnessed a storm quite like it. As the huge black waves broke over the physicists, one of them turned to the other and hissed through trembling lips, "There are thirteen passengers aboard!"

It seemed an augur of evil. The previous night, while still in Penzance, Baring-Gould had sworn he heard the main church clock strike thirteen instead of twelve; and Purnell had eaten no less than that number of pieces of toast for breakfast. But though the vessel pitched and yawed ominously, it came to no grief. The *Mezzotint* docked safely in Hugh Town; the only concession to the fury of nature being that the three-hour journey had lasted seven and that the figurehead of the ferry had been consigned to the furnace when Captain Paoli had seen how low on fuel they had run. We shall discuss the number 13 and the importance of figureheads later. (There is a ghost in this story but it shall not be revealed until the very end.)

The travellers spent the rest of the day on St. Mary's, recovering from their frightful experience. The following morning, the weather being more clement for such a venture, they took another boat to Tresco, landing at the southernmost point of Carn Near, a ten-minute walk from the entrance to the delightful Abbey Gardens. Here, amid the tumbled remains of the priory, are the impressive subtropical gardens, first laid out in 1834. Though many of the seeds hail from no further afield than Kew Gardens, some have their origins in Africa, South America and the Antipodes. You really should try to visit these gardens sometime, it may do you good. But I am not writing a guidebook.

Baring-Gould and Purnell, two fellows of a prosaic turn of mind, ignored the Abbey and made their way straight to the Island Hotel. It was a great redbrick house with a stone-pillared porch; the windows of the house were not many (thirteen to be precise) but they were tall and narrow, with small panes and thick white woodwork. A pediment, pierced with a hexagonal window, crowned the front. Our travellers desired no more than complete peace and solitude; their wishes were explained to the landlord; and, after a certain amount of thought, Wilhelm Magnus suggested that it might be best for the gentlemen to look at one or two of the quieter rooms and pick one for themselves.

It seemed a good idea. The bottom and middle floors were rejected as being already occupied by a group of amateur geologists. Similarly, the top floor had two of its three rooms presently engaged; there was, indeed, a limited choice of only one room – number thirteen. But there was no time for unfounded superstition now; this was the only available room on the entire island and, as such, suited admirably.

There was no fireplace in the room – a handsome stove stood in lieu of more civilised heating apparatus. Something of the character of an oratory was imparted to the room by a broken mast that stood like a crucifix and almost reached the ceiling on one side. Under this stood a sea chest of some age and solidity which, when thrown open, revealed an interior full of brightly coloured shells and seaweed. Baring-Gould was at once much disturbed by the room – the en-suite bathroom contained an old lead-lined bath affixed to the wall. But Purnell pointed out they were far from home and had to make do. They tossed a coin to determine which side of the grand double bed was to belong to whom and then made their way back down the stairs to lunch.

The *salle à manger* was almost full when they reached it. Purnell counted thirteen guests, including themselves. They sat down and awaited the attentions of Wilhelm Magnus. The menu was a curious mix of Swedish and English cuisine; beside each dish was a number. The wine list was composed with similar numerological bent. Feeling determined to loose the grip of superstition from his rational collar and muffle the chill breath of the unknown on his nape, Baring-Gould ordered no.13 on both lists: the smörgåsbord with mushy peas and gravy, washed down with a rare, and not altogether unfruity, Lincolnshire rosé.

Swedes are habitually slow, perhaps, in answering, or perhaps this castaway landlord was an exception. He spent at least a minute looking at his guests before saying anything. Then he came up close to the pair and said, "My friends, I can only say that I understand you; I too was washed up on these shores during an unnatural storm. But here you have made a very good choice; do not expect things to ever be the same. Why have I remained, do you think? Personally I yearn for Uppsala, my home. But I may never return there; I am an exile."

So cryptic was this outburst that both Baring-Gould and Purnell instantly decided to ignore it. Purnell followed his friend's choice and they tucked into the meal. Afterwards, back in their room, they debated the matter endlessly. Finally, no closer to a solution and rather tired of the enigma, they took a walk out across the island in the direction of Appletree Bay. It was a glorious late afternoon; the sun slanted low in the west. Baring-Gould felt ready to dance through the fields of flowers that stood on either side of the road; Purnell reminded him that it was probably illegal to do so. Before long they had reached Valhalla, one of the strangest of Tresco's institutions. This is in reality a sort of museum, whose exhibits consist of the remains of local shipwrecks – chiefly figureheads and the like. They were admitted into the confines of Valhalla just before closing time, but were there long enough to tease their curiosities all the more.

Once inside the museum, the ticket collector or curator (I prefer the latter appellation, inaccurate as it may be) took it upon himself to guide them through the dark chambers of shattered exhibits. He was a hunched sort of man; he was perpetually half-glancing behind him. He recognised the academics at once for what they were and told them, in a low nasally voice, that he too had once been involved in college life. Certainly his accent had less of the Scilly in it than might be expected of a crouching figure that smelt of fish. He looked like an islander; but he utilised words lengthy enough to confirm his previous standing as a lecturer from no mean institution.

"I was a professor of Archaeology," he said; "and came to Tresco to explore traces of early human settlement; but my dinghy was washed onto the rocks in rough seas, and all my equipment lost overboard. Lucky to escape with my life, I thought it best not to tempt fate by attempting a return journey. I have been here ever since." He then went on to discuss the few studies he had since been able to make without his instruments. It was here that he used the lengthy words. Though, as I have already said, I am not writing a guidebook, a little of his speech (omitting the lengthy words) must be alluded to here:

In the annals of folklore, the Scillies are the peaks of the lost land of Lyonesse, a fertile plain that extended west from Penwith before the ocean broke in, drowning all but one of the inhabitants. There was some evidence that Lyonesse had, in fact, existed; that its populace were a thriving merchant people who specialised in brewing seaweed beer and carving dragons out of blocks of salt. This evidence (the curator tapped his nose at this point) was in his sole possession; one day soon he would publish his results. Besides, he had also discovered the tooth of Pytheas of Massalia, the first documented visitor to Britain, who arrived in Salakee, the islands of tin, circa 308 BC. Besides, even if this also proved to be false, Tresco was still a very nice place to live: there were some excellent beaches on the eastern side, many of them looking out to a submarine-shaped rock offshore.

Baring-Gould and Purnell both realised that the little man was trying to convince himself he was happy here. It was obvious, therefore, that he was not. After interrogating him further, Purnell was astonished when he broke down in tears. This was a scene they had little wish to witness. They ignored him until he had regained his composure. To change the subject, Baring-Gould encompassed the figurehead collection with a wave. "There are so many of them. I had been reliably informed there were but a score. Here you have a hundred."

The curator wiped his eyes on his sleeve and nodded feverishly. "That is because thirteen is not an unlucky number on this island, not now." These words had on Baring-Gould and Purnell an effect presumably akin to that of a lightning-bolt. It seemed to them that something was amiss; something awry in the very fabric of reality. They stood and trembled and sought to shake a deep unease from their minds. By the time they recovered, it was time to close the museum, and the curator wanted to go home to his tea; there was no more to be had out of him. They had learned only that he, like themselves and Wilhelm Magnus, had experienced stormy waters when crossing from the mainland, and also that he shared with their Nordic landlord the talent of uttering seemingly meaningless, yet oddly affecting sentences.

Back at the Island Hotel, the Swede in question confirmed the previous status of the hunched fellow. There were, apparently, a number of people on the island who had arrived in a tempest; for some reason this stormy fact precluded them returning home. Apart from Wilhelm himself and the curator, Baring-Gould ascertained that the entire party of amateur geologists who shared their hotel were also of this fraternity, a group that the Swede liked to term 'self-imposed exiles'. Purnell was much annoyed by these revelations. "I certainly do not intend staying here longer than a fortnight," he informed the landlord. "When I am quite rested, I intend to return to my Department."

"We all want to return," Wilhelm Magnus replied, "but a little thought of the consequences dissuades us. There is no room for us back on the mainland now." Here came a strange pause of irresolution, as it seemed; then, with a sort of plunge, he went on: "We are no longer in the world we know. We are in a universe next door!"

"What?!!" It was Baring-Gould (so Purnell tells me) who, ever the hotheaded one, seized a nearby croissant and made as if to strike the hapless Swede. "What manner of nonsense is this? Do you take us for fools?" Only with great difficulty did Purnell manage to restrain his colleague from lunging with the crescent roll. The Swede fell back with a look of abject terror and then muttered something about them all being ghosts, in a dimension that was not their own.

"Explain yourself further," Purnell demanded, and he hinted that he might release Baring-Gould if the landlord did not quickly comply with his demand. The Swede sighed, told them that they had to find out about the whole business sooner or later and invited them into a back room where he kept his own quarters. On a desk were a handwritten book, half completed, and a paraffin lamp, doubtless washed up from some wreck. He bade them be seated and idly fingered the leaves of the book. It was, he confessed, his second work: *The Vampire Book Of Mammoths*. This was a serious subject, and not one to be mocked; evidence of a blood-sucking type of woolly elephant had turned up in the grounds of his Hotel. At any rate, it gave him something to do.

Somehow (and he would not dare to venture any theories about this, not being a scientist) they had all — that is Baring-Gould, Purnell, the curator of Valhalla, the geologists, a Mrs. Bunch of the Abbey Market Gardens and he, the seafaring Swede — drifted into a dimension parallel to the one they had formerly inhabited. The storms they had experienced had knocked them into a cosmos existing adjacent to our own. This new universe was identical to the old one in every respect save one: the unluckiest number was no longer 13. It was, instead, 13½.

"Well it is an idea!" cried Baring-Gould, whose belligerence had been transmuted into enthusiasm by this intellectual notion. "The concept of the multiverse is not a new one." He then went on to explain that quantum theory had given rise to the possibility of an infinite number of universes, each slightly different from the other, that existed simultaneously. Heisenberg, apparently, developed an experiment in which a single photon was directed at a screen with two slits. The fact that the photon could be measured as having passed through both slits at once seemed to indicate that there were actually two universes next to each other, in one of which the photon passed through the first slit, and in the other through the second. This experiment gave rise to the famous Uncertainty Principle. But I am not writing a layman's guide to physics. Seek, if you will, his *Über Quantentheoretische Umdeutung Kinematischer und Mechanischer Berziehungen.*

Eventually Purnell – who hated photons and felt that any theories concerning them were lightweight – was also tempted to consider the possibility they had strayed into another dimension. But how was the Swede to know that nothing had altered save the value of the unluckiest number? And why did this prevent him and the others returning to the mainland? Puffing out his cheeks, Herr Magnus began to illustrate how, over years, his suspicions had been subtly confirmed.

The first thing, he said, was the collection of figureheads at the museum. There were simply too many of them; it indicated that in this world there were a great many more ships plying the oceans than in his own. And the visitors who arrived on calm days (this is a very important difference) were much more affluent and noble of bearing than those who arrived during storms. They were better nourished and in trimmer shape. Thirdly, the coming of the curator had acquainted him at second hand with an ancient text, recently discovered in Hull University's archives. (The curator was a lecturer from those hallowed halls.)

This text was the aforementioned Pytheas of Massalia's lost book, *Travels With My Aunt's Trireme*. As the first Greek explorer to venture into Britain, Pytheas had approached from the south, arriving first at the isles and then crossing to Cornwall. During this crossing he had encountered a violent storm that had buffeted his modest vessel with astounding fury. He had feared for his life; he had raced to the deck in order to ascertain whether they were anywhere near land, when he had a curious, though momentary, vision. He seemed to see an endless seascape of distorting mirrors rising out of the ocean in all directions. It had suddenly occurred to the Swede that this might represent an account of a rare sighting of one of those points where several universes converge. Needless to say, Pytheas made it safely to Cornwall.

"Each parallel dimension would indeed be slightly different," Baring-Gould here interposed; "in some, sheep would have six legs, and in others, mice would be green or cats would be able to talk. But you have not explained why in this one the unluckiest number is 13½ and not its integer. What has a tiresome preponderance of figureheads to do with it?" He sullenly sat back in his chair and took a vicious bite out of the croissant he still held in his hand.

I do not know what is the ideal course to pursue in a situation of this kind. I can only tell you what Wilhelm Magnus did. He repaired to a bookshelf in the corner of the study and took down an old dictionary. Then he opened the volume under Baring-Gould's nose. The worthy academic glanced at the word before him and sneered. "Triskaidekaphobia? Fear of the number thirteen? It is not unusual."

"Yes!" cried Herr Magnus; "but do you know exactly what it entails? Most cultures in the world – our world, that is – have an irrational terror of that number. Here there is no such fear. The number to be avoided here is a whole half greater. Can you not see what this means? In our world, some people stay home on the 13th of each month; they are reluctant to conduct business transactions; they are loathe to travel. There is more illness and consequently, a loss of efficiency in the workplace. Millions upon millions of man-hours are lost every year simply because of this fear – billions of pounds!"

Purnell rubbed his jaw. "I should have thought that fear of the square root of two would have been an 'irrational' fear." But the Swede did not understand the mathematical joke, so he proceeded: "You are absolutely right, of course. Triskaidekaphobia wastes a vast deal of resources. This still does not answer my question."

Baring-Gould was quicker on the uptake. "You are saying that in a world where thirteen is not an unlucky number there would be no such depression in the global economy on the 13th of every month? And thus it would be a richer world than the one we know? You are suggesting that people would be more 'affluent' as a consequence, that they would be 'trimmer' than we are due to a healthier diet?"

Wilhelm Magnus nodded his head, and with growing excitement and nervousness, as our two travellers thought, continued: "Yes and more shipping would sail on such dates; and thus more would come to grief, and the museum of figureheads on Tresco would be more full than it has any right to be. And hotels with thirteen windows would be as popular as those with more or less; and a meal numbered 13 on a menu would not be shunned by gourmets on account of superstitious aversion!"

Purnell frowned. "Perhaps this does illustrate why 13 is not an unlucky number here; but it does not suggest that 13½ has taken its place. And why does it signify the impossibility of you returning home?" He chewed his lip and fixed the landlord with a fierce stare. "If this is some sort of Nordic joke!"

The Swede took a number of deep breaths. "I shall say simply that we are ghosts in this dimension – attenuated echoes of our old selves. We can no longer cope back on the mainland. Just imagine: this world is more advanced than the one we were familiar with. A healthier economy equals more investment in scientific research; this means, in turn, that technology is ahead of anything we have experienced. You may have been experts in your own fields when you left; now your knowledge is less than that of the average undergraduate. The same applies to me. I was once the greatest chef-explorer in the whole of Uppsala. The *Roving Cordon Bleu*, I was called. No longer; in this new world, cooks sail round the world in coracles as a matter of course."

Baring-Gould was disgusted. "Good God, what a man

is this! Yes, I have better teeth than that of any storm and shall brave the waters back, come what may!" And so saying, he took a second bite out of the much-bruised croissant, spitting crumbs with his contempt. He then went on to reflect upon the probability that the writings of Pytheas, Herr Heisenberg and Wilhelm Magnus himself may have been instrumental in bringing about this disaster. "But what of 13½?"

The poor landlord threw up his arms, reflected for a moment in this most solemn attitude; then moving swiftly to a sea chest identical to the one in the travellers' room, he opened it and produced therefrom a large book, wrapped in a white cloth. Even before the wrapping had been removed, Baring-Gould and Purnell had ceased to be interested in the size and shape of the volume. It was a conventional scrapbook filled with photographs of famous paintings, not dissimilar to those as are often encountered in bargain bookstores. The Swede cleared his throat, and with a good deal of effort he spoke:

"Messrs, I can tell you this one little tale, and no more – not any more. You must not ask anything when I am done. This book was washed up from the outside world – that alien place – at the same time as one of the many figureheads. Why is it that 13 is deemed so unlucky in our own dimension? Is it not because that was the exact number of guests at the Last Supper? Take a look then at this – you will find what you seek soon enough. You will then be horribly satisfied."

Baring-Gould and Purnell opened the book and leafed through it. At first the familiar paintings yielded no answers. But then they came across it; one of the most well known of all works of art, it jolted their sensibilities as no other sight had ever done. Identical in every respect to the picture they knew, save in one minor detail. I entirely despair of conveying by any words the impression that this detail made upon those who looked at it. Purnell's face expressed horror and a rare kind of loathing. He pressed his hands upon his eyes in some agitation; his friend, holding up the half-devoured croissant in a sudden cold sweat, began counting his atomic weights feverishly.

For the next two hours the three companions sat and watched the picture by turns. But it never changed. They agreed at last that it would be safe to leave it and that they would return after supper and await further developments. It was certain that neither scientist would be able to sleep that night, and certainly would not dare putting out the light. They accordingly repaired to the *salle à manger* and calmed themselves as much as possible with Sjömansbiff-and-chips, another of Herr Magnus' tasty and adventurous hybrids.

The impatient reader is here wondering when the ghost I earlier promised is going to make an appearance. Let me respond by saying that although there has been little hint of the supernatural in our tale so far, it does in fact permeate the whole substance of the account. It will be best to first reiterate what we have learned: two academics, having survived the stormy seas on a crossing to the Isles of Scilly, discover that they have drifted into a parallel dimension. This universe is identical in every way to our own save that the unluckiest number is not 13, but 13½.

The consequences are that, unfettered by superstition, the wheels of business run more smoothly; the world is a richer place; standards of living (and therefore education) are higher, and our two academics' skills are suddenly redundant.

Baring-Gould and Purnell both managed to conquer their fear and caught the *Mezzotint* back to Cornwall, when next it docked at Hugh Town. It was most fortunate for them that another storm, on the return journey, knocked them back into their original dimension; but the sight they had witnessed in that scrapbook never left them. It affected them both so strongly that they could not concentrate on their work; they were dismissed from Moseley College of Further Education and became tramps, working their way across Europe picking grapes.

The picture had been a photograph of the famous *Last Supper* by Leonardo da Vinci. In our own world, 13 is deemed unlucky because it represents the number of guests present at that meal. In that other dimension, 13½ was deemed unlucky for the same reason… (Dots are believed by many writers of our day to be a good substitute for effective writing. Let us have a few more…)

In Italy, in the convent of Santa Maria delle Grazie, Milan, both Baring-Gould and Purnell were arrested for scratching with dishevelled nails at the priceless original. They were, it seems, trying to strip away the layers of paint to determine that the figure they so feared was not really there. We will say nothing more of what transpired; each of the two men described it separately as half-spider, half-monkey (though not resembling in any way a spider monkey) with a body of fearful thinness, covered in a mass of coarse, matted black hair, with the muscles standing out like wires.

They are comfortable in the madhouse at last, and indeed of all my patients I favour them most highly. I am quite convinced they are not lunatics in the normal sense. If their sight or brains were giving way I would have plenty of opportunities for ascertaining the fact. They do not rant and rave like monomaniacs. It was only this same afternoon they told me what you have just read; but I refuse to draw any inferences from it, or to assent to any that you will draw for me.

(1995)

The Taste of the Moon

Mondrian, the existential spiceman, carries his angst like a basket of fruit balanced on his head. When he trips on the cracked paving slabs, the plums of despair roll out into the gutter. He has been destroying computers for the benefit of sullen consumers. Ancient Electronics Ltd has made him a director. His fingers flutter over the keyboards, one of the few sets of fingers that knows how. A special interrupt is wired to a small charge in the monitor. The word that shatters glass and plastic is stretched like a sucked nipple: "Why?"

Nostalgia is the thing. Every ten years, manners revert to those of the previous decade. Fashions parody themselves to oblivion, like novae in the sky, colours spinning into static spaces. Did computers really explode when asked to process metaphysical data? Even the head of the company is not sure. It was all so long ago. Mondrian does not enquire too closely, he takes the money and saunters.

Nascent Nosegay, his chief rival, scowls at him as he leaves the demonstration tent. "Prostituting yourself again?" Nascent is a purist, refusing to take any job that does not involve spice travel. This is all very well, but Mondrian has a pretension and six aspirations to keep. It is not possible on his wages. And Ancient Electronics Ltd do not make great demands on his time. Next week he must exhibit a stereo, a machine for recycling brief passages of sound whenever someone slams a door. He is up on the jargon already. "Turntable, magnetic tape, double album." Words like popping caraway seeds.

His day job is more difficult. He resents wearing the cumbersome suit. Yet he has a reputation to maintain. He is the best Khormanaut in the whole of North London. Nascent specialises in Biryani, south of the river. So no one at the Greenwich Spice Centre can say for certain who is the real hero. Remarkably, Mondrian is still nervous before missions. It is always a new experience, fresh as uprooted coriander. He does not mix well with the other spicemen. They consider him an example of aloof sociability, baleful serenity.

Weiner, his immediate superior, briefs him on his latest. "Large establishment discovered in Finsbury Park. Tandoori at aphelion, by the smell of it. Plush seating, sitar music. Pickles mostly mango and lime. Rumours of onion ring system. No known poppadums." Always they seem to simmer into existence, appearing where least expected, between honest buildings immobile for years. Because of an allergy to chilled lager, Weiner has never completed a mission himself. Yet he feels for his men, he really does, he is in there with them.

"The name?" Mondrian flexes his tongue. It twitches like a feline ear, but this is a painful analogy. He recalls Schultz, fed cat dhansak in Earls Court. He has seen many colleagues fall by the tableside. It pays to be cautious, though not in hard currency. Nascent scoffs at his obsession with names. There is a spiceman saying: What the fork cannot balance is no affair of the palate.

Weiner is more tolerant. "*The Taste of Asia*. Could be a variable. Some evidence of inconsistent pricing. Big enough to be unstable. Might go nouvelle at any time." He reaches out to touch Mondrian's arm. "There hasn't been a restaurant this large for years. I hate to think what will happen if it collapses. Pizzeria, greasy spoon, Tapas bar." Weiner is a pessimist. He still has nightmares about the Leicester Square Nebula, a sprinkling of white dwarf cafés.

In the common room, the men are polishing their footwear. They do not look up when Mondrian enters. His portrait hangs on the far wall, a lugubrious figure. When they must answer his questions, they address the picture. It makes things easier. There is tension otherwise. Sitting on the espresso machine, dangling his narrow legs, Nascent sneers. "Why not open a restaurant yourself? Explore both sides of the kitchen." Mondrian inclines his great head. He is stuck with his mercenary reputation. He wants to shout at them, tell them about his insecurities, but spicemen are supposed to enjoy anxiety, wear it as part of the uniform. How else will women know they are attractive?

Outside, in the Greenwich evening, Mondrian is at peace. The Spice Centre, on the banks of the river, ignites in the sunset. The gigantic nose rotates high above, mapping the city on the culinary wavelength. A solitary bargee gives his impossibly romantic cry: "Southwark for a fiver." At this point, where the Thames makes a smiling bend, effluent from a thousand unlicensed establishments falters on its journey to the sea. More bargees hove into sight, poles snapping the cooling crust of the curry sauce. Lentils lap at Mondrian's feet.

Making his way to the pedestrian tunnel, he passes the ruins of the pier. Even here, last bastion of authority, freelancers are rife. Among the stubs of protruding timbers, balanced like stylites on the reliable posts, men and women dangle nets, catching the larger pieces of carrot and potato for their own pots. One hag, panning for sweetcorn, nuggets as black as her teeth, gestures with her colander. "Hey, spicer, you've dropped an apple of abandonment." Feeling in his metaphysical basket, Mondrian finds this is true. He is running out of existentialism at an alarming rate. A trip to Camden market is called for.

The tunnel is crowded with ruffians boiling rice. Under every curry there is some Basmati. Mondrian knows how to ignore touts. His stride is purposeful, he shuts his mind to their jeers, the clash of spoon on pan, the turmeric dust storms. On the far side of the river, home territory, he emerges into the Island Gardens. The last industries are milked on this udder of land, tents grouped in concentric circles. In the centre of the commercial Karakoram, the striped marquee of Ancient Electronics Ltd ripples majestically. Dragonflies skim the fabric. The flag, design showing an azure flip-flop rampant, is stiff with pollution, the smoke of charred Naan breads innumerable.

Old Speckled Henrietta, head of the company, is waiting for him at her desk. They have a thing between them. It is not a growing concern, but it is acceptable to both. Like Mondrian, her nostrils are plugged with glums. Her former husband, a hopeless workaholic, used to binge on unpaid overtime, return home in a senseless temper and take her out for meals. Once, he even bought her a bunch of roses. "I have a big mission on Friday night," Mondrian informs her. "If I fail we'll be sucked in." For some reason, she finds this killingly funny.

They hold hands and wander out into the starlight. The moon has embarked on another slow crawl up the sky. "That's persistence for you," he jokes, but she can tell something is bothering him. It is not just pre-mission blues. She bends down and kisses the top of his head, spiky tuft of hair tickling her tongue. He shivers in the warm air. "They say that spicemen weren't always like us. They used to go up there, out of the city. They walked on that crescent."

She nods soberly. "I bet there's something in it. All myths have a seed of truth. I'll look into it. Maybe my company can reproduce some appropriate technology? The past is such fun." Away from the lamps hung outside the tents, her grin is undercooked, too bright. Mondrian squints in her direction, fearful she will drift away on the tether of his arm, taking the limb with her. Her strength and duskiness are what initially attracted him. The muscularity is real, the dark skin an illusion. She is so freckled she is one big freckle.

"I sometimes wonder if there isn't a pattern to it all. I can't accept that each new restaurant operates independently of the others. There must be connections, possibly with non-ethnic retail outlets. No eatery is an island." Embarrassed by his outburst, Mondrian folds away his emotions. He has already thought long and hard about the problem. The Spice Centre are adopting too literal an approach. They calculate total opening hours, estimate takings, analyse atmospheres. Mondrian wants to look sideways, to venture beyond inductive reasoning and the epicycles of Cardamom Calculus.

"You mean jewellers, lingerie specialists, taxidermists?" She has decided to cheer him up by improvising on his mood. He clears his throat and changes the subject by saying nothing, but she has peppered a bland inspiration. Half-empty restaurants are only one kind of institution with no visible means. Others exist on different frequencies. Suddenly it seems the whole metropolis is about to implode, the furthest suburbs collapsing into this huge area of unvisited space, unpressurised life. He picks his teeth for emphasis.

"Maybe. I don't know. Nobody has dared to investigate. The Spice Centre would consider it heresy. Ever since our founder wandered into his first takeaway in Notting Hill, the approach has been rigid. Curry houses or nothing." As he delivers this rebuke of his organisation, he feels a measure of disgust, both with his superiors for ignorance and himself for disloyalty. Old Speckled Henrietta grins at the complexity of his expression. Sweat reclines on his cheeks. He looks to neutral facts for relief. "It's called Spicentricism."

They complete their tour of the Gardens in silence. When it is time to say farewell, Mondrian plucks up courage to touch her breasts. They are soft as hot towels. Wiping his fingers in her cleavage, shaking her sweat from the tips, he shoulders his way back to the Spice Centre, chewing his lower lip bitterly amid the upper lip biters of the tunnel. Things have got darker: pilau rice and other perversions dominate the length. Gobi Aloo has made an appearance.

Walking, he cannot shake away a feeling of doom. Few Khormanauts die in their beds, most retire to hospices with malfunctioning colons. His time will come, he must face facts. This mission might be the final one, the mortal dessert of his buffet life. Would his colleagues applaud when Weiner brought the news? Nascent would attend the funeral, he was sure of that, but only to jeer. He could picture them around the open grave, the empty speeches, the handfuls of powdered cumin cast onto the unleavened coffin. *Requisat in Spice.*

He gains his room without meeting the others in the passages. They spend their spare time in the common room, laughing at Nascent's jokes. Weiner has his own pursuits, though he will never state what they are. Mondrian suspects him of having a second job, like himself. As he waits impatiently to fall asleep, he hears a door close softly and footsteps outside his window. A receding superior makes a distinctive sound. One evening, Mondrian decides, he will follow.

The dawn bastes his forehead in a cayenne glow. He tumbles down to breakfast early, eager to avoid the traditional baiting that precedes a mission. In his case, his colleagues share his reluctance. Lighthearted insults are not the sort they wish to crack his shell with. Belligerent taunts or nothing. They will sleep on.

He takes coffee and checks the time. The morning is his only until elevenses, when he will be required to present himself before Weiner and suit up. Weiner usually has something to say, a reminder of his duties or a potted history of the founder's own exploits. There are just enough hours to take the communal moped for a spin. The antique vehicle, kept as a privilege for pre-mission spicemen, is a symbol of resistance. The one dogmatic herald of the technology backlash.

Mondrian learnt to ride with the aid of diagrams and exercises in balance and embarrassment. The key is waiting for him under his cereal dish, in a brown envelope. In the garage he runs his fingers over the canvas tarpaulin, exposes the rusty machine and settles into the seat. There is supposedly a connection between such devices and the stereo he is due to demonstrate. He cannot imagine what.

He heads north, his favourite direction. Pedestrians part before him like the waters of a Sunday-schooled sea. Waiters move tables and chairs out of his way, panic on their sardonic faces, amazement in the eyes of their alfresco customers. Porters loaded with chillies, fresh and desiccated, stevedores rolling barrels of humus, minstrels juggling falafel, gape at his smoky progress.

In Camden market, he browses among the olives of anguish, plums of despair and apples of abandonment. They are imported from New Zealand, where the climate is perfect for Sartrian posturing. In the dissolute corner of the market, the edge of Chalk Farm Road, the proprietor of a quivering stall calls: "Notions of goodness, a dozen for a quid." On impulse, Mondrian buys a punnet for Old Speckled Henrietta. Slightly squashed, they still represent good ethical value.

He fills up on existentialism. The juice of the strict

philosophy diminishes his fears, though he still does not want to die. Existence precedes essence again, so he can breathe more easy. The journey back, though an exact reverse of the former, takes longer. He is looking out for previous conquests. A particularly sinister restaurant near King's Cross with ever-changing decor, the Khorma Chameleon, has faded to a wisp. The sight renews his confidence.

He returns to the garage of the Spice Centre, where a mock-cheerful Weiner greets him with a nod. "The most enjoyable service of all, so I've heard. Vespas, eh?" He does not wait for an answer, merely checks his watch and leads Mondrian back into the building. "You've got the right stuff. Good heat shield, an emergency napkin for touchdown. We'll talk you through it."

Mondrian grunts absently, his soul oppressed, and yet uplifted, by his basket of philosophy. Turning a corner, they collide with Nascent, who has a bowl of Scepticism. Mondrian's recent purchases spill and roll among Nascent's Schopenhauerian kumquats. As they scrabble on the floor, Weiner mutters his disapproval. "Dignity, boys." The basket and bowl are refilled, the spicemen disengage with a tearing of grimaces, the fibres of a sundered pakora. "Now then."

In the sterilised bedroom, his spicesuit has been laid out on the bed. He dresses with brisk efficiency, checking buttons and cufflinks in the wardrobe mirror. He knots the tie first time, a sober choice. Some of the others prefer zany colours, ostensibly for luck. Mondrian likes simplicity: black turn-up trousers, matching jacket, plain white shirt, dark green socks and tie, red handkerchief and shoelaces. He brushes his hair into the required quiff, straps the yoghurt tank onto his back and calls to Weiner, "I'm ready."

The door opens and he walks stiffly out into a corridor lined with his colleagues. As he passes each sullen face, he notes the absence of Nascent. Unlike him not to form a part of Mission Control, irrespective of who is being launched! Mondrian may despise him, but he respects the man's professionalism. The earlier collision can have nothing to do with it. Raising his fist to his mouth, Mondrian looses a belch; the taste of foreboding rises in his gullet.

Weiner claps him on the shoulder and makes his standard speech: "I know you won't let us down. In the words of our founder, every man and woman is a *star anise*! Perhaps this mission will be the one that cracks the curry enigma? Who can say for sure? But let me tell how our founder evolved his theory. As you know, Sydney Cradle was his name. Halfway through his first Kabuli Chana, an egg in his brain hatched a chickpea of inspiration. The restaurant had more staff than customers. The city, he realised, was full of restaurants hardly anyone ever visited. So how did the management pay the cooks, waiters and dishwashers? This was a paradox. He decided to investigate."

Mondrian sighs. He does not want to hear this again, it is common knowledge to a spiceman. I feel like the reader of a short story, he decides, whose author must impart information that the characters know already. It comes over clumsily. He frowns unsubtly, but Weiner presses on regardless. "His initial survey showed there were more restaurant seats than curry-eating populace. Yet most establishments managed to remain open. Obviously money was being generated spontaneously on the premises by some unknown and possibly mystic process. Our founder knew exactly what this entailed. The economy was being ruined, slowly and steadily, by a *spicentripetal* force."

Weiner taps his nose with a long finger. "Oh yes, but we're not beaten yet. The Greenwich Spice Centre was set up specifically to grate away the root ginger of the problem. Our founder sniffs over all; you are his latest avatar. The day of reckoning is approaching, when cosmic bills will be recalculated and refunds made. Indulge and explore! Glory awaits more golden than any Zafrani Pullao." Standing aside, he ushers Mondrian out into the day.

The launch pad is a fifteen-minute walk from the Spice Centre. In his suit, Mondrian is reduced to a puppet gait. He takes a traditional route, down Norman Road, over Deptford Bridge and along New Cross Road. Mission Control follow at a respectable distance. When he reaches the exact spot, he stops and takes a deep breath. The Spice Centre no longer use countdowns, it unnerves the men. It is up to the individual to pick the moment. With an odd sort of laugh, one that aptly singes his tongue, Mondrian plunges into the urinous darkness.

He does not have to wait long for a train. He is dimly aware of the others boarding a carriage behind him. Holding onto a strap, he braces himself for the acceleration. As the train builds up speed, he turns and sees Mission Control swinging on their own straps, signalling through the glass of the connecting doors. They are making jokes as they lurch wildly all over the place. Despite this attempt to put him at his ease, he still feels afraid. There are shadowy figures beside him, shapes he cannot quite focus on. Do they exist only in his imagination? They too are dressed in suits, yoghurt tanks strapped to backs. As he tries to pin them down, he realises they have always been with him on missions. Why has he never noticed them before?

From New Cross to Finsbury Park is a complex flight path. He will have to change at Whitechapel, taking the District line to Aldgate East, changing again to the Hammersmith and City line for the short run to Liverpool St. From here, the Central line to Holborn will enable him to make the final approach on the Piccadilly line. There are more direct routes, but this one has been calculated as representing the minimal exposure to the perennial underground hazards of cultural vacuum and gamma-poetry. His heart beats wildly as he makes the first change; his accompanying ghosts follow, some of them. New ones join, all seemingly oblivious of him and each other.

Could these be parallel Khormanauts, from an alternative spicetime continuum? It is a staggering concept, yet the existence of dimensions other than the one based at Greenwich cannot be ignored. Suppose there are also Spice Centres at Kilburn or Sidcup or Putney? They might exist in raw form only, just waiting for the right atmospheric conditions to bubble into this world. Mondrian shivers. Some of the faces are stained with lime pickle. Spicemen returning from difficult missions? The idea is absurd; it irritates like a pappad splinter lodged between the teeth. Still they shimmer out of focus, needing a suitable lens, the bottom of a lager glass, to pull their photons together.

The Taste of the Moon

Mondrian decides not to inform Mission Control of his observations. His sanity would be questioned. He reaches into a pocket for his shades and protects his equanimity and his retinas. Sydney Cradle looms in his mind, shaking a finger blistered on the crusts of a million hot Naans. I must persist, Mondrian thinks. But his conscience feels weighted at the wrong end. Something has happened to him; even his nervousness is not of the same order as before. By the time he reaches Finsbury Park, he feels as if a rival has been sewn inside his skin, like a samosa stuffed with cherries instead of chillies. Rising from the tube, tie rolled away from escalator rail, his disgust is too vibrant.

He struggles to orient himself. At first his destination cannot be seen: he has emerged during an eclipse; but as the occluding bus passes, he catches his first glimpse. The restaurant does seem unstable; facade too gaudy, plaster gateway too crumbly. Behind him, Mission Control call indistinct words of encouragement. Once inside, they will still be able to communicate with him, through the plate glass of the re-entry window. But there is a period of raconteur silence when he will be alone in the piquant void: that moment when he passes through the spicelock between the two sets of doors, neither in one world nor the other. Breathing the differently layered air of North London, he struggles to calm his wildly fibrillating taste buds; his saliva mooches.

With a final check on his wallet status, he pushes with icy fingers and enters the spicelock. It is still not too late to abort. A few more paces, however, and he is committed. Now the doorman notices him and opens the second portal; Mondrian steps over the threshold. A sub-waiter is launched from the kitchens, crossing his walk-path at a tangent. "A drink, sir?" Mondrian orders an ethnic lager. This is the pint of no return. He takes a place at a table, twisting the fringes of the red tablecloth with his nervous hands.

In restaurant terms, *The Taste of Asia* is not enormous. There are bigger establishments in Soho: the gassy Mexican giants. But those have only a tiny core and consist mostly of pretentious atmosphere. Eateries such as this are much more dangerous. They generate money too fast; they are centres of activity that warp the entire profession. Mondrian risks a glance over his shoulder. Mission Control are huddling in front of the external menu, pretending to study the prices. They make subtle signs; a hunched Weiner grimaces precise ordering instructions. Bambai Bhajya for Starters, followed by Darchini Aur Suwa-Walla Gajar with a side dish of Piston-Walla Raita and a dozen Bhaturas, all rounded off with Tarbooj Ki Kheer. As a Khormanaut, Mondrian's palate is licensed only to range the mild and creamy end of the spice-spectrum.

A swarm of waiters is captured by his gravity. They steer with the aid of menus and well-directed sighs. Most overshoot and spiral away to the corners of the establishment. One docks successfully and wields pen and notepad. A sudden depression takes hold of Mondrian. He feels a vast impatience; he has had enough of following orders. After all the dangers of previous missions, they are no closer to understanding the secrets of the Curry-Cosmos. A pinch of recklessness is called for. Savagely, with a defiant snort, he requests the hottest meal in the house. For once he will not cry: "That's one mild Madras for a man, one extra hot Vindaloo for mankind." This time he will have the real experience. Departing, the waiter gleams, like a wedge of Badam Paprh.

Mission Control view his disobedience with something akin to panic. Weiner hops on one leg. Mondrian ignores them and concentrates fully on his surroundings. The restaurant, which he initially thought was empty, seems crammed with wispy figures, similar to those he encountered on the tube. A single solid form sits in a dark corner, its back to Mondrian. A fit of trembling seizes the Khormanaut: is he losing his reason? Sipping his beer, he awaits the solar fare.

The kitchen doors swing again; with mounting velocity the plate of steaming lava sputters toward him. With hasty calculations scribbled on a napkin, he predicts its point of collision, clearing the appropriate spot before him. The meal's course is elliptical: a slingshot round the other living diner, then a sequence of wobbles as it passes translucent patrons. Mondrian swallows dryly; if the angle of service is slightly out, the curry will either bounce off to another table or burn up in his lap. He lifts his drink in preparation.

The touchdown is perfect. Mondrian extends his fork and pokes his dinner in the eye. A thin crust has formed over the scarlet sauce; the tines of his implement shatter it into four continents, which begin to drift apart. One tectonic plate sinks into the magma, bearing a culture of carrots and chopped spinach. Steam gouts from the fissure. The fork bears traces from each strata of the feast; a geology of pain. Waiters go into orbit round the table, shirttails lengthening as they approach the kitchen's furnaces, stains and sweat evaporating from the fabric. I am afraid, Mondrian realises. It is possible that a waiter will graze his atmosphere, break into a million fragments of politeness and shower radioactive manners on his head.

With a grimace, Mondrian tucks a sample of his meal into the corner of a cheek. The effect is not quite instantaneous; there is enough time to feel a profound regret. He is aware of Mission Control making utterly frenzied recalculations. A minor change in expenses amplifies right down the line: his final mass will be different. As he attempts to swallow, a rogue lentil, encrusted with cayenne pepper to triple its standard size, detaches from the greater mouthful and spirals into a lung. This is what all explorers of international cuisine fear most: a blowout. Oxygen and legume react explosively. The blast scours his throat, dislodging teeth. His vibrating epiglottis sounds the alarm.

A waiter targets his plight, pitcher of iced water held aloft. Half blinded by tears, Mondrian is oblivious of his presence. Rising from his seat, the Khormanaut strikes the descending pitcher. The glass falls and shatters on the table edge; the liquid is quickly absorbed by the cloth. With this second impact, Mondrian's incisors clatter onto his plate. His frantic report to Mission Control is made with a series of rapid blinks. The loss of enamel tiles is a serious disadvantage for future meals. The waiter flicks a towel at him, though whether in guilt or anger is rather difficult to determine. Mondrian catches him by the collar in an attempt to drag him down, but the spiceman is too debilitated and succeeds only in yanking himself from the table.

Cast adrift in the restaurant, struggling in each other's arms, the pair lose angular momentum and begin to spiral toward the kitchen. There is terror on the waiter's face; Mondrian is too dazed to notice. "I want to know the secret!" he wails. "Tell me the answer! How do you manage to stay in business with so few customers? How do you make enough money? Is there a flaw in spicetime on the premises? Do you have connections with minority retail outlets? Tell me about lingerie shops!" Breathlessly, as they pass the inner tables on their doomed course, the waiter points out the ghostly patrons, who look up in misty alarm.

Mondrian understands the terrible irony. His hunch was right: there really are other dimensions, with rival Spice Centres and Khormanauts. A ridiculous oversight on his part! It is the convergence of these diners, these menu-explorers, which keep the establishments viable. By seeking a reason for the existence of so many restaurants, the parallel spicemen provide that reason. Never has a self-fulfilling process stuffed his mind's belly with such insubstantial provender. "Our fault!" he bellows, struggling to disengage from the waiter.

At last, as the warmth of the ovens starts to baste his brow, he is alerted to his precarious situation. He releases the safety catch on his yoghurt tank and clasps the nozzle. "The glare is too bright. I'm unable to aim accurately. I require assistance! Which way?" Placing his cracked lips close to Mondrian's lobe, the waiter hisses: "South!" The spiceman is bemused. He knows that there simply are no directions in Spice. "When you travel on down toward the ovens," the waiter replies, "and food gets yellow and hot and creamy, then you're going in one direction only." The phantoms are pushing aside their plates.

Mondrian sees a future removed from them by the merest Naan: curry is a black-beaned meal where taste drowns its speech and kisses. Cream a big cream, but spice snuffs it out before it is half down your throat. Gourmets curry, coriander in a flaming matchbox; the dinner is dripping lava, gushing sweetcorn, nothing! In desperation, the Khormanaut presses the lever on his tank. He hates anything to do with south; north is his favourite direction. The retro-blast of the yoghurt should propel him to safety, but the nozzle sputters ludicrously: the tank is empty! With the fatalism of a dishwasher, he sends another desperate message to Mission Control: "Greenwich, cheque please."

They are approaching the chutney-horizon, the boundary between the world of forks and that of cleavers. For the first time, he is aware of other Mission Controls, huddled next to his own. And now the ghosts are busy making their own communications — "Euston, we have a problem!" "Can you read me, Cape Kennington?" "Hampstead, kindly advise!" Mondrian commends his soul to Sydney Cradle and mumbles a prayer. As he does so, the other solid patron in the restaurant activates his own yoghurt tank and blasts from his table, intercepting the helpless pair. He clutches them round the waist and unstraps Mondrian's useless tank.

Mondrian gasps. "Nascent Nosegay!" His old enemy has come to rescue him. As the empty tank is drawn through the double-doors and flashes out of existence, the spicemen lock eyes. Nascent's breath smells sweet; he has obviously changed his diet. While Mondrian ponders this development, Nascent straps his spurting tank to his chest. "Not enough power for all of us," he explains. "Don't grieve for me!" Mondrian demands to know the recipe of this self-sacrifice.

Kicking himself away into Spice, tumbling like a drunkard, Nascent shouts: "I sabotaged your tank! I wanted you to perish! But when we collided after Vespas, our fruit got mixed up. You received one of my Schopenhauerian kumquats; it made you bold enough to risk a Vindaloo. I gnawed on a notion of goodness, which gave me a conscience. It then became imperative to precede you here."

Mondrian weeps, partly from grief and partly from steam. Now he has the reason for Nascent's absence at his launch. The yoghurt tank rapidly carries them away from Nascent's floundering form. To be saved by such a glib fellow! As Nascent vanishes over the chutney-horizon, he closes his eyes. His scream is as brief as the protest of pounded cumin. The scared waiter sees Mondrian's original table; when they pass near, he leaps for it and clings to the tablecloth. This reduction in mass accelerates the Khormanaut to a frightful velocity; he works the controlling valve, but it is jammed. He is unable to arrest his motion as he steers through the tables for the plate glass re-entry window. Mission Control flee in all directions as he connects horribly…

He wakes to find himself in his bed at the Spice Centre,

swathed in bandages. He is quite alone; but he can hear muted voices emanating from the common room. Throwing back the sheets, he climbs to his feet and out the door. The stairs make few allowances for his condition; by the time he reaches the bottom, the conversation has stopped. Weiner glances up as he enters the room. Mondrian blushes. "I've made a complete phaal of myself," he mutters. Weiner nods in agreement. The spiceman rotates his splinted thumbs. "How long have I been unconscious? I've got a stereo to demonstrate. I mustn't be late."

Weiner chuckles. "That was weeks ago. You've lost your job with the company. Ancient Electronics Ltd don't want you. I've taken your place. I was working for them anyway. Old Speckled Henrietta and myself have a thing between us. It's not a growing concern, though." At this news, the Khormanaut wipes his cheeks with his plaster sleeves. "Don't cry!" snaps his superior. "You must have known she was unfaithful. I dropped enough hints to that effect. I told you I was allergic to lager. Old Speckled Henrietta is dark and full bodied." He licks his lips. "She's using me to pick up gold coins with a magnet..."

Mondrian slumps in a chair under his portrait. Weiner ignores him and growls into the picture's ear. "You destroyed Nascent! You set back the Biryani program by a decade! But we're not finished with you. We discovered another restaurant this morning. The biggest yet." Lifting the portrait, he carries it to a window. "Look up there! Seems a colony of spicemen have been living on that crescent since classical times. They finally decided to open a curry house. We'll get you to it before prices go up. We're converting the moped, adding wings, a pressurised cabin." The real Mondrian lumbers over and squints into the lunar glow, soft as ghee. He silently mouths the question, "The name?" With a sneer, Weiner whispers it to the picture, but not to him.

(1996)

Lunarhampton

(i)

The city was tugging at her elbow.

It felt like that, as if the fumes, litter and rain were conspiring to irritate her. She liked cities, but this one mistrusted her. Flyovers clapped hands above, falling away in exhausted parabolas, shadowing her car but doing nothing to keep the elements at bay. The convertible was a bad idea, she realised, as she changed lanes to avoid an ancient tanker, windows tinted like a blind man's glasses, which kicked up whole puddles of oily water to baptise her anew.

On the edge of her vision, she was aware of addicts skulking in the shadows of tenements, needles catching her headlamps and signalling like heliographs. Was there substance in these messages, ironic insights from beings who closed down veins like television channels? She passed a huddle of towers and a figure lurched onto the road before her, syringe impaled in a wrist, clutching something in a clawed hand. He seemed to tread on the pools, feet gripping the surface tension. Swerving to avoid him, catching his disappointed wail, Melissa Sting wondered if this was not a junky but a patient from some eviscerated asylum, saturated with so much lithium he was lighter than water.

In her mirror, she watched the man dance between the

vehicles. His movements were jerky as he lunged at speeding windscreens. With a start, she recognised his weapon as a sponge: he was a squeegee merchant. She awaited the collision with an abstract pity, but it did not come; he was too agile. Soon her view was blocked by other drivers: a sedan attempted to overtake her on the inside, losing its exhaust as it glanced off the safety barriers. Brown smoke merged with the drizzle and was beaten into dead rainbows in the choked gutter. A second car struck the exhaust and flipped it into the air. It curved over Melissa and landed on the grassy embankment between pavement and road.

A depression, the first of the day, enveloped her as she approached the city centre. It was nearly noon, but still dark. Though this was her first visit to Birmingham, myths of its soullessness had filtered into her sceptical consciousness. Now she had to acknowledge the truth of the stories. The environment was self-parodic, and thus essentially baroque, with tangled junctions crumbling like plaster scrolls, effluents in the canals swirling into complicated filigrees. From above, the megalopolis surely resembled a shattered portico to an extravagant tomb. Once inside it was difficult to avoid the reek of putrefaction, the taste of bruised faith. The grandeur was a stamping boot.

Only when architects allowed children to scribble on their designs, she reflected, would they understand what they were producing. Modernism tries to oppose nature, a futile battle. Lines that are clean on a page turn dirty on a street, walls succumb to graffiti, glass collects grime. Without constant attention, reality and theory divorce and it is always reality that wins custody of the populace.

Architecture must work with decay rather than against it, improving with neglect. Living in a fake Gaudí house, Melissa had verified the adaptive qualities of the organic aesthetic by refusing to make repairs.

When she was feeling in a didactic mood with herself, it generally boded ill for the remainder of the day. She turned onto potholed Digbeth High Street and accelerated past the Coach Station. If Birmingham really was a tomb, then this was the actual site of the corpse: a heaving jelly of decomposing humanity, a gateway between this unsatisfactory world and the comparable hells of Wolverhampton and Coventry. As if lying in wait, a bus pulled out and tried to block her path, but she roared ahead. Like Charon ferrying souls, the driver was a bony fellow, long teeth grinding in frustration as he missed his target. His debased passengers stared at her diminishing form, tarnished coins for eyes. And for an instant, she had a metallic taste on her tongue.

(ii)
She skirted the giant Bull Ring, where cattle had once been tortured to improve the flavour of the meat. Now shoppers were baited in their place by the commercial hooks of shoddy goods and pseudo-bargains. Beyond this monstrous precinct, the Rotunda kicked the grey sky like a broken femur. She cruised down New Street, proceeding as far as Victoria Square, where she stopped on a shattered pavement below the library, which she mistook for a multistorey car park. A guard came to escort her into the Council House, which had somehow lost part of its dome.

The interior was filthy, strewn with old papers and cigarette filters. The guard ushered her into a room full of charred furniture. Holes in the roof allowed the rains to tumble in, slicking the mosaic floor.

A council official sat behind a desk in a corner of the office. The guard bowed stiffly and departed, leaving Melissa to pick a route among blocks of fallen masonry. The official shifted uncertainly, as if he had forgotten the appropriate greeting. He began to stand, thought better of it and offered a limp handshake. Behind him, nailed to the wall, dripped the new city flag, a tricolour composed of various shades of grey. Under his shirt something bulged and rustled.

"Ms Sting? I'm so pleased you could make it," he muttered, stroking his pockmarked face. "Please sit down."

He indicated a chair piled high with storm-damaged cardboard files. Melissa stood silently until, with a deep blush, he leant over and swept them aside. Easing herself onto the damp leather, she waited for him to say something else, but he was too shy or indifferent, it was impossible to decide which. At last she announced:

"The Lunar Commission expect my report within the week. I trust you will issue me with full security clearance?"

He was offended. "That is not a problem. All our documents will be turned over for your inspection and, naturally, you will be allowed into our research zones. We're ahead of schedule."

Melissa grinned. "That's what they all say." Turning up her collar, she huddled into the seat. With an apologetic cough, the official passed her a twisted umbrella, which she struggled to open. During this hiatus, he cleared his throat again.

"Allow me to introduce myself, Ms Sting. I am Alleneal Asherley. Not my real name, of course, but a pseudonym chosen by committee. We believe it safer not to become too informal with outside agencies. However, this initial meeting between us requires a gesture of trust, so at this point I wish to make a statement. Birmingham City Council is only a month away from founding a working moon colony."

Melissa was unable to suppress a laugh, but compassionate enough to stifle it when she saw the pain it caused him. "This is news indeed. The front-runners are still developing their ecology systems. They're having trouble with the hydroponics."

"We don't want to recreate Earth, Ms Sting. Our colonists have been adapted to cope with existing conditions."

A violent desire to be sarcastic overwhelmed her. "What will they say in Newcastle and Oxford? There'll be rioting in the greenhouses!" She lowered her voice to a whisper. "Bookies are giving you odds of a trillion-to-one against. If what you say is true, you will be able to clean up and retire to Luton."

Alleneal raised his eyebrows. "What other municipal authorities see fit to spend money on is none of my concern. And as you should be aware, Ms Sting, no council worker, or Lunar Commission agent for that matter, is permitted to gamble on this project."

Melissa brushed her damp hair out of her eyes. Better not to waste time trying to decide whether he was an imbecile or joker. Probably he was both: council employees trained themselves to be inscrutable, hiding their motives even from themselves. After an awkward pause he fumbled in a soggy cardboard box under the desk and retrieved a bottle of blended whisky. She drank only malt and refused his offer of a glass, watching carefully as he filled one for himself and rotated in his swivel chair to face the faded flag. Squeezing water from one frayed end into his tumbler, he swirled the mixture in his mouth and gargled.

Keeping his back to her, he confessed: "We were hoping you wouldn't come until we'd finished. I wanted to spring a surprise on your masters. A way of getting our revenge. You said we'd never be able to do it, you hurled insults. The Commission wounded us, Ms Sting, I can tell you." He glanced over his shoulder. "We are not all simpletons, you know. I have standards, like any other councillor."

"Well, your municipality has a reputation for incompetence. So many other projects have been mismanaged…"

He swivelled in his chair, so forcefully he completed a full turn, his words phasing in and out of audibility as he passed her. "So that is your justification? Past mistakes have nothing to do with me!" He made a second attempt, ending up at right-angles to her. "I was appointed only at the commencement of this scheme."

"I appreciate that. As you seem so confident, perhaps you will show me the finished plans for your colony?"

He tapped the bulge beneath his shirt. "A map of the settlement has been prepared. It's supposed to be a secret, which is why I keep it next to my body at all times. You may view it, but I would prefer to restrict access until the end of your appraisal."

"This is rather eccentric. Will I also be dissuaded from asking how many colonists you intend to sustain?"

He was dismissive. "Oh, all of them…"

Melissa sighed. "Yes, of course. What I meant was how many citizens do you intend to establish in your first settlement? Do they constitute a representative sample of your electorate? A breakdown of figures would be useful, based on social status, educational qualifications and ethnic origin. Do you possess such figures?"

"I object to your patronising tone, Ms Sting. It is you who fail to understand. As an egalitarian authority, we protect the interests of all our people. We intend to settle everybody."

Before Melissa could protest at this absurdity, shouts from outside interrupted her. A sputtering grew louder overhead. She glanced up and saw, through the broken ceiling, an aeolipile descending through a bank of dark cloud. There was something wrong with its engines: the globe was tipping over, dragging the capsule at an unnatural angle. She jabbed at this sight with her umbrella, just as the contraption vanished from her field of vision. "One of yours?"

Alleneal was at her side in an instant, fists clenching, flecks of spittle creaming his words. "An intruder, Ms Sting! I've given orders to shoot down all aerial spies. Where are the municipal troops? They ought to be on standby. Come with me: hurry!"

She followed him out of the building. On the steps, a

ragged group of men were gathering, shouldering various firearms. Melissa was amused to note the age of the weapons: bolt-action rifles and shotguns from the last century. Some guards even held blunderbusses and muskets. "Get into line!" cried the councillor. "Take aim!"

The aeolipile vanished behind the Anglican Cathedral but bobbed up a minute later, reeling towards its Catholic counterpart like a convert. The capsule crashed against the edifice, showering stained glass over a malnourished procession of worshippers. Then the whole thing lifted and changed course again, coming back towards Colmore Circus. Waving a used handkerchief, Alleneal screamed: "Fire!"

Melissa clamped hands to ears, an unnecessary precaution. The guns jammed or misfired, bullets rolling lamely out of barrels. A mob filled Victoria Square. While excited faces peered upwards, pickpockets worked on the gullible, lifting empty wallets and cancelled food vouchers. The aeolipile, a common sight in most towns, seemed a novel diversion here, as if the hydrogen-filled spheres had never eclipsed Birmingham's moon. The weight of past centuries suddenly pressed on her: this scene was an example of primitive street theatre.

Reinforcements arrived from the Town Hall. A ballista complete with rocket-powered harpoon was hoisted onto the roof. Rusty pulleys strained to lift the device, which was positioned on a balustrade. The aeolipile, oblivious of the danger, tumbled towards the Science Museum. By the time it reached Cornwall Street, the ballista was primed. Without waiting for the councillor's orders, the engineers released the mechanism, sending a bolt of blue flame in a steep arc toward the invader. Melissa thought it was climbing too rapidly, but the engineers had calculated well: dipping suddenly, as if pulled by an invisible hand, the harpoon caught the apex of the orb and lodged in the fabric.

The explosion was followed by an exuberant cry, which Melissa found more startling. It was emanating from the mouth of Alleneal Asherley. For the first time since she had arrived, the city was illuminated properly. The aeolipile did not fall at once: the burning envelope peeled away and exposed the skeleton, a delicate lattice. Too beautiful for these skies, she thought glumly. The councillor was bellowing into her ear: "Keep our secrets safe, we will! Bloody foreigners!"

She ignored him and frowned as the capsule broke free and plummeted to the ground. A wild cheer went up from the crowd. Wisps of ultramarine fire dispersed on the greasy air. Melissa angled her umbrella to protect herself from the soot and molten shards.

"There might be survivors," she pointed out. "I suggest we find out immediately. My car is parked over there."

"Good idea, Ms Sting. We need live prisoners."

Melissa pushed her way through the crowd to the spot where she left her convertible. She had expected the hubcaps to be missing, but it was the rest of the vehicle that was gone. She discarded her brolly with a scowl. When the councillor reached her side, panting loudly, he betrayed a perverse pride. "Best thief in the country, the Brummie opportunist!" Melissa glared at him as her four hubcaps span like buttons and came to rest, one by one, with a mocking rattle.

(iii)
They travelled in the councillor's limousine, with two bodyguards and a chauffeur, to the site of the crash. Glowing bolts from the balloon had embedded themselves in the pitted road. Tyres squealing, they clattered up Newhall Street, the limousine protesting at each gear change. The vehicle had been requisitioned from the mayor, Alleneal explained. As she wiped her window with a sleeve to peer out, he added, "Everybody makes sacrifices for the cause. We're a proud race."

The frame of the aeolipile had been scattered over a wide area, but the capsule had come down in the middle of Church Street. Men in woolly hats were stooping over the pod, working at the shell with crowbars and chisels. In their striped and colourful headgear, they resembled mutant bees collecting pollen. They fled when the limousine pulled up, gaining the safety of doorways. Melissa jumped out and approached the craft. It had been completely stripped. At the heart of a bare frame, two figures sat strapped into smouldering chairs.

They were relatively uninjured, blinking in surprise. Ordering them cut free, Alleneal turned to Melissa. "Now we'll learn what our enemies are up to. A happy accident, Ms Sting!"

"They require treatment. Aren't you going to call an ambulance? The Commission disapproves of punitive neglect."

"You have no authority on matters of provincial security. They are spies and will be treated accordingly." Reaching into the web of struts, he slapped one of the occupants on a blistered cheek. "Why did you enter our airspace? What was your mission?"

"Engine failure," the figure mumbled. "Blown off course."

Melissa recognised the accent as educated Cardiffian. It was common knowledge the Welsh capital was having difficulties with its propulsion units. Alleneal was dangerously paranoid, she concluded. And yet she was powerless to restrain him as he instructed his bodyguards to arrest the aeronauts. While she debated what action to take, a Black Maria arrived and the hapless prisoners were bundled into the rear. Triumphantly, the councillor returned to the limousine.

The woolly-hatted men started to emerge onto the pavement. She did not relish being left alone in their company, so she climbed in beside Alleneal. The chauffeur trundled onto Edmund Street, heading back to the Council House. The return journey seemed to take longer. She tapped her fingers on a knee and asked the councillor, "How did you know it wasn't your own aeolipile? It was unmarked."

"A straight answer, Ms Sting. We don't use them."

Staring at him in disbelief, she realised he was serious. "Then you have developed a new kind of launch vehicle? This is remarkable. What is it called? Can you describe it to me?"

He rubbed his unhealthy eyes. "It is simple, Ms Sting,

the guiding principle of all we seek to accomplish."

Reluctant to divulge more, he lapsed into an affected gloom. Before they reached the square, his natural enthusiasm broke through again. "We showed those liars and saboteurs! You can't mess with our council. Might as well slit your own perfumed throat."

"Waste of hydrogen, though," said Melissa.

"An academic point, Ms Sting. We have no interest in such fuels. We use gunpowder to achieve our objectives."

This was too much for her. He was plainly testing her patience. "In the past hour," she protested, "you've made a number of fatuous claims. Unless I've misheard, you intend to transport the entire population of Birmingham through space with the aid of firework propellant. I warn you not to insult my intelligence."

Alleneal tapped his nose. "Be patient, Ms Sting. I will personally conduct you on a tour of our facilities and explain every aspect of our lunar bid. When you study our moon-buggies you'll be convinced. A whole fleet of them! It will verify everything."

"When does this tour begin?" she demanded.

"I have urgent business with my fellow councillors this afternoon. It is vital to interrogate the intruders."

"You're not going to provoke a war with Cardiff?"

He waved aside her fears. "Our citizens are not capable of fighting anyone other than themselves. I simply wish to determine whether we have managed to keep our preparations secret. With access to our ideas, rival councils can accelerate their own programs."

Melissa accepted this. She examined her hair. Although

the internal heaters were blowing warm air into her face, her auburn locks refused to dry. The water had a peculiar adhesive quality. She wondered if exposure to the local rain was the source of the councillor's skin complaint. His cheeks were suggestive of selenic landscapes, repellent yet fascinating, brutal as the geology of Emmental. His rinded lips curled, rupturing the illusion. She tumbled out of his orbit.

"I've arranged for you to stay in one of our safest hotels," he was saying. "My chauffeur will collect you tomorrow morning. Remain in your room, Ms Sting. Some odd people about."

She considered this advice. At the Council House, he left her alone in the back of the limousine. It proceeded down Hill Street and into the Chinese Quarter. Eventually, the chauffeur pointed out the façade of the Arcade Hotel. This was supposed to be one of the smarter areas, but the desolation was merely more pretentious. Eroded theatres and nightclubs exhibited scars and graffiti like drunken sailors; fractured restaurants bled steam like dying turbines. It was an extra worry to be guided into the hotel lobby by the chauffeur: she might have to come to his aid. He fled before she could refuse him a tip.

Her room was at the top of the building. Long and narrow, it seemed a microcosm of the city's mentality. Insects scuttled when she turned on the light; the furniture bristled, a wooden conspiracy of puritans; a sagging bed took her weight with a nasal moan. Her report would stress the apparent running down of infrastructure to pay for the moon project. She had encountered diversion of council funds before, most notably in Leicester and Norwich, but never on such a massive scale. Did Alleneal really enjoy the support of his people?

If he was trying to distract her with ludicrous statements, he had succeeded only in making her more determined to carry out her task. She was eager to verify his claim that Birmingham had an alternative to the aeolipile. These were standard equipment for space travel. Other methods of reaching extreme altitudes existed, but they were more expensive and less efficient. At the beginning of the century, when state-funded space programs were overtaken by private enterprise, a large number of designs had taken to the skies: the astroplane, the roton, the scramjet. But the aeolipile rendered them obsolete, a single-stage craft that carried its fuel in an inflatable envelope, using it in this form to elevate itself into the stratosphere before conventional rockets cut in to complete the escape of the planet's gravity.

Like so many achievements in aviation history, the aeolipile was an invention of two brothers, Hans and Eric Pfaall. A giant hydrogen bubble mounted on pivots, it made use of the Magnus Effect: the tendency of an object moving sideways to rise when rotated along its horizontal plane, depending on the direction of the lateral movement. Engines protruding at right angles from the envelope took power directly from the enclosed gas, mixing it with oxygen in a combustion chamber. To protect the crew from a possible explosion, the capsule was fitted with parachutes and slung under the sphere on cables, at a safe distance from the fuel. As the aeolipile rose and the globe deflated, the capsule was gradually winched closer. When the orb attained its service ceiling, the remaining hydrogen was pumped into the capsule, which disengaged and blasted off into orbit. The Pfaall brothers had been killed in a prototype, but the apparatus was highly reliable.

The device was such an integral part of astronautics it was assumed every council involved in the lunar colony competition would use them to carry equipment and materials into space for the construction of orbital stations. Portsmouth and Leeds had recently started work on their bases. Newcastle and Oxford had completed this stage and were already preparing for the next step of establishing a foothold on the surface of the moon. Melissa could envisage no other way of doing it, but Birmingham Council expected her to believe that gunpowder, clumsiest of propellants, was an alternative. She wondered if this was becoming a typical Brummie fiasco, comparable to the abortive Olympiad bids.

Her train of thought was interrupted by a stampede in the corridor. She stepped to her door and secured it, a moment before it was violently shaken and a voice demanded admittance.

"I will hold a fiver for you!" it boomed.

Melissa was prepared for the native attempts at intimidation. In a voice no less aggressive, she called:

"And I'll break an arm for *you*…"

The panhandler moved away and Melissa reclined on the bed. For the rest of the evening, the hotel reverberated with distant oaths and sobs. She listened to indefinable sounds located in hidden cavities behind the walls, a decay both human and inanimate. Sleep evaded her and she sat by the mottled window. Soon after midnight, a series of muffled explosions tickled the city. An oscillating rumble flirted with the edges of sound, like the snoring of an unemployed giant.

(iv)
The following morning, and each day thereafter, the limousine picked her up at the hotel and drove to carefully selected city sites. Alleneal was always nervous, a student sitting an exam, confident of his ability but uncertain whether his methods would be palatable to the invigilator. As they roamed the urban decrepitude, Melissa wondered when he was going to play his trump. They passed through the gutted suburbs of Bournville and Edgbaston, which the councillor appeared to regard as personal triumphs, examples of an unspecified progress. At every crater, he fingered one of his facial pocks, as if they were analogous to the larger ruination. She found his cryptic messages infuriating.

In Aston, he gestured at the expanse of powdered brick and sawdust, the legacy of a particularly violent cataclysm. "This suburb can be seen with the naked eye, Ms Sting. No need for telescopes to appreciate the beauty of these radial fissures."

To Melissa, it looked like the result of badly laid carpet bombing. Was Alleneal hinting that Birmingham had engaged in unlicensed warfare? But she still believed his assertion that inter-municipal aggression on an organised scale was impossible in the Midlands. And no other council had reported a military engagement.

"An accident of some kind?" she asked.

Disappointment showed in his expression. "A carefully orchestrated operation, requiring dozens of workers and tonnes of explosives. Haven't I made myself clear yet, Ms Sting?"

"Apparently not. But I'm all ears."

His response was a shrug denoting both irritation with her naivety and satisfaction with himself for preserving a mystery. "You'll realise the truth before long. Let me show you the ongoing work." He tapped the chauffeur on the shoulder. "To Sarehole Mill!" Turning back to Melissa, he chuckled. "It's like a jigsaw. Concentrate on the edges first. Comes together in the middle of its own accord."

"I think I understand. To encourage people to relocate to the moon, you destroy their homes and places of work."

"Places of work? Oh, Ms Sting, you're a romantic!"

They drove south in silence. At various points throughout the city, sheets of blackened fabric from the aeolipile glimmered in the drizzle, caught on lampposts like the sails of ships in mourning, or draped over tenements like the awnings of repossessed shops. Finally, reaching Cole Bank Road, they stopped to watch a group of surly labourers demolishing what was apparently a famous building. Charges were set in the edifice, a ponderous corn mill. The detonation itself was a less dramatic affair than the aeolipile incident: the mill leaned over and briefly regained its feet before sprawling in a polluted pond, cleared of algae for the purpose of receiving its body. Alleneal explained the details in muted tones, as if suffocating the facts.

"Your earlier remark about fireworks was most apt, Ms Sting. There are many local factories producing gunpowder that we have pressed into our service. The workers daren't protest on pain of public flogging. We have had few problems with forced labour."

"Just what sort of official are you? This is barbaric behaviour for a councillor. Not even in Hull…"

"Obviously, when our colony is fully functioning, I shall no longer be content to remain a standard councillor. I intend to award myself the title of *Conducator* and rule by decree."

"I often think total devolution was a mistake," Melissa sighed. She decided to press him on seeing the actual project hardware. "I thank you for the tour of the city. The craters and social collapse have been most instructive. However, my report must not be delayed. I wish to view your transportation and surface hardware."

"How can you entertain doubts?" Alleneal spluttered. His tormented eyes took in the urban landscape, accepting its pain and tragedy with an obscene stoicism, a father who witnesses the circumcision of a terrified boy. "The noose of desolation is tightening. Soon even the Council House will be torn down. A total wasteland."

"With all respect, these perverse civil operations hold very little interest for the Commission. I was specifically charged with grading the viability of your colony tender."

He was amicable again. "I know this, Ms Sting. Allow me to show you our fleet of moon-buggies. They are fine beasts, heavy and powerful. The best way of sculpting lunar seas."

Chewing her lip, she allowed herself to be ferried back to the city centre. The councillor fumbled in the glove compartment for a torch. The rains were in benevolent mood, each greasy droplet falling slowly enough for Melissa to avoid. She sidestepped from limousine to National Indoor Arena, a structure that was plainly sick, bulging like a raped wife. As if tuning in to her thoughts, Alleneal twisted his nose. "Pregnant? Yes, expectant mothers are our chief export."

They passed the bored guards, who barely offered them a glance. She saw how the structure had been disembowelled and turned into a cyclopean garage. The interior was unlit and Alleneal played games with his torch, angling it under his chin and illuminating his horrible face from below. As his hand trembled in the low temperature, and the halogen bulb cast a shifting glow over his cheeks, tiny shadows moved inside his dimples and pockmarks. Melissa was reminded more than ever of the moon: a lunar day, sunrise to sunset, fleeing across his visage as the beam rose higher and abruptly turned away to prick a ludicrously small hole in the void. Down on the floor of the hall, metal gleamed.

"Bulldozers?" she hissed. "You'll never be able to lift these into space. Your jokes become more crass."

He touched her elbow. "Buggies, if you please. These are my babies, Ms Sting, the key to my future tranquillity." He breathed on her neck, a moistening of the clue, but she was too stubborn to work at the hint. It was a relief to return outside, to flee the stench of antique diesel and damp earth on caterpillar tracks, oppressive as the odours of a roadside allotment. Alleneal watched her warily.

She snapped: "It is clear you are trying to obstruct my mission. My report will not be sabotaged by such foolish tactics. You should revise expectations about claiming any bonus."

He seemed hurt. "You are closing your eyes to your surroundings, Ms Sting. It's all here, you know. We're on the threshold of a new age, one we've been chasing for decades, without even knowing it. Birmingham has finally woken. Our traditional strengths no longer shame us. We know how to exploit our most valuable resource."

"And that is?" she asked bitterly.

He rolled his eyes upwards, leaving rotten eggs in his sockets, and pressed palms in an attitude of prayer. "Entropy." He held the stance for a full minute, before scratching the emptiness above his head, as if he wore an invisible halo infested with fleas. Exhausted by the messianic fervour of his pronouncement, he staggered away. "I must rest. Tomorrow, I will show you Moseley and Olton, the venues for serenity and crises." Hunched, but with supplicating hands, he left her, a series of hops too athletic for one in his condition.

Trapped by the threatening stares of natives, she returned to the limousine. The chauffeur followed the familiar route, but now everything looked different, more open and yet cluttered with the jagged peaks of dilapidated buildings. The horizon was nearer: the Chinese Quarter was hidden by the curvature of the city, looming into view with a terrifying clarity. She stormed into the Arcade Hotel and shut herself in her room. Behind one wall, a prostitute entertained a sterile client, mouthing an obscene checklist of erotic controls.

The city was not insane, as she had suspected, but simply following its instincts to a logical extreme. This might have happened in London, but the separate boroughs maintained equilibrium by pulling in different directions. Here, the tension was all directed inward. Birmingham seemed ready to snap in on itself. Time to leave: she needed to gather only one piece of evidence to complete her report. She would have to confront the councillor directly and demand a copy of the map hidden under his shirt. If he refused, she would exercise her authority and muscles, tearing the sackcloth monstrosity from his back.

There was something in her shoe. When she bent down to remove it, a cloud of soot puffed in her face. She had a use for this abducted filth. In the cracked mirror, jumping at each eruption out in the city, Melissa rubbed the dirt into her hair and face. She ripped her own shirt, worked holes in her trousers with her little sharp teeth and scuffed the polish of her shoes against a radiator pipe. Now she looked like a local: only the multiple earrings were missing.

On the streets, she passed unnoticed. Demolitions were taking place everywhere. Girders and blocks fell more slowly than they should, almost gently enough to be caught in her hand. The iron and concrete struck the pavement silently. Melissa ignored the quiet and concentrated on a group of young delinquents, approaching with unsheathed stubble. She was ready for them and launched a preemptive strike.

"Can you spare an ingot for a cup of tea?"

They shied away and she was free to continue her journey, removing her smirk and pocketing it for later. At the Council House, she brushed past the apathetic guard and entered the mossy travesty. The only light came from a phosphorescent slime that coated the walls. Pausing on the threshold of Alleneal's office, she placed her ear to the rotting door. A peculiar chattering came from inside. Eye to keyhole, she watched him plucking at his face with tweezers.

Was this how all councillors groomed themselves? Turning away, in a fit of embarrassment, she reached a spiral staircase and went down. Her unease intensified with each step, as if she was descending the helix of the council's DNA, the code that controlled the growth of the municipal nervous system. At the base, she found herself in a corridor. She passed a dungeon with a lock rusted almost all the way through. Inside, leaning over a trestle, the Cardiffians were comparing injuries. "My shoulders are more dislocated than yours!" Rising to their broken feet, probably smashed by council hammers, they started a brawl, adding a second layer of bruises to insulate the lower.

A second dungeon held her convertible. She tried the door: the iron bars crumbled in her grip. The vehicle was covered in parking tickets, a petty, as opposed to pretty, wedding dress. Alleneal was a thief as well as a liar, but he had left the key in the ignition. The voices of guards echoed along the passage. She had time only to free the prisoners or the convertible, not both. The decision was less painful than it should have been. As she jumped into the driving seat, she reflected that justice is simply a covert weighing of beauty.

Clogged with local air, the engine protested as she

started up and drove straight through the remaining bars. The rust coated her like the pepper of a robotic chef, spicing the corners of her eyes as she swerved tightly into the corridor. She roared in the opposite direction to the voices: soon the passage began to spiral upwards. She was gratified to discover it emerged in the library: she cruised down the aisles, packed with cankerous bookcases and exenterated computer terminals. Tramps and students sheltered under collapsed shelves, offering her no more than a toothless smile. Other vehicles waltzed among the sundry literatures. It really was a multistorey car park: she could trust her perception once more. She clattered down the stairs.

Leaving the building by the main entrance, she parked outside the Council House. She left the engine running, giving the convertible the appearance of having already been stolen and abandoned as inadequate. She did not pause at the councillor's door this time, but strode in. He was sterilising his tweezers in blended whisky. Resignedly, like a moon regarding an oncoming eclipse, he turned his hatching eyes towards her. His questioning shrug was very eloquent.

"You stole my property," she cried.

"Councils do not steal, Ms Sting. They confiscate. We had to ensure you remained with us for the whole week. Perhaps I should have been more open, but I am unused to dealing with females." Dropping the tweezers in the whisky bottle, he sighed. "Especially not sassy redheads. I never engage in relationships, Ms Sting. I find you somewhat alarming. Emotion is noise in my brain: I am a councillor."

"I'm just the same as everyone else."

He shook a finger. "Oh no, Ms Sting! You won't pull that particular shade of wool over my eyes." In a more conciliatory tone, he added: "The car is a minor issue. We all make sacrifices, we all have fears. My dear mother was startled by a monkey. She was pregnant and the shock affected her womb. This world is an absurd place."

"Enough nostalgia. I demand to see the colony map."

Instead of protesting, as she thought he would, his fingers jumped to unbutton his shirt. Below, he wore a string vest: his chest was very hairy, trapped under the grubby net like a fur coat. A scroll was fixed by a ribbon to one of the vest's interstices. Untying it, he gave it to her and cradled his skull in his hands.

Breaking the seal, spreading the parchment on the desk, she moaned. "This is a street map of Birmingham."

He giggled. "Take a closer look, Ms Sting." He allowed her a second perusal. "Did you read the names? The old suburbs have gone. The craters and plains have more suitable appellations."

She traced the parchment with a finger. As if a moon chart had been superimposed on the urban map, exotic words stretched across the prosaic boroughs. She pronounced the names self-consciously, mindful of her poor aptitude for dead languages: "Aristarchus, Mare Nubium, Ptolemaeus, Mare Imbrium, Eratosthenes, Albategnius…"

The councillor interrupted her by clearing his throat and slotting three fingers into his largest pocks, as if preparing to bowl his head. Melissa felt she was not his target, but the skittish city beyond. "The Midlands. The final frontier, boldly gone."

She removed her hands from the map and it snapped back into a tight cylinder. "But what is the point?"

"When I was a boy, Ms Sting, I regarded the future as a benefactor. I looked forward to the shining cities we were promised: gleaming towers connected by aerial walkways, frictionless monorails, a populace free of the degradation of hunger and poverty. We would all be wearing togas and discussing philosophy in spacious parks. I thought that by the beginning of the new millennium we would be living on the moon. A crystal dome for a sky, a purple sea, an alien forest."

"You should have tried to make friends."

"You don't understand. The disappointment stayed with me. When the First Space Age ended, the real moon was derided. Instead, we seemed to want our inner cities to turn into substitute lunar landscapes. Was that a cheaper way of getting there? I believe it was. This subconscious need influenced councils more than you might imagine. I inherited the policy, but knew it for what it was. By that stage, it was irreversible, so when space was rediscovered, and the moon colony competition was announced, I chose to accelerate the whole process."

"Hence the bulldozers and explosives. An amusing effort at twisting the rules, but to no avail. The Commission is very strict on this score. Birmingham is not an eligible moon."

"Consider the similarities, Ms Sting! Both are unavoidable, lack an atmosphere and shine by reflected glory. To deny us the victory would be churlish. Our citizens are the perfect colonists, resigned to bleak and unforgiving environments. Did you know our junkies have started to cut their heroin with an oxygen compound?"

"You are insane. My report will recommend instant disqualification. You'll be grounded for a century."

"There's no leaving us now. The project is too far gone. The limits of the city are finished. How will you get beyond Solihull? Your car is not pressurised. You'll bleed to death through your nipples!" He thumbed his own chest, as if needing to convince himself of the possibility. "It will be a municipal stigmata." He pondered this thought, which seemed to provide solace, like the dream of a ladder to a stylite. To puncture it, she delved into her pocket for her smirk.

"What will you call the colony? A new name is essential. Birmingham is inappropriate. How about Moonchester?"

He recoiled, confused and miserable. "Ms Sting! Such questions will be decided by committee. It is presumptuous…" He grinned unpleasantly, wagging a finger. "You must call it home from now on. There's no running away. The cosmic radiation will kill you."

She turned to leave. "You've confused semblance with reality, image with modus. A city sculpted to impersonate a moon does not automatically become that moon. You are a lunatic!"

He appreciated the joke. "But the way things *feel* is more important than how they actually *are*." Again, he rotated his proboscis, tuning in to her recent thoughts. "If you felt our city was tugging at your elbow, then that is surely what it was doing."

Before she reached the door, she stopped and asked, "So what's your real name? Is it less comfortable than your pseudonym?" Glancing at her elbow, she was shocked to notice a few unravelled strands. Alleneal was trembling, chomping on nothingness.

"My mother was startled, Ms Sting. She was carrying me at the time. The monkey came from behind a curtain in the Repertory Theatre. Some say there is no link between the incident and my condition. Our family has a noble heritage. We have dominated Birmingham for generations. The Rattle clan is respected and feared. I pluck my face every day: soon I will try electrolysis. The surface of the moon is devoid of laughter. The gravity of my problems has been lessened."

Standing up, clutching the flag behind him for support, he mustered every ounce of dignity and announced: "I am Simian Rattle, *Conducator* of Lunarhampton." He sagged and wept into the woodworm, unaware or uncaring that Melissa had already departed.

Outside, the rain had stopped falling. Globules of moisture drifted sideways over the pavements. At last the sky was clearing: ribbons of cloud strangled denticulated peaks. Bouncing toward her convertible, delirious as a bubonic puppet, Melissa desperately tried to laugh, while a million heliographs flashed from crater rims.

(v)

To reach escape velocity, she knew she must never take her foot off the accelerator pedal. The mountains merged into a wall, a grey tongue. Her ears played a staccato rhythm:

pressure was leaking from her improvised canopy. She had picked up one of the flapping sheets from the aeolipile and wrapped it round her chassis. She hoped the fabric was tough enough not to burst. Speed and style were the vital factors. Overhead, despite the sun, stars burned in a black sky.

On the horizon, at the end of the road, a movement caught her eye. A tiny object was bounding towards her, growing larger at an astounding rate. Each leap was the width of despair. At last she made out a human form. It had a bucket on its head, connected by a length of hosepipe to an oxygen cylinder. A syringe glittered in a wrist. It was the squeegee merchant, charging with drawn sponge.

They connected silently, his body rotating over her bonnet and off at a steep tangent. He left a soapy smear across her windscreen and she watched in her mirror as he gyrated into outer space, stretching a palm to accept payment. One way of clearing them off the street, she thought. But she made a symbolic movement toward her pocket. It was too late: he was already an orbital beggar. An inverted meteor, harbinger of failure, he vanished in a subsidised explosion.

The speedometer was exhausted, lying horizontal on its right side, but her velocity increased. There was less friction, less of everything here, but now she knew she would make it. If a city wants to tug at your elbow, be firm with it. Do not permit yourself to be bullied. The music of the spheres washing in her head, Melissa allowed herself to dream of an asteroid shaped like a fake Gaudí house. It lay out there somewhere, in the void, beyond the adventures that awaited her on the alien worlds of Redditch, Bromsgrove and Kidderminster.

(1997)

The Expanding Woman

It was the year Klingon became the official European language. Laura and I were present when the police broke down the door of the last Esperanto Institute to resist the change. There was fierce fighting in the cellars and gun smoke poured from the external vents. The global, pacifist dreams of Zamenhof had finally been upstaged by a joke. Not that the decree was issued in a spirit of fun. It was simply that a federal society required a common tongue and Klingon was the obvious choice. A modern bureaucracy must always place economics before taste.

The fact that Klingon was cheaper to standardise throughout schools was largely due to the enthusiasm generated by the more neurotic pupils. Nobody had ever wanted to learn Esperanto, despite its phonetic spelling and absolutely regular verbs. It lacked glamour. Klingon, with its gruff militaristic timbre, appealed equally to the bullies and the bullied. It had originated as a cult among obsessive, solitary disciples of escapist science fiction in the closing decades of the twentieth century, growing rapidly in popularity on the campus, where new phrases were exchanged by timid freshers huddled in padded anoraks.

We watched the scrap until hunger drove us away. As we took a short cut across the hovertrain tracks, Laura turned to me with an exclamation of surprise. In the dying light, only the gleam of her myriad nose rings confirmed her identity. I am not suggesting that paranoia is a necessary survival trait but any attempt to fit in with the new world order should be applauded. If the federal government intended to give every advantage to the misfit and sociopath, it made sense not to discourage such latent qualities in my own psyche. I squinted in the direction of her seemingly detached finger, extended to the shadows.

"What's the matter now?" I demanded.

She gripped my elbow, bruising the bone. "Something's there, animal of unknown species." I like the way she talks when startled, panicky yet rational. There was a snort in the weeds.

I stumbled over the rails. Vandals had sabotaged the electromagnets with disruptors made from anvils and loops of wire taken from bundles of forged banknotes collected by the police. Regular raids on the remaining National Health hospitals unearthed millions of fake eurodollars printed by starving nurses in Radiography departments. After confiscation, these were incinerated by fraud squad flamethrowers, but the technetium strips that survived were dumped on landfill sites and retrieved by scavengers who haggled with them on council estates.

"It took the wrong evolutionary path," I hissed, still referring to Klingon, but Laura assumed I meant her unnamed monster. A coil snared my foot and I sprawled, trousers ripping at the knee. She helped me extract myself from the tangle, hurling it aside.

Homemade disruptors rarely derailed trains because express services were fitted with scoops to catch the devices. I had discovered an easier way to interfere with commuter schedules, a technique of manipulating my environment that served to reduce stress. I would make use of it later, after humouring Laura in her belief that a beast was stalking our realm. I could see almost nothing in the gloom but groped my way vaguely to the spot from where the snort had emanated. It was quiet now. Laura was irritated with my poor night vision, my scepticism.

"Didn't you see it? It was enormous and hairless."

The embankment was suddenly pitted with frozen light. NARCISSAT had risen in the east. A vast mirror designed to relieve the winter darkness of the Shetland Isles, it had been cracked by a meteor and sent spinning in an erratic orbit that covered London.

"I note a footprint. I agree it's somewhat large."

"Surely a human couldn't make that?"

As the satellite passed overhead, catching the shattered remains of the Greenwich Millennium Dome, I knelt and tested the depth of the print with my hand. I chewed my lip in disgust.

"I believe it's the spoor of the expanding woman."

Laura sighed in disappointment. She knows exactly which urban myths inflate house prices and which bring an area into disrepute. The Genetic Circus had been in town during the summer. Had an unhappy exhibit chosen to flee into the overgrown gardens of our district, media interest would have generated considerable investment from outside. The expanding woman can generate nothing but calorific value.

The expanding woman owns a chip shop. Over a period of a month, she doubles in size, giant chins swelling like udders. Her maximum width has been estimated as that of a piano. The type of piano is never specified. I have rarely seen the expanding woman at perigee, when she eclipses her husband and children. She is always civil to customers. Her chip shop is an example of insidiousness. Many locals, even the greasiest ones, avoid our street because of its noxious allure.

I have a theory. I believe the expanding woman submits to extensive liposuction during each new moon. The fat that is removed is used to fry the chips. Also, she sustains herself by eating the garbage in our bins. This may explain why the expanding woman is so confident of taking early retirement. She has no need to buy cooking oil or food. If the operation is performed with makeshift equipment, bicycle pump and garden hose, for example, the savings must be substantial.

Laura nodded and we descended through the nettles, over a wall into our yard. The rusty swing cast an ominous shadow across the untidy lawn, telling the time with its relative slant. NARCISSAT has largely replaced the sun as the luminescence of choice for outdoor timepieces, though the recent adoption of metric minutes means we have less opportunity to idle in our gardens. I unlocked the rear door and we entered the kitchen. The house was playing up again, nervous system sparking. I have doubts about the benefit of printed circuit wallpaper.

While I watched teevee, Laura set about reprogramming the scrambled domestic functions. The News Channel offered an account of the Esperanto rebels and the battle. The report was in English with Klingon subtitles. Soon it would be the other way around. A journalist in a pale suit stood outside the Institute while faint explosions echoed from within. Tatters of green flag whipped his ankles. The walls were daubed with messages in clotted blood, something that neither Laura nor myself had seen. As the story progressed, I grew increasingly concerned. Helicopters circled and settled on the roof, disgorging soldiers.

"Laura, come and look! We're being interviewed."

She joined me on the sofa and frowned. "That's not right. We didn't talk to anyone. They must have generated computer doubles!" She was more infuriated by the fact her doppelgänger had the wrong accent than by the process itself. I snapped the teevee off.

"What happened to reality after the millennium?"

She shook her head. "We had to make it different, you know. How can we go on otherwise? It's a joint effort."

"I suppose so. But living constantly in the future is exhausting. I just hope it's worth it in the long run."

Laura chuckled and went off to brew a drink. She knows I will never regress, despite my complaints. There are communities who have reverted, but they hold no interest for me. She returned with a pair of peppermint tea bags dangling from her earlobes. The joke depressed me. I decided to retire to the spare bedroom, the one that overlooks the hovertracks. If a mysterious creature really was loose in the neighbourhood, I wanted to make certain it left my vegetables alone.

Laura removed one of the tea bags and popped it into her mouth. She will never allow a malfunctioning kettle to deprive her of a nightcap. I turned away and wearily climbed the stairs, glad to be free of her vice. I was once addicted to her fresh wit and menthol sense in a similar way, but something had happened. She was no longer the female I knew. Perhaps my earlier doubts about her identity were based on subconscious insights rather than my nurturing of neuroses in preparation for learning Klingon grammar. But if she had been an impostor since the day we first met, how would I be able to verify the difference?

News Channels were able to create convincing replicas, so there was no telling what governments were capable of doing. I had often suspected the majority of Londoners were copies rather than originals but it never seemed important. Now, in my own house, the possibility was chilling. In Laura's case, there was an extra dimension to her disparity, elements of unearthliness that suggested an alien source. I imagined the population split between official doubles, sanctioned by the Federation, and agents planted by extraterrestrial authorities.

Having worked for the Environment Ministry in the Somerset lagoons, tagging bison with radio-collars, I was acutely aware of the attachments affected by my fellow humans. Naive visual statements were not enough to explain the continued popularity of body piercing. Nobody could remember why the trend had started, so many decades ago, though some cited tribal instincts in revolt against the present. What if Laura's nose rings, and those of her kind, were monitoring tags for intelligences from a distant galaxy? Control through fashion, a trick.

NARCISSAT was already setting, tumbling toward the

flooded counties of the west. I stood by the window and watched the mirror dispensing bad luck all the way to the infected towns of Wales. When the light was gone and the shadows thickened on the embankment, I detected a vague movement in the thistles. Was this Laura's monster? I could hardly deny something ravenous had been at our bins, yet the expanding woman was reason enough for the disorder. I had no desire to multiply entities beyond necessity, especially when the entities were horrid.

I opened the window and leaned out. The window box betrayed various signs of recent activity. In the moss that separated the petunias there was a miniature crop-circle. On this modest scale the usual explanations for the phenomena — whirlwind, hoax, mating hedgehogs — were more absurd than the possibility that an alien spacecraft had used the location as a landing strip. I brushed the scarred moss with a finger, wondering again about the print on the hovertracks. Filled with a sudden urge to revolt, I called down in the forbidden Esperanto:

"Kiu vi estas? Kien vi iras? Ne iru en la gardenon!"

Along the street, other windows were raised. I waited for soldiers, searchlights, the paraphernalia of trouble. Distant voices mumbled, fell into silence again. Bored with the irony of it all, I retreated, sitting on the bed, shaking. How long could any of us keep this up? The pressure to ignore the date and begin a straightforward life was immense. At last I rose and fled, down to the living room.

Laura was ransacking a cupboard for a torch. "The animal is outside and it's talking to itself in Esperanto."

"I am inclined to doubts," I sighed.

"No, I heard it. Come on, we'll get it this time."

I trailed her through the kitchen and into the garden. Looming over the far wall was a giant head, tongue lolling in a steaming mouth, horns curling forward over oily lashes. Fireflies perched on its lips, burning the dusk like flecks of luminous spittle.

Laura hid her face in her hands. "It's grotesque!"

"No, I think it's a cow," I replied.

"What are you talking about? They were outlawed nearly twenty years ago. Is someone illegally breeding them?"

"I guess so. No other explanation. There'll be a reward if we catch it. Which of our neighbours could it be?"

We approached the creature warily, stepping lightly on the volcanic dust that coated the path. It seemed docile enough, watching us through the widest eyes I have ever seen. But before we reached it, a thunderous rhythm paralysed our resolve. Something new was coming closer, confusing the experience. Across the tracks, visible as a deeper absence of light, a gargantuan shape crushed the sky. It was the expanding woman, sheathed in stiff leathers, a Stetson pulled down over her brow, mounted atop her husband. She tugged the reins looped round his neck and he increased his pace. In one huge hand she swung a lasso.

Laura frowned. "I can't see any futurism in this."

"Nor I. We better leave them to it."

We crept back into the house and held each other in the little room under the stairs. She was close but cold.

"Laura, suppose the expanding woman is just fat? Not a myth at all, not a living urban legend, but a human being?

She may be the last genuine person on the planet for all I know. I mean, everybody is trying so hard to be what the century wants that we've lost ourselves. What if there is nothing mysterious about her great size?"

She draped her arm around my shoulder. "Don't give up now. Would it help if I came up with a scientific explanation? Perhaps she's a mirage, a woman whose image has been magnified by a convex lens of polluted air. It's all that benzene in our atmosphere."

I grimaced. There was less free oxygen available these days, a fact with one unexpected benefit. Fewer cell-damaging oxidisers had increased the life expectancy for anyone who survived the toxins. I already felt a chain of years bearing me down. To be born in a previous century is hard enough, a previous millennium is unbearable. I remained sullen and Laura lost patience, her nose rings signalling.

"What did you expect? Did you think ordinariness was ever a choice? How can we continue living simply when the date is futuristic? Blame the numbers, everybody has to work for them."

"But I'm overdosing on imagination!"

There was little more she could do for me. Yet some comforts thrive in complexity. The teevee can offer much.

In the spare bedroom, I wait by the window with the remote control. During a party last month it fell into a bowl of rum punch. It has never been quite the same since. It can now influence the hovertrains. I check my watch and raise the device, aiming it at the tracks. The Philadelphia to Waterloo express is due any minute now. It amuses me that after three thousand miles of transatlantic tunnel, a voyage can come to grief in an Ealing allotment. With the appropriate buttons I can make a train pause, fast forward or rewind. Tonight I intend to try an experiment, something truly futuristic. I will change channels.

(1998)

All Shapes Are Cretans

"All Cretans are liars,"
– Epimenides the Cretan

The college contains a chapel that is never visited. We were bored one night and decided to explore the secret recesses of the building. Wrather remembered a key on an obscure library shelf; I recalled a hammer in a dusty storeroom. His arguments were more persuasive. The lock turned with difficulty but the heavy door swung quietly on ancient hinges. I was surprised at our sense of exhilaration. The interior was not at all creepy. We lit the warped candles at the altar and waited for the flames to settle. There was no dust and very few cobwebs.

Wrather was not a religious man, at least no more than myself, but the strange simplicity of this chapel, its unambiguous mystery, induced in him an appropriate mood. We discussed a supreme being, solitary but perhaps not lonely, who had created everything, including feelings of isolation. We neither believed nor doubted the qualities of this deity, merely questioned what they were. Vastness in any category must be reduced to analogy, or no serious attempt to comprehend why it may never be properly understood can be made. I raised the subject of omniscience, the ability to know everything.

Smiling to himself, Wrather announced, "The shape

that a person creates during their whole lifetime simply by moving: imagine its complexity! But the mind of God can grasp this figure as easily as a human can visualise a circle or a square. That is omniscience."

I was too weary to nod my agreement. An abrupt tiredness had replaced my excitement. I stood and waited for him to recognise my condition, which bordered on paralysis. He stepped forward and the spell was broken. I was trying too hard to absorb the unnatural but not unwelcome ambience of my environment. I wondered if his assertion was original to him. From the way he winked in the magical gloom, I suspected not. We left the chapel and locked it behind us. I have never been back since, but we returned the key to its shelf. It is still there.

Shortly after this incident, Wrather was offered a position in a private university in Iráklion. He accepted less for reasons of an increased salary than the opportunity to escape our dismal climate. He preferred warmth to dripping eaves. Over there, it was possible to sleep on the roof under the stars. He welcomed this fact, though he had no intention of testing it. He did not want the fuss of a leaving party, so he deliberately argued with his colleagues during his final week. I was too busy to regret his departure. We had never been close friends. We had almost nothing in common.

My career remained undistinguished for the next ten years. I was neither satisfied nor bitter, but one morning I entered my office and found him sitting in my chair. He was engaged on a global lecture tour that included this college. He expressed disappointment that I was unaware of his schedule. I answered that I never took an interest in such events. In a nonchalant tone, he informed me of his importance. He had become famous in his field. Then with a false modesty that was unpalatable, he blushed.

"It was partly your doing," he said. "The breakthrough is all mine, of course, but you provided the clue."

"What have you discovered?" I asked.

He stood and gripped the edges of the desk. "The geometry of human morality. The shape a person makes over their entire lifetime determines the character of that person: good or evil."

I spoke truthfully. "That is remarkable."

"Indeed. The research involved was enormous. I selected people already renowned for travelling as my subjects. Even so, only those who had made records of their movements were of use. Precise data was often impossible to obtain. I could not hope to chart the exact shape of a lifetime without approximations. I settled for nodes at regular intervals along that figure. For instance, I might discover that Subject X had travelled from London to Buenos Aires and from there to Santiago, Bogotá, Kingston, Miami, Atlanta and New York. That shape is easily plotted. But it would be much more difficult to determine which streets in those cities had been walked down: which parks, theatres, shops and hotels had been visited. Those are the *epicycles* of the overall shape. The mind of God does not disregard them merely because they are insufferably small and complex."

"There is no solution to that problem," I said.

He chewed his lip. "But an attempt can be made

to achieve greater accuracy. Perhaps Subject Y is more meticulous than X. He has detailed the streets and buildings. He has noted every room he has entered. But still the motions he made inside those rooms, the shapes created as he walked from one side to the other, are unknown. Even Subject Z who *has* recorded these tiny voyages from wall to wall, across landscapes of carpet and floorboard, cannot possibly have itemised the even smaller journeys through space of every muscle, the involuntary twitchings and tics during sleep."

"A subject would have to be followed from birth to death," I replied with a snort, "or tagged with electronic sensors."

He grinned hugely. "That is exactly what will happen. For the meantime, my approximations must suffice. But the real revelation of my work is that behaviour is intimately linked with the geometrical qualities of the final shape. Good lives tend to have more curves; bad lives tend to have more corners. The weight of my evidence is substantial."

"What will you do with such information?"

"That is the main purpose of my lecture tour. I propose to experiment on *living* subjects, men and women still in the act of creating their lifetime shapes. By analysing the part of the shape they have already made, it should be possible to extrapolate it into the future, to complete the figure and work out now whether the person is good or evil."

I felt uneasy. "And what then?"

"The evil ones can be locked up before they do further damage."

"Monstrous!" I exclaimed.

"Ah, you are worried about the ethical consequences of a flaw in my reasoning. That is understandable. The actual area covered by a subject is irrelevant. The outline is what matters, whether it encloses a single room or several continents. I am aware that errors might exist in my research, but I am prepared to take the risk."

"For the benefit of the human race?"

"Absolutely. But now you must excuse me. I came to see you only to express my gratitude. A chance remark of yours inspired me to follow this line of investigation. Excuse also the pun. Would you like me to mention you as a footnote in my forthcoming book?"

I politely declined the offer.

He left my office with a swagger. I thought he was trying to insert as many curves into his walk as possible.

My career came to an end, gradually and naturally. I had always waited impatiently to turn into an old man and now my body and feelings were in fragile harmony. I remained aloof from society and its developments. Nobody troubled me at the college. The eaves continued to drip. The chapel remained unvisited. My memory of Wrather did not fade but it changed into something indistinguishable from the inanimate parts of the environment, the shadowed stones and smell of redundant varnish. I occasionally found traces of him in textbooks, the notes he had made in the margins.

It was my last day before retirement. I had not argued with my colleagues. A formal banquet awaited me in the refectory. As I hobbled across the lawns, I passed a figure hunched over the fountain. He was not drinking. He looked up and there was anguish in his face. His clothes were expensive but his gestures were poor. I paused and waited for him. When he approached, I warned him that my private world was sealed. I did not read newspapers. He nodded curtly. He seemed almost relieved that my reaction to his presence was so undramatic.

"I altered the workings of society," he said.

I shrugged. The statement seemed ludicrous. "What of it?"

"The effects have not yet reached this remote campus in an isolated country. But they will. Much of the world now lives under radical laws. You know what I mean. People with suspicious shapes are incarcerated. The experiment began with the lower classes. It was a great success in Iráklion. So it spread in two ways: across the globe and up the social strata. The middle classes are currently the new subjects. Even academics are scheduled for inclusion in the project."

"I have no opinion on this," I responded.

He raised a feeble hand. "Wait! Last week I finally analysed my own shape. There was a surprise awaiting me. It was evil! My shape is evil. Do you understand what this means? If I am evil, then so are my deeds. What is my greatest deed, the one that defines my life? The creation of the scheme! The link between morality and geometry."

"That link is therefore wrong?"

"Yes, because it is evil. The scheme is bad. This suggests that innocent people have been imprisoned."

"That must be a heavy psychological burden," I said.

"Not that. Worse. I have no idea whether I should be distraught or merely bewildered. My efforts have all been in vain, but if the scheme *is* bad, and my system flawed, then I am *not* evil and the scheme is right, in which case my shape *is* bad, which means that the system is flawed and I am *not* evil and…"

I broke his sentence with a wave. "An endless loop."

"And so I am bewildered."

I rubbed my chin. "You seem to be trapped in a variant of the Liar Paradox. A man confesses that everything he says is a lie. Is he speaking the truth? If so, then he is lying about being a liar."

"Epimenides invented that puzzle," he sighed.

"Possibly," I answered. "It has been attributed to many sources. It was even misquoted and misunderstood by St Paul in the Bible. The philosophical point was completely overlooked."

Wrather smiled thinly. "I know. Titus 1:12. We no longer need the chapel, do we? But the question is this: do I feel depressed or not? I can't work out my fate. There is no solution."

"None," I agreed. "Farewell."

I left him standing there in the sweat of his own indefinable self. A loose thread from my shirt tickled the nape of my neck. I pulled it out and cast it from me. The wind, soft and damp, took it away and dropped it on the lowest step of the refectory building. There was noise and lights behind the door. I glanced down at the shape made by the thread. It was a series of complex loops. The outline of a single morning or minute for a man or woman. For myself, the shape of years. I have never seen Wrather since. I sit in my chair without a care or cosine or tangent in the whole world.

(2001)

The Innumerable Chambers of the Heart

As she lay awake one night, Viviana suddenly realised that the tapping noises inside her radiator were deliberate messages. For several weeks she had assumed they were the products of unsatisfactory plumbing. Everything in the apartment creaked or gurgled or found some other means of audible protest. Now she attempted to make sense of the code. It was simple enough, for each letter of the alphabet was represented by a different rhythm. With short sequences of notes clustered into words, somebody was hoping to establish contact in this vast labyrinth of loneliness. There was desperation in the plea, but also, strangely, an element of humour.

The apartment block was the largest in existence. It dominated the eastern horizon of the city and blotted out the dawn. Not even the architects knew how many rooms it contained. Rival firms had worked independently on the designs, which were finally superimposed on each other and constructed simultaneously. It was still a mystery whether this had been a mistake or not. The geometry of each floor was confusing and inhuman. Passages intersected at unlikely angles. There were stairways that ended in blank walls. The exploration of the entire structure had never been achieved by any individual, though several had vanished into unknown volumes in the undertaking.

The authorities had moved the inhabitants of the central slums into the block in a single night. This difficult operation was illuminated by floodlights suspended from cranes. There had been a war. The residential areas were smashed and unsafe. The people converged on the gargantuan building, invading its emptiness and filling it with their own little voids, the dead emotions inside them. As they selected their rooms at random and switched on the lights, the round windows formed a growing constellation on the immense façade. But this pattern became mundane as it became more regular. None of the countless glass circles displayed any variation of brightness or colour.

Eventually the monotony was broken as the residents made efforts to individualise their apartments. Lampshades or curtains softened the glare as perceived from outside. Plants on windowsills filtered light with their leaves and tinged it green. Viviana had arranged mirrors in her room and in the corridors outside in a manner that uniquely personalised her own space. She had discovered an obscure skylight at the rear of the building, at the end of a passage that led nowhere. Her mirrors reflected and bounced the sunrise through the width of the hive and out again through her window.

Dawn now became a solitary red ray that slanted from her room down into the rubble of the city. She guided this beam with her silvered angles and her new duty made her feel special, but it did not cure the isolation. Only the messages from her radiator managed that. Somebody was knocking on the pipes in another room, hoping the sound would be carried along the hidden network of gargling conduits and deciphered by a potential friend. It was impossible to judge how far these rhythms had travelled to reach her, how many bends they had negotiated, how many times they had split along the branching pipes, rejoining at further junctions and finally bursting out with all the implacable joy of an acoustical trick in her tiny domain.

The messages were sent by a man. Viviana was certain of that even before she taught herself to interpret them. It should not really matter, but it was a relief. They were tinged with passion, subtle but powerful, in the same way that a casual shrug is adulterated with only a twinge of despair. The sender did not have professional poetry in his heart, for his phrases were often awkward, but he was definitely reaching out for a woman and her tenderness. She listened for several days before responding. The workmen who had constructed the apartments had lost many tools in the various rooms. At the back of a fitted cupboard, she found a heavy spanner. She swung it thoughtfully in her hand for a minute, aware she was about to cross a threshold. Then she struck her radiator sharply and waited. Her ears tried to follow the sound along the pipes, but they could not twist and diverge at such speed and they returned to the sides of her head.

The ensuing pause seemed to last longer than her senses could bear, but this was an illusion, for she remained hunched over the radiator. Then the single note returned. It was a replica of her own message, one of the simplest greetings. Are you there? Suddenly his poetry had been reduced to something plainer, more real, human and intense. Once again she wielded the spanner. Who are you? And now her heart, not her ears, raced along those pipes, as if her loneliness had fallen into arteries and veins to be dispersed throughout the organism of the building. But there was no real warmth in the arcane spaces that contained all the plumbing. Despite the lagging, those conduits were always chill, a fixed web that washed itself from the inside as part of its purpose, a solid representation of the cold water, its direction and destination.

Where are you? I am Viviana.

Yes, you are. That must be so. I am here.

You might be anywhere.

Same as you. I am looking for someone. For you.

For me? The search is over now.

Perhaps it is. Yes, it is.

This relationship of words without mouths, hopes without shapes, began to deepen almost immediately. She felt comfortable with this secret man, with his responses to her questions, sentiments and interests. They were in phase both intellectually and emotionally. It is impossible to fall in love at a distance: this fact is common knowledge. But what is the maximum range at which the real feeling can still work? After all, he might be in the adjacent room, or in one of the other apartments along her corridor. Perhaps their messages took an unnecessarily long route through the monstrous building simply to span a few metres of opacity, in the same way that an explorer at the mouth of a labyrinth may be separated from its terminal chamber by a single wall. But the loops and twists are not wasted if they are negotiated successfully, whether by foot or word.

Viviana did not fully believe the force of love is directly related to linear distance, but if this man *was* housed in her vicinity it would make the whole process both less and more mysterious. Less because it is conventional for love to develop among couples who are in physical proximity. More because the improbable nature of their meeting, via the plumbing instead of face to face in the corridor, indicated that destiny was a reliable phenomenon. Despite the ambiguity of the magic, she was satisfied. But she doubted he was close. The apartment block was simply too huge. Almost certainly he was far away, eclipsed by thousands of cells of huddled families. She suggested that they try to meet, and he agreed.

The difficulties inherent in this enterprise were beyond the dreams of the architects of the complex. Her apartment was one level beneath the highest floor, on the left or northern edge of the façade. She knew where she lived, but he could not even guess his own position. There were no windows in his room and no skylights in his ceiling. He often heard footfalls above and below his cell, and other human sounds behind his three walls. His door opened onto a narrow corridor that slanted steeply upwards and joined a wider passage. From this information, Viviana wondered if he dwelled near the very centre of the building. It was feasible. There were no obvious landmarks that they could use to pinpoint his location in relation to her own room. And there were no maps of the maze.

Once they tried to meet by leaving their rooms simultaneously and walking towards the heart of the block at a specified rate. The moment they moved from their radiators, all contact was lost. The unreasonable corridors led her past closed shops to a place she had no desire to visit, a courtyard filled with deserted stone benches and a crumbling fountain. This was where all senses of desolation came to rest. She was near the roof, because she heard the sour rain striking the ceiling, which was high in darkness. She had planned to descend, because the core of the hive lay below her original point, but the passages had ushered her their own way. Somehow she managed to retrace her steps, shaking with exhausted frustration as she collapsed on her bed.

The next time, they agreed to meet outside, by the main entrance. This should have been easier, but it turned out there was no such thing, or if there was, it was no larger or different from hundreds of other portals which graced, or disgraced, the length of the edifice. She stood in her best coat, utterly alone, like a woman at the edge of the world, her back to the concrete, with myriad windows above and to both sides. She waited. The ruined city, mostly levelled, stained rather than filled her gaze. Separated by enormous distances, sodium lamps on tall posts turned nothing of significance an unnatural yellow. From unknown regions, a faint sound of machinery saturated the damp landscape. Industry at play.

She returned to her room and sent him a desperate message. There was no answer, but later he signalled to her that he had waited at the designated spot, but had selected a different side of the building. Then he seemed to change his mind. Now he explained he had felt too ill to attempt the adventure. Viviana frowned. The mistakes in his behaviour, the discrepancies here and there, made her uneasy. A suspicion started to grow in her mind. He wanted to flirt but always pulled back before the point of commitment. He was afraid of something. First she thought it was his own emotions. Gradually she deduced it might have a less vague outline. It would be able to loom more alarmingly than an extreme change of heart. A scruple with a shadow.

They always announced themselves to each other with that same call. Are you there? On many occasions, his messages broke off in the middle of a sentence. She had assumed this was an undesirable property of the plumbing under certain conditions: a faucet might have been opened elsewhere, drawing his words with the water away from her, diverting his passion. Now she wondered if the true cause of the interruptions had a more anatomical explanation. Even when he did communicate with her for long periods without a pause, there was a furtive slackness in his rhythms that she had not noticed before. He was not striking his radiator with vigour as she did, but tapping it gently, almost with a muffled instrument, with desire that was in fetters. His adoration for her followed the rules of a forbidden game.

On the shortest night of the year, she was awakened by a metallic voice. She stumbled to the window and peered out. Loudspeakers on trucks roared up at the apartment block, huge chunks of fragmented sound reverberating from the cheap concrete and feeding back into the amplifiers, so that a wail rose in volume and made the landscape scream, which was a perfect substitute for the panic in the voice of the announcer. The building was being evacuated. Lines of people were already streaming from the numerous exits. Viviana dressed hurriedly and left her room. She had no idea which way to run, but soon chanced on a staircase which spiralled down. At the bottom she found a door that gave out onto the chaotic scene. She joined the mass exodus, tripping in her slippers. The residents stopped when they reached the location of their former homes. Then they turned and watched.

From snatches of gossip, Viviana worked out the reason for this extraordinary operation. The apartment block had apparently been raised directly over a caldera, a subterranean volcano. The seismologists at the university had calculated it was due to erupt. Most of the occupants had left their lights on, to ease their escape from the cells, and the whole edifice blazed like some ancient computer at the limit of its ability, horribly magnified. There was stasis and drowned stars. The crowd lingered until the cold weakened and the first pale light of dawn, blocked by the enormous domestic silhouette, changed the odour of the air. Viviana sniffed. Then all the windows snapped to grey. The generators in the basement had stopped working. The caldera had burst inside the building. First the lowest level of rooms filled with lava, the molten rock glowing and swirling behind the reinforced windows in too many variations of a drunken wink. Then the second level began to fill and the grey returned to red.

Relentlessly, one at a time, every cell in the block received the flickering liquid. The room which was last to be filled, through some trick of corridors and conduits, belonged to Viviana, though it was not the highest. When it was the only grey square left in the matrix of fire, the sun rose behind the building. The mirrors were still intact and her pane anticipated its own fate with a more ethereal red. The single ray that shot out pierced her directly in the forehead. She felt its dim warmth and an ironic smile altered her face. Then it died, for the lava had taken over. The caldera was exhausted. The molten rock cooled and hardened, and the walls of the structure, weakened by the pressure and heat, crumbled away. A replica of the apartment block was left in its place, slightly smaller but solid throughout, with all the furniture and fittings, the plumbing and its romantic possibilities, vaporised and trapped like love in gestures, embedded and mingled indistinguishably.

Viviana realised she was holding something heavy. It was the spanner. She must have instinctively snatched it up when she fled her room. She looked around. There were many people of every description. Families, couples and solitary individuals. She wandered among them. Her route was random, but she had a purpose. Somewhere amid all this humanity was her man, her untouched lover, the same person who had done so much to kill her loneliness and lift her hopes out of the truth of her situation. She would find him now. However long it took, she would meet him at last. Although she had no idea what he looked like, she knew exactly how to recognise him. She had their greeting call. Are you there? She had that, and he had a head. Ignoring the single men, concentrating on those who were with wives and girlfriends, she meticulously began to call for him.

(2001)

Pity the Pendulum

Sick, were you? Thought your agony was long? Nothing that happened to you was truly comparable to our ordeal. Certainly, they gave you a tour of the torture chamber, insisting politely but very firmly that you try out every device. Primitive machines on the whole, with few moving parts. No sense of time down there, in the flickering glare of the braziers; and too much pain to count the seconds. Completely unlike the dungeon where they cast you later. Cold reason under the blade of the pendulum and your life became a clock, simply because you were fortunate enough to avoid falling into the pit on your first foray into the darkness. Between these two extremes there was the sentence of death, the catching of your swooning body and its conveyance into the square room of iron and slimy stone. The idea of this was for you to awake and perish when you went wandering.

But you cheated them. And so did we. For us all it was mere chance, an accident, that we tripped *before* reaching the edge of the pit and so discovered its existence. Sprawling at length, chins on stone but lips and noses and brows resting on nothing, bathed in the chill updraught and odour of rotting fungus. That is how it was. And how it annoyed them! They prefer their victims to be stupidly unlucky, to confirm an inferiority in matters of mind; for these priests do not believe faith to be a quality of the heart. No! For them it is a symptom of pragmatism and the purse. Prisoners who demonstrate too much intelligence, whether abstract or purely instinctive, are thorns in their white lips or scorch marks on their pristine robes. But in truth their own brains are desiccated things, mummified in those ridiculous cloth pyramids that serve as hoods.

Luck is not a sign of cleverness, but taking advantage of it most surely is. That is how you insulted them. To defy the Inquisition is a small matter: it is expected of foreigners and heretics. To offend their sense of control is a major incident, a guarantee of causing those inhuman parasites sleepless nights. The ghouls reckon that true retribution for our imagined crimes should be divine; and when it cannot, which is the general case, then accidental and absurd; and if not that, then symbolic. But that is a poor third and they resent being forced to employ it. Thus the pendulum is kept locked away most of the year; if not quite forgotten then never mentioned, or alluded to only by hints at secret meetings, a clicking tongue or a wagging finger. Much more agreeable to talk about cosmic justice, dooms both causal and casual!

So we all went through the same procedure. I know you are still too disturbed to wonder exactly who we are. Let me simply state that we have witnessed more of subterranean Toledo than yourself. A diversity of characters, our little group, with men from many countries and professions. All are special heretics, deemed beyond even the remedy of cleansing fire. They burn their enemies at the stake as an act of mercy. Since they are destined for Hell, it is kinder to introduce them gently to the torment of flame, rather than suffering them to plunge straight from comfort to agony. But for us they have no pity at all: death by moral horror is worse than extinction by physical pain, however prolonged. Thus runs the dark theory of our Inquisitors. We have the pit and no audience, save the devils that stage our dooms. There are peepholes in many locations on the walls and ceiling of the dungeon. When all are in use a prisoner may feel no less bounded by eyes than bricks and iron; and the sensation is more grotesque.

Toledo is an ancient town, as you may appreciate too well, and its layout resembles a web shredded and re-knotted by a wild wind. The craggy surroundings hold it back from expanding far beyond its original limits. Before the Inquisition was established here, it was a model of cosmopolitan tolerance, but when they came they expelled the Jews and Arabs. All but one. An unknown architect, possibly of Moorish descent, was commissioned to construct this hidden world, a honeycomb of cells, chambers and passages deep below the streets. And so the Inquisition funded a model Hell in the direction of the real one. They caused their old machines to be carried down here and designed others still more horrible, inspired by the cloying shadows and rejection of surface values; but they did not know all the secrets of the architect. For every tunnel he was forced to build, he added a second for his own amusement; and for every dungeon, a way out, sometimes leading to a worse fate, for he was as warped as his masters. Then it was finished and so was he.

For the actual labour, the madmen of Toledo were rounded up and given tools. At the end, they were sworn to secrecy and scattered over the land. The architect was cast into the lowest dungeon and used to test its singular properties. First he was allowed to stumble around in the dark, but he knew about the pit and kept away. So they entered and drugged him and he awoke under the pendulum. The rats ate his bindings and he escaped. As with the rest of us, he was then pushed toward the hole by the contracting walls. The plates of iron are held in place by long bolts that pass right through the masonry. Here, on the other side, they are fitted with braziers, and when these are loaded with burning coals the heat is conducted along the bolt to the interior of the dungeon. Thus the hellish manner in which the plates, and the awful figures carved upon them, glow and hiss.

The walls are moved inward by means of a giant clockwork device. It is a slow process, not merely because cruelty delivers itself over long heartbeats, but due to the gross weight of the moving parts. The desire in the breast of the victim is always the same: to embrace the searing iron and scald himself senseless with the steam of his own boiling blood; and to continue that blackening clutch until the skin peels away and the fat bubbles out and the nerves and sinews ignite, snapping and curling like threads of cotton dangled over a candle. Still more: to press tight against the glowing metal until the skeleton itself is stripped free of flesh and must fall apart, waiting to be swept into the pit by the relentless walls. Anything other than to plunge into the hole alive!

But this voluntary death is never managed, for the reflexes always pull the body away from the heat; and the heretic will dance back, until there is no ground left, and on the edge he will totter and over the side he will sprawl into the phosphorescent pit, its cold circumference brushing his face with the stalks of monstrous fungi, the rats on their tiny ledges turning their backs on his grimace. The contempt of vermin is supposed to be the introduction to a new set of terrors, considerably worse but unknown, for even the Inquisition dares not speculate beyond this point. For them, there is water at the bottom, but whether deep or shallow, ancient beyond stagnation or replenished by underground currents from rivers or distant seas, remains a mystery; and rumours that broken spars from lost ships sometimes surface there, with the bubbles of drowning sailors, are discounted as the events of dreams.

Thus was the fate of the architect after he cheated the pendulum. Pity this poor device! For it is among the Inquisition's most symbolic dooms and yet it continues to fail to deliver the fatal stroke. How those ghouls must grind their teeth behind their hoods when they are forced to draw it back up and set the walls in motion! The braziers must be fired: coals must be conveyed from a bunker and stains on their white robes are inevitable. And the winding of the enormous spring! How tedious and annoying! No wonder they resort to this measure only at the final extremity, the ultimate stubbornness of an ungrateful heretic. And the architect had created all this himself: perhaps to mock them with the effort required to complete the procedure. Or else to mock, and save, himself. White lips? No, his were black and not at all thin. He shared a love of deviousness with his tormentors; but he felt neutral about devils. He had doubts about their existence and these grew as he was numbered among their brood. But now he was plummeting into his own abominable trap.

He tumbled through the nets of the tangled mushrooms, snapping stalks and sending clouds of spores into the air to swirl pointlessly. He acknowledged the rats and the manner in which they snubbed him; but he also passed something else, an item unknown to the Inquisitors, a large mirror fixed to one of the walls of the pit at an angle. In the light from above, which was only the unhealthy glow of the overheated walls, it resembled a pool of frozen blood, suspended in the act of spinning, a coin of death. He turned his head and briefly beheld another perfect circle, the entrance of a tunnel, also tinted red as if with insubstantial gore, but dimmer along its length, and though he understood the meaning of both mirror and tunnel they still astonished him, for the breaking of his mind under torture had made him forget his hopes and doubt his own cunning.

The plunging of his form continued, but his fall was broken by a real net and he bounced and settled, dazed and childlike, closing his eyes against the spores which drifted down and coated his damp forehead. It was peaceful here but safer to move. He swung himself over and jumped to the floor, jangling the bells that hung from the circumference of the net. Then he stooped under an arch into an adjacent chamber. This was his sanctuary. A chair and desk stood in one corner. A candelabra and a tinderbox was on this desk; and next to them a slim book bound in brass clasps upon which rested an inkwell and quill. Drawing a heavy velvet curtain over the arch, he groped his way to the chair. Here he caught his breath before daring to ignite the candles, which gave off a glow less ubiquitous but more universal, in simplicity and human warmth, than the burning dungeon walls.

He had anticipated his betrayal and his preparations for escape were elaborate, but it was essential to curb his impatience until the time was right. It was best to remain in this sanctuary for several hours, for the immediate aftermath of a plummet into the pit was the one time the hooded tormentors cared to examine its interior in any detail. Already the walls were being drawn back. The grating of the huge winding mechanism came to him through the ponderous walls like the decelerated laughter of some unimaginable chthonic beast entombed in the stone. Then he heard a faint spitting. The coals that provided heat to the metal plates and sculpted figures that adorned them were being extinguished with pails of water. Sooty, smoky work! When the dungeon was back to its original dimensions and the walls cooled to darkness, a trapdoor in the ceiling opened and a lantern was lowered on a cord.

Without flinching, his judges inspected the empty dungeon and noted the remains of the pitcher of water and wooden frame positioned directly beneath the pendulum, both crushed to charred dust. But still not wholly satisfied, they caused the lantern to descend further, toward the mouth of the pit, but not so far that any of its lateral beams were blocked, for a bright pit in a gloomy dungeon was too perverse a notion even for their depraved minds. In fact, when the lantern was still several feet above the circular chasm, they held it steady and took turns to peer into the forbidden depths. This rare treat lasted no more than a minute, for even the most fevered of religious imaginations can find little extra heresy in slimy walls and rippling water and the matted backs of diseased rats. They are secular abominations. Time to reel the lantern in and abandon the dungeon to forgetfulness, an easy task to accomplish, for it is a nullity rather than an object, an absence in the bowels of Toledo, and only when its sides are clamped together, the carved figures grinding in private embraces, perhaps seeking to melt and fuse together, may it be said to have true substance.

But the architect remained in his sanctuary, for it was possible the lantern would be lowered again by an Inquisitor more suspicious than his fellows. There is always one. Only when the excitement following the execution had started to become the smooth blandness of a seldom-shared anecdote might it be safe for the prisoner to attempt his escape. Until then he took up the quill, dipped it in the ink and opened the book of blank pages. For the eyes of those who came after, he told his story, explaining how he designed this dungeon for his masters and then became its first victim, but not before secretly adding a way out. He wrote with careful strokes; and by the time he had finished, the long candles had burned to half their length. He blew them out, pulled back the curtain and fumbled his way across the base of the pit. The net was above him. He passed under it, avoiding the bells. On the far side, there was a shallow groove in the wall of the pit, wide and deep enough to accommodate his starved body. Reaching out, he grasped the first iron rung.

Taking a deep breath to steady his trembling arms and legs, he began climbing, slowly and painfully but with a rising joy, passing the net and feeling the thick cord of its edge rubbing against his back, setting the bells swaying but too gently to make them chime. Every fifth or sixth rung he paused for a rest. Then he reached the level of the mirror and eased himself into the mouth of the tunnel, crawling faster and faster toward freedom. If an Inquisitor now chanced to open the trapdoor and lower a lantern, he would be convinced the architect was not just a heretic but a sorcerer, for it would appear the man was crawling vertically *down* the inside of the pit, head first but not quite like a fly, for it was his elbows and knees which adhered impossibly to the stone. This shocking vision would persist until the architect reached the end of the tunnel and passed through the surface of the water and vanished without a bubble. But the Inquisitors were all in bed and saw nothing and their nightmares were insignificant.

What next happened to the architect must be envisaged with less precision, for now he found himself among vaults of peculiar shape and ventilation shafts that wormed through the earth in such convoluted figures that the breath which they issued in horrible gasps and sighs was at least one week stale. These vaults led to others or to passages and stairways until a labyrinth was born through the simple act of stumbling onward. Many of these routes led to dooms or frustrations and all were completely dark. Nor would it have been helpful to take the candles with him, for inflammable gas had leaked down from sewers and the deep coal bunkers and settled in pockets; and a naked flame was likely to ignite them and collapse the roof fatally on his bid for freedom.

First the vaults would be empty, but in time the occasional object might appear to stumble against, a lonely barrel or wheelbarrow, then items at more frequent intervals and doors between the connecting chambers, and a general feeling of moving closer to the level of real life, a slackening of oppression, a lessening of imagined weight. Then the first faint glimmer of natural light, painful to eyes nourished for so long on shadows, and the first taste of fresh air in the nostrils, still clogged with dried blood, and cobwebs in corners and footprints in the thick dust, ancient but human. Now coffins on strong shelves of stone and the ornate sculpture of a crypt for the wealthy. Shreds of rotting tapestry and more vaults beyond. This channel: a crack through the sundry worlds of the underground city.

Numerous wine cellars, dull bottles full of untasted, strange sediments nestled in mouldy racks from floor to ceiling. After these, a room with glass walls containing dead plants in terracotta pots, but choked on the outside by gigantic weeds; a long forgotten hothouse which has subsided into the earth. Then flooded rooms and stairs which sag with every step, the light growing brighter and brighter. Finally the ground floor of an abandoned house near the edge of the city; and out into the streets and the dawn. But whether the architect departed Toledo or remained, survived and flourished, or was destroyed by bad luck or arrogance, perhaps stabbed by a robber before the sun fully rose, is unknown. The Inquisition was not responsible for his demise: that is all we may safely conclude.

How many other victims followed his full destiny is also a mystery. There might have been a dozen or twice that. The dungeon with the pit was used once a decade on average, for such was the frequency of special heretics in Toledo during those vile centuries. As for the lesser heretics, they were still merely crisped at the stake in a public square at the rate of one a week. A swallowing by the abominable hole, whether by stumble or closing walls, was always an experience reserved for an elite of spiritual villains; and yet there must have been *some*. The net came as no surprise to the architect but to them it was probably the most astonishing event of their lives. Yet they did not panic. They found the arch and the candles and the book and read the story within. They followed its instructions and climbed the ladder and crawled down that other tunnel and passed into the labyrinth of vaults. Many probably chose the wrong route here and perished in ways beyond conjecture, but a few surely made it to the surface again.

Then came a dark age over Toledo, but it was the kind that is welcome to ordinary men and women, for it was a temporary lull in the power of the Inquisition, an eclipse of darkness, a veiling of horror, which though not as wholesome as the creation of light is yet a relief to threatened hearts and brains. The Inquisition did not lose authority or influence, nor was there a lack of funds or recruits, nor a reduction in political support from ambitious merchants and cardinals. It was a stifling of *will*, as if a black cloak was cast over a black flame. The

Inquisitors grew decadent, interested in material pleasures, men of the flesh. They turned corpulent, indolent. They cared less about punishing blasphemy and more about consuming food and wine. The torture implements were employed infrequently; burnings became rare. And the dungeon for special heretics with its pit, pendulum and trickery was forgotten. It lay neglected beneath the other cells, the narrow passage which twisted down to it blocked by an enormous scarlet clock, a gift from a corrupt prince or duke.

The centuries passed and the horror was diminished, if not extinguished, and the lowest dungeon, always unknown to most, became unguessed by all, though some dim memory was passed on as whispered rumour among the highest levels of the order, but doubted to the point of disbelief. Then there was political upheaval in a foreign land. Europe was shaken by one man and a vast army was baptised in the blood of revolution. The old regimes were threatened and the Inquisition feared for its existence. First nervous about the future, then deeply insecure, finally hysterical, it clung to life by reawakening its traditions. Burnings suddenly increased, albeit in private courtyards rather than public squares; and the renewed demand for victims was almost insatiable. Rust was scraped off the implements, the boots and screws and claws, and the red mist of blood boiled into steam by pokers drifted up the alleyways at nights and condensed on misshapen windows.

How it was that the passage to the lowest dungeon was rediscovered and the pendulum polished and sharpened, and the clockwork mechanism wound tight, and the braziers loaded with coal, has not been documented. Nor was it revealed to me at my trial. I was condemned for voicing my belief that all men are equal, the doctrine of the enemy power. I could not protest, for I was guilty. At political meetings I wore the cockade, the badge of dissent or treason, depending on your perspective; but I defied my judges to the last. I cried out that even the angels of heaven should be overthrown, for they too were aristocrats! My tormentors in their musty robes, no longer white but stained dark grey by soot and sweat, trembled visibly at this outburst. Yes, they labelled me a special heretic. So I was carried past the toppled red clock and into the subworld of grander and more horrible cogs and springs and slow motions to measure moments.

There is no need to detail my sufferings. They were the same as yours. I avoided the pit, escaped the pendulum and finally endured the closing, stifling walls. Into the pit I plunged. I did not shriek: I was beyond expression. I was no longer Juan Segismundo Rubín, if indeed I had ever been, but a limp puppet liberated from a cruel play by a twist of vicious mischief. I fell with the ruddy glow above me, anticipating a long drop. Then I passed the mirror and landed on the net. Because I am quick of brain I guessed much at once. I realised this was not another ruse of the Inquisitors but something opposed to them. The bells on the circumference of the net had been cunningly tuned to mimic the sound of splashing water. I did not lie there for long but jumped to the floor of the pit. I discovered the arch, the sanctuary, curtain, desk, candles and book. I read and understood all. I waited for the lowering of the lantern and its withdrawal. Then I groped my way to the bottom of the ladder.

But now my hope was taken away again, for my fingers touched only the stubs of the lowest iron rung. The secret ladder was gone! It had turned to rust and flaked away over the damp centuries. My only route to freedom now existed as powder around my feet. I gnashed my teeth and wailed. I shook the bells violently in my frustration and the lantern came down a second time. This brought me to my senses and I crouched very still and waited with shallow breath. A full hour passed before the light was drawn back up. I inched my aching body across the floor to the sanctuary. Here I collapsed on the chair and wept quietly. Then I began laughing, for I was not insensitive to the irony of the situation. Eventually I exhausted myself with these exertions of despair and fell asleep.

Strangely I awoke refreshed and determined to survive. I remembered that a few lumps of mouldy bread and meat had also been caught by the net, like deformed insects on a giant spider's web. The previous prisoners of the dungeon above had been fed by their captors and clearly some of these morsels always found their way into the pit, perhaps hurled there in disgust by the victim, for the bread was extremely poor quality and the meat was heavily seasoned almost to the point of inedibility, doubtless to inspire a raging thirst as part of the torture; or else they had been kicked accidentally into the hole by the prisoner while he roamed free in the darkness at the beginning of his incarceration. But this food was my own, for I had no immediate predecessors, and the closing walls had pushed it into the pit, cooking the meat and charring the bread to toast in the process. I crept back out, retrieved these leftovers and treated myself to a loathsome feast.

Driven to extremes by my situation I reserved a few crumbs of food as bait for the rats. They came and I caught one. I hesitate to confess how I consumed it. Raw meat is not a delicacy in my culture. I reserved a fragment of this supper to entice yet more rats, and so on. By pressing my tongue to the inner walls of the pit I drank more than enough water to satisfy my needs. My health was by no means perfect and I developed a fungal infection that irritated my skin with excessive intensity, but I welcomed this as a distraction from the monotony of my furtive existence. Whole days were passed in scratching myself from the soles of my feet to the crown of my head, though there were always regions beyond my reach. As if by instinct I saved the candles and dwelled in thick gloom. Probably I feared to inspect what lay under my fingernails.

I now believe I dwelled in this abominable but somehow heroic manner for a few weeks at most, though at the time it seemed a span closer to years, before I was given the opportunity to play the host to an unexpected guest. I heard a demented screaming from above and it was familiar because an identical sound had once issued from my own lips. A secret door opened in the walls of the dungeon and a new prisoner was cast inside. The door closed with a groan. I wanted to call up to this latest victim but it was very risky to reveal my presence too early. Ears may be pressed to peepholes as well as eyes. The fellow wandered about and avoided falling into the pit. When he fell asleep they came again with drugged food. He awoke and consumed this and fell into a stupor. When he recovered he discovered himself strapped directly below the pendulum. This he also avoided and so they closed the walls together. The familiar pattern.

He plunged into the pit, struck the net and settled there. I emerged from my sanctuary, reached up and pressed the palm of my hand over his mouth. Then I helped him down and led him into the extra chamber. The tinkling of the bells finally ceased and it sounded as if a pool of agitated water was calm again. While we waited for the dungeon to be expanded back to its maximum size and for the lantern to descend, I shared the secrets of the architect with my new friend. I explained the design of the pit. Its true depth was fifty feet but its apparent depth was closer to three hundred. Just under one third of the distance from the lip to its base, fifteen feet down, lay the mirror and the mouth of the horizontal tunnel, the passage unknown to the Inquisitors. It was the length of *this* tunnel that gave the impression of a dizzying vertical distance to any observer from above, because they were really looking into the mirror, which reflected the interior of the supplementary passage at right angles. The arrangement of the peepholes in the ceiling was not absolutely symmetrical. The one above the mouth of the pit was slightly offset. Thus while it appeared to any Inquisitor that his line of sight was perpendicular to the shaft, he was actually able to stare only into the mirror, and that in relative darkness; and this optical trick was sufficient to satisfy the entire order that the pit was absolutely lethal.

We remained together in the sanctuary, eating rats and scratching each other, in an intimate but chaste fashion, until we were joined by a third victim. Because of the political situation in the upper world, the Inquisition was growing frantic. It was more eager than ever to blame its troubles on men with ideas. There was a glut of special heretics. Again the secret door in the dungeon was opened. Stumble, pendulum, hot walls. He was a big fellow and I thought the bells on the net might jingle themselves longer and louder than any water could. But the lantern was lowered and raised in short order. Our new companion was strong and his intake of rats was enormous. Feeling the power in his shoulders I began to toy with an astounding notion. I shared this idea reluctantly, fearing it would be greeted with derision, but it was received with cautious enthusiasm. It was an authentic chance. We had hope again.

There are certain fiestas in this land of Spain, which is a kingdom of performers and acrobats, which involve men making towers and pyramids with their bodies. They stand on each other's shoulders. There is skill and stamina and determination to succeed; and these displays take place in town squares or in wide courtyards. Never in a pit. But there is no rule to prohibit prisoners from balancing in a like manner until the highest man may reach up and grip the lip of the horizontal tunnel and pull himself into it. And even if such a rule existed, who better to break it than a troupe of special heretics, acrobats of the intellect? I had already contemplated taking down the net and turning it into a rope, but what was there to cast at? The mirror would not support my weight and the mouth of the escape tunnel was free from projections. The rope could not catch on anything. No, the only way was to send up a man first and have him lower it down for the others. The lightest would be first; and as more joined him in the tunnel, so more arms might be employed to pull up the heavier men.

This plan became the guiding principle of our lives. The distance from the base of the pit to the mouth of the tunnel, as may be calculated from the measurements I quoted earlier, was approximately thirty-five feet. Seven men were enough to reach that height. We had three; soon we were four. We prayed for others. The rate of executions increased. Special heretics almost became common. Not every prisoner cast into this dungeon took his place as one of our number. Several did not escape the swinging blade. Then we pitied the pendulum less, because it wept tears for itself, saving us the bother, and these tears were of blood; or so we supposed. The hunks of bisected torso were reclaimed by the Inquisition and the crescent of steel was hastily blessed, then drawn up. We remained profoundly silent at these times, though not once did anyone peer over the edge of the pit, or even approach it within a dozen steps.

We continued to dine exclusively on rats, but some of us deliberately ate less than others. We wanted a gradation of strength in our human tower. The fellow at the bottom would be expected to bear an enormous amount of weight without buckling. He gorged himself while the rest of us ate in relative moderation or starved ourselves to varying degrees. A fifth and then sixth recruit was added to our company. This last was an inhabitant of Corsica who brought us news of the situation in Europe. The man who was rampaging across the continent, overthrowing regimes and looting museums, was one of his countrymen. Even Toledo was threatened with invasion. We rejoiced at the thought of the destruction of the Inquisition and also at the realisation that one more prisoner was all we required to make good our escape.

When he came, we would lose no time. Turning a net into a rope is easy. So too the rest of the plan. The strongest man lifts the next strongest onto his shoulders, while the third climbs up them and takes his own position, ready to receive the fourth, who has higher to climb to reach *his* shoulders and wait for the fifth. The sixth was myself. The newcomer, rope looped about his shoulder, persuaded of the excellence of our scheme and wishing to contribute to our fiesta of liberation, climbs up all of us, one at a time, his fingers jabbing our uncomplaining throats and mouths, to my shoulders. Here, stretching up, the lip of the tunnel is just within his reach. With a mighty effort he pulls himself up and enters the mouth of the passage, then turns and lowers the rope to me. Joining him I help anchor the rope for the next man down, and he helps for the next, and so on, until all seven of us are inside the tunnel.

Along it we must crawl to the circular blue curtain that gives the appearance of being a pool of water from a distance, especially when it ripples in a breeze from one of the ventilation shafts behind it. As we pass under it we may discern that the cloth is really double; that there is a second curtain which might briefly reveal itself if the first parts in too strong a current of air, and that on this other drapery is painted, with formidable skill, a few broken spars and bursting bubbles. Beyond this the labyrinth of vaults and passages and stairways, and if luck is with us, emergence in the ruined house and the clean air of Toledo, on the Paseo de la Ronda, at the edge of the city, beyond the smokes, and a short walk across the bridge of Saint Martin over the River Tajo, and freedom and open country and wayside inns and wine and music and señoritas, all the best things we have missed, and sunlight and the stars and friendship and the celebration of natural and simple pleasures.

Yes, we waited for the man who would make all this possible. We waited; and then you arrived. You were the seventh, our saviour. You were silent when they deposited you in the dungeon. Clearly you had swooned during your trial, perhaps as the sentence was uttered. Your body was carried down the obscure passage and abandoned in this miniature hell. The robes of the Inquisitors were no longer white. Too much exposure to coal dust, soot, blood and sulphur had stained them the colour of a cesspit. With the wars raging around the city, the hysteria of the order had reached its peak. Like a fever it was due to break, but in the meantime the sheer number of heretics to be dealt with, both normal and special, left no time to clean their garments. When you awoke you wandered about. What else might you do?

First you completed two circuits of the dungeon, going one way and then the other. I suspect you felt a strange relief you were not within a *tomb*. Next you lurched directly across the middle of the chamber. We reasoned this from your footsteps and prayed for you to fall into the pit, but you stumbled just before the edge and discovered it. We dared not call up. Then you did something that nobody before you had ever attempted. You dislodged a piece of masonry from the inside of the pit and let it drop. The stone bounced and rattled between the walls, making the hole sound deeper than it was. It struck the net and set in motion the bells that chime like water. A trapdoor opened in the ceiling and the beam of a lantern flashed down. The Inquisition wanted to check if you had fallen. You had not. The trapdoor was closed.

Convulsed with horror, you crawled back to the relative safety of the wall. After a time you fell into an exhausted sleep. Then we heard them enter through the secret door and leave the drugged food and water that is one of their most tasteless tricks. You consumed it and under the effect of the unknown substances you did not feel them return and manipulate your body. They strapped you to a frame and lowered the pendulum ever so slowly over you. Not once did you scream; not once did we cry out any words of encouragement. We heard the slide of the blade through stale air, more delicate and relaxing than it ought to be. But you were not relaxed. At this time we knew nothing about your character. Would you escape the blade or would you be cleaved in twain? We hoped for the former but we had seriously depleted the number of rats in the preceding weeks. And they were the only way out of the bindings that held the victim to the wooden frame. Sharp little teeth.

But you were as resourceful as us and there *were* enough rats. You smeared the remnants of your food over the bandages, as had we, and the rodents gnawed you free just in time. Now came the final stage of your imprisonment and a considerable amplification of our hopes, for no man had ever eluded what was to happen next. The pendulum was drawn up by unseen hands in conjectured disgust. The coal bunkers were plundered and the braziers loaded with fuel. A flame was puffed into a blaze with bellows. The heat was transmitted along the bolts to the metal panels on the inside of the dungeon. Gradually these grew brighter and your place of incarceration became visible to you. Then you noticed the small gap running along the base of each wall and you guessed that this was to enable them to move together without jamming on the stone floor. For despite the slime, the clockwork mechanism was not powerful enough to overcome *that* amount of friction.

Here we must mention the fact that the Inquisitors regularly dusted the sculpted figures on the metal plates with sulphur. Thus they glowed in a more hellish fashion than they might otherwise have done, serving as a prediction of that realm where the souls of the prisoners were shortly to find themselves for eternity. One consequence of this that the Inquisition had not anticipated was the fumes that rose up from the walls and passed through the peepholes and swirled among the torturers above. Sulphur fumes are toxic and doubtlessly contributed in a small way to the dulling and disordering of their wits, so that they were just a little less capable of guessing the existence of survivors in the pit itself. And yet in no way did this mean we might reduce our precautions and call out to you not to be frightened.

As the walls moved closer, you lurched around in a

dreadful panic. The heat seared your flesh and eyes. You endured this pain for as long as you imagined yourself capable. Then you decided to sacrifice yourself to the cool waters of the pit. You tottered on the rim and looked down. Our hearts rejoiced! You were coming to us! The last section of our tower was ready to jump into our hands. But something else happened. Our plans were spoiled. A freak accident and a misunderstanding was the ruin of us. The stone you dislodged earlier and let fall had shattered the mirror. The real base of the pit was visible to you. This should have filled you with joy. You should have greeted our presence with silent jubilation and leapt in willingly. But we made a mistake. You recoiled in terror.

We were frustrated by this circumstance but we shrugged it off. You would have to come to us one way or another, for when the dungeon was completely closed there was no place to stand. We knew this. You did everything within your limited power to postpone this moment as long as possible. A few minutes ago, you had been willing to throw yourself into the pit of your own free will; but now only the unstoppable pressure of scalding metal would ever accomplish what we desired. You shrieked but the walls did not pause. Our hearts swelled with ecstasy. One more step and you would be ours! The missing piece of the tower would belong to us. With the rope in your hands you would climb up to the hidden tunnel and help us to also reach that level. Together we would test our further luck in the labyrinth, where we might perish by taking a wrong turn, quickly or slowly, depending on what doom we encountered, or else pass through safely to freedom and happiness and life, *the most protracted doom of all*. But this irony troubled us not.

Now there was no space on which your feet might balance. The closing walls had passed over every inch of solid floor. There was only the pit left. You were in the very process of beginning to fall. Gravity had claimed you. It remained only for your body to gather velocity in a downward direction. Although you had not yet started to move, the balance of forces working on you had changed. One blink of an eye and you would be committed to us. Surely it was too late for our hopes to be denied? How could such an inconceivable thing happen? But it did. There was a discordant hum of human voices! There was a loud blast as of many trumpets! There was a harsh grating as of a thousand thunders! The fiery walls rushed back! An outstretched arm caught your own as you fell, fainting, into the abyss. It was the arm of General Lasalle, or to give his full name, Antoine Chevalier Louis Colbert. The French army had entered Toledo. The Inquisition was in the hands of its enemies.

All very well for you, but for us a disaster! They carried you out and took care of you. But they did not hear our cries. They sealed the entrance to the dungeon with explosives. We hoped you might alert your new friends to our plight but clearly you did not. Nobody came to rescue us. We are still here. Possibly you were too traumatised to ever speak again. Or else you do not believe we are men. Yes, this second option is more likely. When you voluntarily approached the pit to hurl yourself in and looked down, what did you see? What was it that drove you away, screeching? We were impatient for you to join us. We had already taken down the net and converted it into a rope. To save you from breaking your neck, to ensure you a landing no less soft than if it was still in place, we clustered together, all six of us, and held up our arms to catch you. *That* is what you saw when you gazed over the rim. With the mirror broken, you observed the pit as it really was; but this shattering of one illusion merely created another.

Instead of an abominably deep hole with water at its bottom, you beheld a shallow chasm full of the grasping hands of tormented souls or demons. Impossible for you to judge which. It must have seemed we were rising up to claim you, or else that the sinners were stacked thousands deep all the way down to Hell. Our excited faces were like masks of menace, our welcoming smiles and winks like cruel or hungry leers. We were not men to you but ghastly apparitions. Now we are simply *unmentionable* memories. The dungeon has been silent ever since. We no longer scream or weep. In the sanctuary under the arch, at the desk, I lit the stubs of the remaining candles and with the last of the ink wrote this account on the handful of blank pages left in the architect's book. It will never be read. The final flame is about to flicker out and so I now bring this story to its perpetually dark, famished, lunatic, but logical conclusion.

(2003)

333 and a Third

"There are no spare rooms left."

It was a familiar reply and Boz turned on his heels but the landlord reached out and clasped his shoulder with an enormous hand.

"You can have the cupboard under the stairs."

Boz hesitated a moment and then followed the landlord over the threshold of the door into the lobby of the building. It was the best offer of the past month, a month of walking the streets and ringing doorbells. Space was at a premium in this city right now and available rooms were scarcer than unicorns. The landlord turned on the lights in the stairwell and pointed upwards.

"It's near the top. I shouldn't really rent it out, but I feel sorry for young men in your position. There are three hundred and thirty three apartments in this block, so I guess we can just call yours number 333 and a third."

"I'm not expecting visitors or mail," said Boz.

The landlord shrugged and they ascended the flights of steps together, puffing hard by the time they reached their destination. Boz peered at the door of the cupboard. It was low and small and he would be required to crouch to pass through it, but he was grateful for any form of accommodation, however cramped. Everything in his life had worked out fine apart from not having a home. He had money in his wallet and a full belly but no place to stay. This one problem soured all the good things.

"I'll draw up a contract and you can sign it tomorrow. Here's the key."

Boz accepted the tiny metal object and inserted it into the lock. The landlord had already wheezed off down the stairs and was gone before he opened the door. The cupboard contained a few blankets and a pillow. At the rear were an old vacuum cleaner, a dozen plastic bags and two large cardboard boxes. With a heavy sigh he squeezed into this space and fell asleep. The deep exhaustion of more than four weeks living rough, cold and damp and an easy target for violent drunkards, had caught up with him.

He woke slowly. It was pitch dark and his muscles were aching. He thought about the city and the new building regulations which made it impossible to construct new housing. The authorities were determined to stop the metropolis sprawling outwards any further, nor did they want the skyline encroached upon more than it already was, so building higher was no solution. Boz understood this desire to preserve the city the way it was. It was a beautiful city, as cities go, with courtyards and patios and balconies and roof gardens.

Not having enough space in the cupboard to stretch out at full length, he had curled up in a foetal position, legs hugged to his chest. Now he had terrible cramps. He decided to move the vacuum cleaner, bags and boxes out into the corridor for the remainder of the night. He could always replace them in the morning before his landlord returned. As he moved these objects, he was astonished to discover that they concealed an opening to a tunnel. A faint glow came from its depths and he felt a light breeze on his face.

"How far back does it go?" he wondered.

There was only one way to find out. Crawling on his hands and knees he proceeded down the tunnel. The glow broke apart into a number of individual specks of light like stars and the tunnel itself grew wider and taller. Soon he was able to stand and walk. Wherever he was headed, it was not into the building. This was not a service duct that wove between clusters of water and gas pipes, bundles of insulating fibre and electrical fuse boxes. He savoured the distant scents of honeysuckle, cooking and wine.

The sides of the tunnel were no longer bricks but mossy stones and worn railings. The ceiling had vanished. Somehow he was in a street, the street of a city not his own, a city equally as beautiful, with a castle on a crag and tall houses clustered below it. The stars were lamps on poles. He passed under an archway and impulsively resolved to remain here, not to go back, not that he could ever retrace his steps because he had already forgotten the way he had come. This city was no worse than the one he had left and his wallet was bulging. First he would find a proper place to live.

"There are no spare rooms left."

Although he expected this reply, Boz did not turn away immediately. He asked the same question he had asked all the other landlords.

"Don't you have a cupboard under the stairs?"

The landlord licked his lips and hesitated before

nodding and leading the way up the flights of steps to the designated space. Boz heaved a sigh of relief. He had found his escape route after another month of rough living. This city was as pleasurable as the one before it, but its charms and opportunities could not be fully appreciated by one who had no place to rest his head at night. Once again homelessness was the fly in the ointment, or something larger than a fly, a crow or vulture.

"I shouldn't really rent this out, it's against regulations, but I know how hard it is for young people these days. I sympathise, really I do."

Boz accepted the key and opened the door. Now his search was over, he was able to relax and enjoy his memories of his brief stay in this unknown metropolis. The first thing to delight him was the discovery that the inhabitants spoke the same language as he did, though with an alluring accent. In return he appeared exotic to them. This city was identical in size to the one he had known but the layout was changed, as if the buildings and streets had been shuffled and replaced on the landscape in a different order.

Boz had a special fondness for the districts nearest the river, the stone bridges and restaurants festooned with coloured bulbs, the steep cobbled lanes and little squares full of musicians and dancers. And that girl on the scooter. But always the fact he lived nowhere spoiled everything. He had even tried to get a job where he might be allowed to sleep safely on the premises, in a kitchen or warehouse, but that was not acceptable behaviour here. Without a place to return to, he was nowhere. His life was on hold, romances had to be abandoned, all his future was suspended until he found a room.

No rooms were to be had. Now he had been given a cupboard instead, but he could hardly be expected to bring a girl back to a cupboard. It was not a home at all, but it represented another chance elsewhere. His wallet was still mostly full, he had spent only a fraction of his savings, and he still had hope. As soon as the landlord was out of sight, he moved the vacuum cleaner, bags and boxes into the corridor.

The opening was there, complete with the faint glow, the glow of the merged streetlights of a third city. He crawled into the tunnel, stood when the ceiling was high enough and began running. Soon he was running down a street, biting scented air. A song emerged from an open window above him, a girl brushing her hair in the moonlight. He slowed his pace, sauntering along with his hands in his pockets, whistling her melody.

A man clutching a newspaper came the other way. Boz stopped him and asked, "Where might I find a place to live in this city?"

"You'll be lucky," replied the man. "There's nothing much here."

To confirm this assertion he showed the newspaper to Boz, opening it to the section where landlords advertised properties. The page was blank. Boz sighed and the man tried to cheer him up by saying, "You have an interesting accent. The girls will love that."

"Not if I have no place to go."

The man shrugged and moved on and Boz went the other way, appreciating the sights and magic of the city, even while another part of him was downcast. Could he meet a girl and move in with her? That option seemed dishonourable and was probably impractical. Better for him simply to start searching now, ringing the doorbells of apartment blocks. If he did not find a room he might still find a cupboard under the stairs, an escape route to the next city. And this process could continue until he ran out of money and cast his empty wallet into the gutter.

The night passed uneasily. The days that followed it passed in the same manner. He grew to know and love this new city but he was never established here. There was wine and food, music also, and a girl. But nothing stable. During daylight hours he enjoyed living, being in the city, but in the evenings he searched for a room. He was always on the move, tense, without a base, aimless, unable to relax.

"No spare rooms? What about a cupboard under the stairs?"

At last he found one and he said goodbye to this city, another month of his life, as he tramped up the steps. The vacuum cleaner was there and the other items too and he moved them out of the way and plunged into the tunnel. The tunnel became a street, the street of a city with yet another reshuffling of buildings and squares. Already he knew it was as full as the previous two. He could hear the city breathe, a breathing composed of the flexing of the floorboards in every room, all occupied. He knew that another month of searching lay in wait, the growing of more stubble in shadows while he waited for morning and the warming rays of the rising sun.

He called to a girl on a street corner, "Excuse me, Miss,

but do you know…"

Of course she did not. Suddenly he was overwhelmed by a vision of his destiny. He saw himself passing through city after city without settling in any of them, searching for and finding cupboard after cupboard under a sequence of nearly identical stairways. A future of crawling into tunnels, hurrying down them until they became streets, and then a snatched form of life, taking pleasure between slabs of anxiety, closed doors and rejection. He checked his wallet.

"I have enough money to last another forty or fifty cities. I won't stop yet, I'll keep going as long as I can. If I don't find a place to live, I'll just keep looking for the tunnel to the next city. When I have only enough money left to pay for my funeral, I'll climb the highest tower of the city I'm in, wherever that tower might be located, and I'll throw myself off. That way I'll have rest and respectability in death if not in life!"

He struggled to open his eyes. Where was he? A gloomy chamber with a pungent odour, some sort of cleaning fluid. Had he found a room at last, a real room, a home? He was naked and stretched out on something hard, not a bed. As his eyes opened fully, the memories settled back slowly in his juddered brain. Many cities, many streets and restaurants and girls. He had been searching for somewhere to live for years. He had explored dozens of cities that were variations of just one city, so many that he had lost count.

There were other people in the chamber with him. An ache throbbed through his bones, fading and then suddenly flaring up, the pain concentrated at a point on his chest. He remembered what he had done, the final moment of despair, the sensation of falling. And yet clearly he had survived. Was he in a hospital? All those wonderful things, his experiences, degraded by the fact he had no roots, and now this? Was he going to be stuck in a hospital for weeks or months? He blinked and waited for his eyes to adjust properly.

The men standing over him did not look like doctors. They wore heavy cloaks and very tall black hats that almost scraped the ceiling. One held his wallet, another was clutching two electrodes in gloved hands, electrodes connected to a machine that hummed and spat in the corner. Boz felt there was an association between this machine and the burning sensation in his chest. The man holding the wallet nodded down at him and said:

"Pleased to meet you, we are your undertakers. You have just enough money to pay for a funeral, we've counted it, a single note and a few coins, it comes to 333 and a third crowns altogether, which is exactly our fee. But there's a slight problem, a minor hitch, and we couldn't just get on with the burial. So we brought you back to life to discuss something with you, to make a proposal. We all think it's a neat solution to our difficulty."

"Tell me," gasped Boz. His words emerged thin and dry and his efforts to sit up came to nothing. He knew he would never feel more alert than this ever again, but it did not seem to matter. The reply to his question was a murmur but he heard it and managed to roll his eyes in exasperation.

"There are no spare coffins left. But there's an old tea chest in the attic…"

(2004)

The Candid Slyness of Scurrility Forepaws

Hello there! I'm sure you don't really want to hear about my childhood, so I'll just briefly mention one incident that was crucial to the development of my career. On the eve of my seventh birthday, my father summoned me to his study for a lecture. I entered the enormous room with a certain amount of trepidation, for my father was a remote and gloomy figure, frequently absent on long sailing voyages. His study was crammed with souvenirs of his travels and I was particularly impressed with the grinning masks hanging on the walls. He sat at a large mahogany desk and I took the chair opposite him and waited patiently.

"The world is a chaotic and unhappy place," he began, "and it is best to prepare at a young age for the problems it will cause you. Justice is a lie and fair play simply doesn't exist. Women are beautiful but cruel and ask too many awkward questions. Friends are treacherous and laugh at you behind your back. Dogs and cats are even worse."

He continued in this manner for a long time, listing things I was certain to encounter and dismissing them with contempt. Although his cold fury was fascinating, the list seemed endless and I found it impossible not to yawn. He frowned darkly at this.

"You're not an adult yet and doubtless harbour traces of

hope and optimism in your heart. That's understandable. But let me tell you something — I've travelled the globe and visited every country and culture in existence and not once have I discovered anything other than greed and disappointment. That has been true *without exception.* Shattered dreams are the rule."

He resumed his list and I hastened to interrupt him. "With respect," I said, "you've made your point and I accept it."

He nodded, torn between anger at my audacity and relief that his words had not been wasted. Pouring himself a tumbler of brandy he sipped the liquid slowly. "Very well, I'll skip the remainder of the list, even though it contains such important items as Finance and Toothache. But there is one thing worse than all the others."

I leaned forward and met his gaze. "Pray tell."

His voice became sad. "It is being accused of something you haven't done. Getting the blame when you are innocent. That's the bitterest pill of all! And it will happen to you, as it happens to everyone, unless you work hard to preclude the possibility. Make sure you are always guilty, that you really are to blame. Get into all sorts of mischief, cause all kinds of trouble. Be ambitious and imaginative but don't neglect the details. If you live according to these principles, you'll never be condemned unfairly. I want you to promise me you'll be an unrepentant rogue until the day you die. It's the only way of avoiding miscarriages of justice."

I solemnly made that promise and he added, "It's customary at this stage to beat you to ensure you remember this lecture, as Cellini's father beat him when they saw a salamander in the fire, but I'm much cleverer than that. From the moment of your birth I anticipated a need to arm you against the world. That is why I named you Scurrility. This name will always serve as a reminder of your vocation as a villain and mischief-maker. True, you will be exposed to ridicule from your peers, but this would have happened anyway considering the surname I bequeathed to you. Now leave me to brood alone and close the door behind you. We owe it to ourselves to be bad."

The following day he embarked on another voyage and never came back.

The mischief I indulged in for the next decade was fairly minor but I was simply awaiting the greater opportunities of adulthood. One of the first consequences of my father's speech was that I stopped trusting my mother. She had informed me that the word 'scurrility' meant handsome and smart in appearance. With the aid of a dictionary I discovered that my father's definition was more accurate. At school I became the bane of my teachers and fellow pupils. A flair for chemistry resulted in many small explosions and much petty damage to property. Nothing could ever be proved against me, for I was as lucky as I was careful, but the teachers avenged themselves by awarding me low grades in examinations.

I left school with few qualifications but I refused to let this fact hinder me. I took a job in a jam factory and saved my wages with dedication, for I had a scheme in mind that required considerable capital. While I worked, I amused myself by adding flies to the jam. I collected large numbers of the insects by visiting the kitchens of restaurants and hotels in the guise of an Inspector of Hygiene and asking for the contents of all the flytraps to be given to me. They never refused. Walking to work with pockets full of flies seems less funny now than it did then. I added a single fly to every pot, using my thumb to push it deep into the jam before screwing down the lid.

I was constantly occupied with inventing new annoyances and torments for the people around me. I dialled telephone numbers at random during the night. When using an elevator I always pressed all the buttons just before getting out. In the supermarket I became an expert at striking the ankles of other shoppers with the wheel of my trolley. I always used the slowest and most complicated method of payment in any queue. Naturally there was only so much I could do alone, but I didn't allow an appreciation of my limitations to deter me from making at least one attempt every day to lower the quality of life for my fellow citizens. I was a dependable scoundrel.

It is true that none of my tricks and acts of sabotage were original. But I had made plans for a truly unique piece of mischief that could only be implemented when funds permitted. I bided my time and continued to save and I wasn't dissatisfied with what I did achieve. I became an expert at making the neighbourhood dogs bark after midnight. Every time I passed a laundry I entered and added fistfuls of tissues to the pockets of trousers waiting to be washed. In pubs and nightclubs I enjoyed dropping cigarette butts into drinks, especially cans and opaque bottles. I was never caught and I guess I began to consider myself invulnerable or invisible.

One morning I was rudely awakened by a persistent hammering on the door of my apartment. I dressed to answer the call and found myself facing two men in dark suits with insincere smiles. They pushed their way inside and closed the door behind them.

"You are Scurrility Forepaws," one of them said flatly.

"That is correct," I replied with a forced sneer, "and I'm already late for work."

"You are employed at Gulliver's Jam Factory," the second man declared. "We know what you've been up to."

I suspect a part of me had always assumed I would be caught one day. There was no point denying my guilt. So I answered coolly, "Flies are very nutritious."

They shook their heads together. Both men had expressionless blue eyes and I considered loaning them two pairs of dark glasses. "Not just that. We know everything."

I was alarmed by that statement, for it implied I had been followed and spied on for a long time without my suspicions being aroused. Knowing how corrupt the secret police were rumoured to be, I wondered if I should try to bribe my way out of this predicament, but at the same time I reasoned I couldn't afford to pay an unofficial 'fine' without setting back my favoured scheme, the one I was saving for. I had no intention of being deterred from a life of mischief because of this failure. It was simply a lesson for me to be more subtle in future. With a short but wholly authentic laugh I extended my arms and waited for the closing of the handcuffs on my wrists.

"It is your duty to arrest me. I'll come quietly."

The first man announced, "We aren't policemen. We want to offer you a job."

The second man said, "We've been impressed with what we've seen of your mischief so far. We represent an obscure organisation dedicated to the spreading of chaos throughout society. We need people like you. Will you work for us? The wages you will receive are ten times the amount you are currently paid. All you are required to do is to continue being a nuisance. Indeed as this is a full time post, you'll have many more hours each day to cause trouble than you presently have. What do you say?"

I was stunned. The chance to earn a living from what I intended to do anyway was almost too much for my mind to absorb. I needed to sit and breathe deeply for several minutes before I was calm enough to respond to the proposal. They watched me indulgently.

At last I gasped, "I accept! You won't regret taking me on. I'll be a punctual and conscientious rotter! I'll always be sly and deceitful too — trust me!"

I resigned from my job at Gulliver's Jam Factory the following morning and commenced working for my new employers on the afternoon of the same day. I never learned much about the organisation I was now a member of. My wages were delivered regularly in an envelope pushed under my door and I had little direct contact with any of my colleagues. An occasional visit from one or other of the blue-eyed men took place, but these were no more than routine checks on my progress. They rarely answered questions about the nature of their secret society. I thought I detected one of them referring to the organisation as 'The Scamps of Disorder' but I was probably mistaken. The mystery of the whole business appealed to me.

My acts of chaos remained modest for another few months. I offered sweets with tiny fragments of silver foil clinging to them to people with lots of fillings in their teeth. I smeared vaseline on doorknobs and taps. I hung enormous untuned wind chimes around the city during the stormy season. But soon I had raised enough capital to turn my carefully nurtured dream into a reality. I founded a magazine. This was my unique piece of mischief, my apotheosis. It doesn't sound like much but it was the character of the magazine that made it so unhelpful to my fellow citizens. It was called *The Suicide Review* and it did exactly what the title promised — it reviewed suicides.

Imagine the malice of that, if you will! It is bad enough for the family and friends of a person who has just taken their own life to cope with the shattering reality of the loss, but when that loss is treated as an example of popular art, analysed and criticised in a public forum, the anguish is amplified with the addition of horrified incredulity and frustrated rage. My publication was a supreme monument to tastelessness and exploitation. *The Suicide Review* was not only profoundly morbid but perversely enthralled by the most facile and shallow aesthetic values. Glibness was deified. I employed writers who were clever but insecure and addicted to withholding sympathy from their subjects.

I'd expected to make a loss, for I cared only about causing strife and hadn't taken profitability into account, but to my amazement the magazine prospered. It paid for itself many times over. It became a sort of fashion accessory for self-conscious artistic types. Publication was increased from monthly to weekly and I became a wealthy man. Writers of renown began asking to join my staff. I remember the day the famous journalist Wormhole Kidd simpered into my office and begged for employment. He had worked for *The Bohemian Examiner* for the past ten years, cementing his reputation with a prose style that disparaged everything. The entire contemporary arts scene was said to be balanced on his sneer.

"I love your magazine," he babbled. "It's just so conceptual!"

I welcomed him into the fold and our sales increased dramatically. I never instructed my writers in how to handle the latest suicide because the main rule was instinctively known by all — always give a bad review. Because they were 'cool' they never dared to show tenderness, humanity or generosity. Wormhole Kidd pushed them even deeper into postmodern cynicism. They did everything ironically and therefore could never be accused of making a mistake. Wormhole's first review was a small masterpiece. A girl jilted by her lover had thrown herself out of a window and impaled herself on the railings below. Wormhole condemned her death throes as a set of clichés and ridiculed the derivative angles made by her twitching legs.

During this time I felt a warm glow in the pit of my stomach that had two different sources of heat, in other words I felt a powerful double satisfaction that merged into one sensation. I was proud of myself for exceeding the probable expectations of my secret employers and also I was delighted not to have let my father down, wherever he was. I had truly lived up to my name, my first name I mean, not the family name, for I have no clear idea how to behave in a manner consistent with the word 'Forepaws'. I was extremely pleased with myself and it was at this point, perhaps inevitably, that my first setback occurred, though I didn't perceive it as such at the time.

My magazine received an envelope addressed to the editor. I opened it and saw it was a suicide note from a man who wanted it published — the moment it appeared in print he would kill himself. *The Suicide Review* had published the farewell notes of unsuccessful suicides, usually with a commentary attacking the poor literary style of the note, and these reviews had sometimes encouraged the survivor to make a second and more successful attempt. But we had never published a note prior to the deed. I wrote back explaining it was not our policy to give publicity to pseudo-suicides. As well as implying he was a coward and a charlatan I also mocked the wording of the note itself, declaring it the work of an idiotic hack.

A few days later I received a second letter, or rather a second draft of the first. The man had reworded his suicide note as if my criticisms had been serious and well intentioned. I saw an opportunity for a game. I handled this duty myself instead of passing it over to Wormhole Kidd or one of the other reviewers. I wrote back with even greater contempt. As expected I soon received a third draft of the suicide note. This foolish amusement continued for many weeks. It was the delight of the office. Once when

I entered the café where most of my staff members took their lunch, the place burst into applause. Wormhole was eating a thick ham sandwich and greeted me with a wink.

"I'm practising vegetarianism — ironically!" he cried.

We laughed together but with a superior sort of laugh to show we were above straightforward humour. After all, the joke might eventually turn out not to be funny and we needed to protect ourselves. I think it was at this time I first noticed the girl in red sitting at a table in the corner. She didn't work for me and was obviously just a normal customer. She was with a man, her fiancé as it happened, but I could tell from her eyes she was planning to give herself to me. Constant mischief-making had left me with little time for relaxation. Physical activities of the horizontal kind had never figured largely in the agenda of my life. I decided it was high time they did.

☙

Her name was Belinda Bourbon and even her underwear was red. It was her favourite colour. She liked to have her ears nibbled and her own teeth were charmingly crooked. She broke off with her fiancé the moment he discovered our affair, to prevent him taking the initiative. She thought she knew a lot about me but it was mostly society gossip and conjecture. I excited her because I was a rogue, no other reason. She always generalised her own beliefs and urges. She told me that all women were biologically programmed to find villains attractive. She craved a wild life and seemed to think this consisted of ingesting illegal drugs and performing standard acts of exhibitionism.

There was no danger I would allow romance to divert

me from my career. We walked hand in hand, watched the stars together, drove above the speed limit on country roads. I agreed with her that our behaviour was risky and cutting edge. I even nurtured her illusion that cycling topless through the city streets was an act guaranteed to shock and distress pedestrians and motorists. I sometimes found it difficult to stifle a yawn in her company but she suspected nothing. When I judged she was genuinely in love with me, I told her that we needed to talk. I had something to confess. We sat on a bench in the park and I lowered my eyes as I spoke.

"Belinda, you know I love you, and it's for this reason I must come clean. I can't deceive you a moment longer. I'm not really a rogue at all. I'm a sweet, kind man, a gentle soul full of tenderness with a yearning for world peace. I have a social conscience! Please forgive me. Please find it in your heart to continue loving me. I don't think I could live without you."

She broke off our relationship the following day. She could no longer trust me. I had betrayed her, tricked her into thinking I was a complete bounder whereas in fact I was a mature and reasonable individual. Not only was the relationship ruined but all her memories of our outrageous antics had been soiled. She wished me the very worst luck for the future. This result was delicious. Some men fake their own deaths, others fake their own lives, but I had gone much further. I had pretended to fake my own fakery! In some ways I consider this to be my finest piece of mischief.

I was so satisfied by the outcome of this affair that I neglected my correspondence with the writer of the suicide note. Indeed I paid only infrequent visits to the offices of *The Suicide Review*. My other mischief-making activities also dwindled in number and intensity. I had been suffering headaches and muscle cramps prior to my relationship with Belinda and these were gradually growing worse. I finally arranged to see a doctor. He examined me carefully, studied the tips of my fingers with a magnifying glass and clicked his tongue thoughtfully. Then he consulted a large textbook on one of his shelves. The word 'Poisons' was embossed on the spine of this volume and I shivered.

"Do you have many enemies?" he asked me casually.

It soon emerged I had absorbed a large amount of arsenic through the ink of the letters sent to me by the hopeful contributor to my magazine. His rewritten suicide notes were really an attempt at assassination! I was impressed as well as horrified by this subterfuge. It served as a timely reminder I was not the only scoundrel in the world, that some others were naturally vicious rather than simply fulfilling a vow never to be good. I had accidentally saved my own life by breaking off the correspondence. My system was weakened but not fatally. I would fully recover in time, but it was essential I give up work and take a complete rest. Those were the doctor's orders.

Taking time off work was easy enough, for I never needed to report to my employers. I felt sure they had other ways of monitoring my progress. I had enough money to last me many years when the wage packets stopped. My mind was peaceful on that score. But another thought began to obsess me. Without my constant mischief-making, the quality of life in the city must improve. While I was recuperating and not spreading chaos, life had to get better for everyone else. With one less 'Scamp of Disorder' to make existence miserable, a tangible rise of standards had to be observable in the coming weeks. I entertained myself by imagining some of the positive things that might happen.

I had various images in my head, involving people helping other people, little acts of empathy and support. One of my favourites involved the daily traffic jam in the complicated circuit of roads in the city centre. I visualised a perfect gridlock with all the vehicles stuck behind each other unable to move even the smallest distance. Suddenly the doors of the cars opened and all the passengers got out and walked forward to the next car ahead. They entered these other cars and closed the doors. In this manner they shifted themselves one position forward. A few minutes later they repeated this action. Continuing this process, all the commuters would find their way out of the monumental jam.

This was a bizarre fantasy, of course, and it relied on people not caring who sat in their vehicles provided they could sit in somebody else's. It was an elaborate metaphor for the concept of sharing, I suppose. As my health returned I decided to talk long walks. To my bewilderment, life in the city had not improved at all during my absence. If anything, it had got *worse*. Everybody wore sour faces and walked with aggressive but also somehow dejected strides. I remained flabbergasted. Had all my previous wickedness been in vain? Had I wasted my life, betrayed my father and lost Belinda for nothing? The world without Scurrility was more scurrilous!

How could such a thing be? An answer was provided by a chance encounter with one of the men who originally recruited me. I was standing on a bridge gazing at the river when he came up and stood behind me. He knew what my trouble was and spoke first.

"Don't feel too gloomy," he said. "The reason why life has got worse rather than better since you took time off work is because you have stopped causing mischief to other mischief-makers. Do you understand now? You were a villain to everyone around you. But some of those people were also mischief-makers. You aren't the only rogue in this city, Mr Forepaws, nor are you the worst, not by a long way. But your acts of mischief, which were always directed at random members of the population, frequently sabotaged or interfered with the plans of other scoundrels, hampering them and accidentally helping to make the world a finer place."

The irony was unbearable. I digested it slowly and muttered, "You mean to say that if I hadn't dedicated my life to mischief there would be more mischief in life?"

He clapped me on the shoulder. "It's all part of the rich pageant of disorder."

He moved away and I wept a few tears before embarrassment dried them in their ducts. I looked at the people who passed me on the bridge and I wondered which of them were rogues like me, or rogues even more dastardly. Possibly every single inhabitant of the city was a member of the same secret society. I'd never learned how many scoundrels it employed. Or perhaps they were members of different secret societies devoted to the same purpose? Who could tell? It now seemed very likely there was no such thing as an innocent person. It was much more plausible that we were all mischief-makers of varying degrees of skill, hindering each other and chaos in the name of chaos.

A few weeks later there was another knock on the door of my apartment. I opened it and found myself facing two men but not the two men who visited me before. They didn't try to push their way inside. I asked them directly if they represented 'The Scamps of Disorder' or some other organisation committed to strife and badness. They shook their heads. On the contrary, they were agents of a secret society devoted to regularity and order, the exact opposite of my former employers. I invited them in and made them cups of coffee while they explained the reason for their visit. It was unexpectedly connected with my father.

"We knew him quite well," one of them revealed, "but he was a very private individual. He liked to conceal his activities from everyone."

"We were in business together," the other man clarified.

I remembered the long sailing voyages my father had been apt to take. The first man said, "We came into possession of one of his journals. He misplaced it and it remained jammed in a dark corner of a ship's cabin for many years. Anyway, when we finally got hold of it, we read it carefully. It turns out that on one of his travels he discovered a land where everyone is happy and peaceful and nothing is ever a disappointment. That's where he's living now."

"So he lied about the universal misery of the world!" I cried.

"Well his name should have given you a clue — Fibber Forepaws."

I sulked. "My mother told me that the word 'Fibber' meant golden haired and noble chinned. You just can't trust anyone at all, can you?"

The men smiled gently. "Except in that land your father discovered."

I sighed. "What do you want of me?"

"Nothing much. It's just that as his son we thought you should be kept informed. But we do intend to make a proposal to you. We are fitting out a ship at this very moment on behalf of our organisation. We plan to sail to that perfect land. Our own world could learn a lot from them, don't you think? We intend to bring back their ideas, their way of life, their peacefulness and happiness. Do you want to come with us? Such a voyage might well be a victory blow for our organisation, for regularity and order. It could destroy chaos. We are offering you a chance to join the winning side, to become part of history. What do you say? It could be magnificent!"

I considered deeply. "Very well. But don't you think it would be a good idea to take some gifts with us? Something to demonstrate our good intentions?"

The men were ecstatic. "What do you suggest?"

"Something simple but effective. I know for a fact that Gulliver's Jam Factory has just gone bust and closed down.

They will be selling off their remaining stock very cheaply. A thousand pots of jam should do the trick."

We shook hands on the deal. After they left I performed a little dance.

Scurrility, you sly rascal!

(2005)

Ye Olde Resignation

When Celia Radical saw the size of the nostalgia storm in Betjeman Gardens, she was astonished that nobody had reported it sooner. The typical suburban setting had been profoundly affected by the winds of yearning. Couples stood on tidy lawns chatting and smoking cigarettes. There were even some bicycles on the streets.

"Living in the past!" she muttered ruefully as she checked the readings on her retrospectometer. Under the rose tinted glass the dials had stopped spinning. The eye of the storm was located in the kitchen of one of the dwellings. She wove her way between the figures and rang the bell of the house in question.

The door opened and Mrs Diode peered out tentatively. She wore several strings of beads looped about her neck. "At last! It's getting worse, you know. My husband has been wearing a cravat all morning and I've had this terrible impulse to dance a Charleston. Is there anything you can do?"

Celia sighed. "Show me the eye," she said. She followed Mrs Diode through the hallway into the kitchen. As she passed the open door of the lounge, she glimpsed a man with a dark kiss-curl pasted to his forehead winding up a clockwork gramophone. "Mr Diode?"

Mrs Diode nodded. "Best not to disturb him. I think he has absorbed more nostalgia than I have. He hardly talks to me anymore. Prefers to read newspapers and tune the wireless."

Celia placed her retrospectometer on the floor and felt under the sink. The eye of the storm blinked at her apprehensively. "Why didn't you blindfold it earlier?" she demanded.

Mrs Diode cleared her throat and shrugged her shoulders. She fitted a cigarette into a long holder, raised it to her lips and then changed her mind. She started polishing the leaves of an aspidistra that had forced its way through the floor.

Celia fixed the blinking eye with a cold stare. "It looks to me as if someone has been batting their lashes at it. You should bear in mind that's not only highly illegal but also rather reckless."

Mrs Diode blushed and became restless. Ignoring her, Celia quickly hypnotised the eye and sent it into a deep sleep. Then she carefully extracted it with tweezers and dropped it in a black bag. "That will be 350,000 credits," she said.

"What's that in old money, dear?"

"Seven pounds, four shillings, two pence," replied Celia.

She picked up her retrospectometer and made her way out of the kitchen back through the house. In the lounge, the clockwork gramophone had been replaced by a slightly later valve model. "You're lucky this time," she told Mrs Diode, who was following her. "The effects seem to be wearing off already. Be more careful in future."

Mrs Diode nodded. She pressed something into Celia's hand. Celia looked down and saw food coupons.

"Get yourself some butter and powdered eggs," came the whisper. "I know you'll keep quiet about this. Go on, take them, love."

Celia frowned and returned the coupons. "I want you to understand that it is a criminal offence to attempt to bribe an employee of the Style Council. I may have to suggest you contact a solicitor if you persist in this blatant disregard of fashion ethics."

"Let me tell you about my nephew," Mrs Diode began.

"No thanks, I'm busy," said Celia.

"Ah, you sneak!" Mrs Diode turned away in disgust, removing the bubblegum from her mouth and adjusting her beehive hairdo. The decades were falling back into place rapidly. Celia reached the front door and rubbed her eyes. The winds of yearning were dying down. The environment was shimmering and changing even as she looked.

Outside, a skiffle band was growing its hair.

Back in the office, Celia collapsed into her swivel chair and waited for it to massage her neck and shoulders. "I'm tired of working out in the field," she told her assistant. "So tired!"

Jules Oviform was sympathetic. He patted her hand and flashed his new smile at her. He rarely failed to amuse Celia: she had spent a small fortune on his French accent and love of garlic. The voicebox and tastebuds had been grown together in a tank and grafted on at a private clinic. Celia had chosen him for his entertainment value.

"People can be so obtuse," she added. "I met a housewife today who flirted openly with a big blue storm eye. Thought she could have some harmless fun! She let herself and her neighbours regress back to the 1920s before doing anything about it."

Jules raised Celia's hand to his lips and kissed it. "I only have eyes for you. And not just eyes but croissants too." Celia withdrew her hand and wiped it with a handkerchief.

"What worries me is where the rogue style goes after it disperses. Is it all accumulating in the atmosphere?"

Jules made a comic face. "Ah, *mon cheri*! Such ideas!" But Celia was in no mood for his buffoonery. She switched on her secretary and began to forge ahead with her report. Paperwork depressed the machine as much as it depressed her. To enliven the process, the secretary occasionally queried the accuracy of her version of events.

A chime sounded and Celia threw up her arms in despair. "What now?" she cried. The chime was a summons from Big Boss Barium. This usually meant more problems. She stood and made her way out of the office onto the moving walkway of the corridor.

Big Boss Barium was sweating in his plush room, his huge bulk suspended from the ceiling on a system of wires. He greeted Celia with his customary sneer. The neons on his oversized pinstripe suit crawled with council slogans. "Sit down, Ms Radical."

"There's nowhere free," she replied.

"Exactly!" he roared in triumph.

The room was filled with large rubber balls designed to break his fall if the wires snapped. Big Boss Barium glowered for a full minute in silence and then he spoke again, his chins wobbling alarmingly as he rumbled the words in her direction. "I've had a complaint, Ms Radical. A complaint concerning you. I want you to know that the Style Council takes such matters very seriously."

"Who made the complaint?" she asked.

Big Boss Barium chewed his fat lip. "The Chief of Police, El Greco Cooper himself! He rang through a few minutes ago and demanded to know why you were poking about in Betjeman Gardens."

"I was doing my job," responded Celia.

Big Boss Barium shook a finger smudged with chocolate. "Mrs Diode is one of his favourite aunts. We don't take action against the friends and relatives of the police force. We can afford to let a few nostalgia storms work themselves out naturally. I suggest that you return the eye to her kitchen immediately!"

"I sent it to the crushers half an hour ago."

"Can't you call it back?"

Celia shook her head. "It's already jelly."

Big Boss Barium held his head in his chubby hands. Pulleys groaned and squeaked as he sobbed. "There's such a thing as being too efficient, Ms Radical. This is all becoming a mess."

"El Greco must learn to live with disappointment."

Big Boss Barium flew into one of his melodramatic rages. They were bad for his health but sometimes earned him a bonus. Celia knew that one of the rubber balls contained a secret critic who judged these rages and arrived at a monetary figure. As the wires twanged and whistled and the vast blob of flesh bounced and span over her, dribbling foam, she decided to take the easy way out.

"Fine. I'll make a replacement."

Big Boss Barium shuddered to a halt. "You will?"

"I'm dedicated to my job but I'm not a particularly ethical person. My morality is fake, for intimidation purposes. Nobody is better at swelling up hugely with artificial righteousness."

"We all have our individual bloats," Big Boss Barium agreed.

"I'll open the refrigeration units where the jellies are kept and mould a new eye from a big blue scoop."

"That will be a very sensible thing for you to do," said Big Boss Barium. He was convinced he had won the bonus and was already planning to spend it on more ultra-high calorie food, which in turn would damage his health more, making his next melodramatic rage more alarming and droolly and more worthy of a bigger bonus. This cycle would accelerate towards a spectacular blubbery doom.

"I'll do it right now, with your permission."

"Of course!" He waved a shapeless hand and allowed her to depart his presence. He had no love for his employees, no outstanding loyalty to the Council. His only concern was not to come under the adverse scrutiny of his superiors, the Style Gurus, or to make an enemy of the President and his Police Chief. El Greco Cooper was the sort of man who arrested autumn leaves for crunching underfoot without an entertainment license. It was imperative to keep on his right side: but that side was as thin and sharp as a scalpel.

Celia urged the walkway to maximum speed and returned to her office within seconds. "Jules!" she called.

Jules Oviform appeared at her side. "*Mon cheri!*"

"We have an unorthodox job to do. We're going behind the crushers to pilfer some eye jelly."

"How bohemian! How *fin de siècle*!"

"Then we're going to shape it into a new eye and plant it under the sink in a domestic kitchen."

"How *escargot*! How *Victor Hugo*!"

Celia nodded. It was going to be all those things and more. Opening a filing cabinet and selecting a winter scarf and mittens, she hurried down the tunnel that ran behind the crushers. These garments matched her colouring not at all and suited her in no degree. The Style Council was full of confiscated goods. And all of them were bad.

The walls of the tunnel were decorated with murals depicting packets of frozen peas and carrots, tubs of ice cream, bottles of beer and other refrigerative subjects. Celia and Jules proceeded to a chamber that resembled a garage. This was the deepest part of the Style Council. Here stood the Five Famous Freezers.

Celia opened the first freezer and removed the ice tray, turning it upside down and pressing the bottom with her thumbs until the frozen key worked itself loose. This key provided access to the second freezer and *its* ice tray and frozen key, which in turn opened the third freezer, and so on. These security measures were deemed cool by Style Gurus the world over. Even Guru Futuro approved.

The fifth freezer was directly connected to the crushers. Its door was rarely opened. Big Boss Barium preferred not to know what the jelly inside was doing. All those pulverised storm eyes gave him the jeebies. He could live with heebies but had a dread of jeebies. Celia felt no such qualms as she opened the lock.

The inside was empty! This was worthy of a gasp!

Celia was amazed. The container that should have held a milky white jelly streaked with blue, green and hazel, the end result of a thousand storm eye pulpings, had gone. In its place was a note. She snatched it and read it aloud with a frown:

"*I am a terrorist organisation and I have stolen the storm jelly in order to build a massive nostalgia bomb. This bomb will be detonated at noon on the President's birthday.*"

"But that's today!" simpered Jules.

"Don't be ridiculous. The President was born under the sign of the Toerag. The sun is still in Hoops."

"He changed the law. Didn't you hear? He passed a rule saying that from now on *every day* is his birthday."

"What's the time?" Celia roared.

"Ten minutes to noon! Goodbye *mon cheri*! How I adored you!"

"We must show this note to Big Boss Barium," said Celia. She closed the freezer with her foot and ran back up the tunnel, Jules clattering along behind her. Then he stopped dead.

"Footprints! I know who the culprit is!"

Celia span. "What do you mean?"

"See these footprints, *mon cheri*! They must belong to the person who proceeded us to the eye jelly."

"But there aren't any footprints!"

"Exactly! That proves that the man who made them did *not* walk down this tunnel. He must have come some other way. Among all the agents of the Style Council who is the only one who never walks? Big Boss Barium! This evidence is incontrovertible."

"I'm not sure about that," responded Celia.

Jules seemed on the verge of tears but Celia had no time to comfort him. She continued along the tunnel, reached her office and then mounted the walkway to Big Boss Barium's office. She knocked on his door with a minute to spare. "Enter!" he bellowed.

He was swinging and sweating when she came into his presence. Jules remained in the corridor, timidly peering through the open doorway. Big Boss Barium scowled and juddered.

"Did you manage to make a replacement?"

She shook her head and passed him the note. He read it and frowned so deeply the folds of skin above his eyebrows came down and obscured his vision like blubber goggles. He traced the words with his fingers instead and then crumpled the note in his fist like an empty chocolate wrapper. "This must be a hoax," was his conclusion.

A giggle escaped from one of the rubber balls. Celia and Big Boss Barium exchanged glances. Now everything was clear! This explained why there were no footprints in the tunnel. It suddenly seemed obvious that a hidden critic would aspire to be a terrorist. Big Boss Barium leaped across the room, dangled high and peered down, trying to work out which ball had emitted the telltale sound.

He hovered over one ball, rubbed his chin, chose another. He cocked his head, angling his ear carefully but the critic remained silent. Then Big Boss Barium grew impatient and bounced violently on his cables. This action worked off his frustration but it also created catastrophe. With a horrible pinging sound, the cables snapped. Big Boss Barium plummeted to the ground like a dropped house.

He landed on one of the balls. It broke his fall but it happened to be the ball with the critic inside. And the critic happened to clutching his nostalgia bomb. There was an awful sound, a squelch not merely of bones and fat but aeons. Suddenly winds of yearning were everywhere, a thousand storm eyes unleashing their fury all at once. Celia blinked in horror at the changes in her environment. One moment she was wearing a toga, the next furs. Then she felt an abrupt chill and gazed down. What was keeping that fig leaf in place?

After the prehistoric mists had cleared, Celia went looking for Jules. He was squatting at the base of a vast tree. Sap dripped from a gash in the bark and slowly covered him.

"Move away," warned Celia, "or you'll become trapped in amber for eternity and be expensive to collect."

He glumly shuffled to her side, tripping over his newly acquired long beard. "My odour is unbearable!"

She sniffed. "You'll get used to it. Where's Big Boss Barium? What are these grooves in the earth?"

"He has been dragged away on ropes, *mon cheri*."

They followed the grooves through the Cenozoic forest until they reached a rocky plain. A flint tower stood precariously at the summit of a low hill and here they found the President and El Greco Cooper going about

Ye Olde Resignation

their familiar business. The President was attempting to juggle three sabre-toothed tiger's teeth, failing to catch them properly and cutting his arms in the process. El Greco Cooper was standing in a muddy puddle swinging a club awkwardly.

Still fully concentrating on the flying fangs, the President nodded at his Chief of Police and said to Celia, "First I declared mud illegal and he clubbed every puddle around here. Then I declared clubs illegal and now he's trying to club his own club."

"Very amusing," commented Celia as she passed on.

Jules began complaining about the condition of his feet. He didn't mean blisters but the fact that his toenails weren't nicely manicured. Celia ignored him and continued until she came to a cave. Just inside the entrance stood a large pot and inside the pot bobbed Big Boss Barium with wild carrots and asparagus.

"It's boiling in here!" he groaned.

Celia and Julia managed to overturn the pot and release Big Boss Barium. But he wasn't able to rise without his wires. He just sat there like a magnified globule of mucus.

"Who did this to you?" Celia asked with only minor interest.

"A pair of cannibals. I couldn't get a word of sense out of either of them. They were positively Pliocene!"

"I think you're exaggerating," remarked Celia.

Big Boss Barium shrugged. "I'm just glad you rescued me in time. They'll be back soon. They went to collect some salt from the nearest ocean. I find that grossly insulting!"

"I think we're in the region of Betjeman Gardens," said

163

Celia.

"But 40,000 years ago!" whimpered Jules. "What if another nostalgia storm takes us even further back? We might end up in the time of the dinosaurs and be eaten completely raw, without flavourings of any kind. Have you considered that scenario?"

Celia shook her head. "We've gone back to the limits of nostalgia. Storm eyes can't survive here. Nostalgia is only possible when social change is apparent. During this particular era the relevant changes that occur are so gradual they aren't noticeable. Society will remain pretty much the same over a lifetime. To put it more simply, nostalgia does not exist at the present time!"

"There is nothing to feel nostalgic for," agreed Big Boss Barium, "because everything remains the same."

"By the same token, the effects can't wear off," she confirmed. "We are stuck here permanently. Feelings of nostalgia can't disperse when they aren't there in the first place!"

"I'm scared, *mon cheri*. Don't you have any pity for me?"

Celia laughed. "As you well know, the Style Council only employs agents who don't have normal emotional responses to changing events. I have never felt nostalgia. That's why it's safe for me to tackle storm eyes. I'm immune to the effects."

"I wonder how the Style Gurus will cope as hunter-gatherers?"

"Anything can become fashionable," Celia replied.

Big Boss Barium raised a fat finger to his lips. "Hush! Someone's coming. It might be the cannibals!"

Ye Olde Resignation

Two figures bounded into the cave. They were dressed in strips of bark and badly cured fish skins.

"Mr and Mrs Diode!" exclaimed Celia.

The female figure pressed something into Celia's hand. Celia looked down and saw cowrie shells. "Get yourself some Mammoth lard and Teratornis eggs," came the whisper. "I know you'll keep quiet about this. Go on, take them, love."

Celia sighed. "I'm tempted to resign my job."

"You can't do that!" protested Big Boss Barium. "You're our finest agent, certainly the most emotionally stunted!"

"Back in the future I was special," she pointed out. "One of the privileged few never to feel any sense of yearning. But here I'm just like everybody else, because nobody feels nostalgia now. I don't think the Style Council needs me anymore."

"You can't resign!" repeated Big Boss Barium.

A sudden roar from outside the cave distracted them all. They went out into the light, blinking at the object that was descending from the sky. It resembled a child's drawing of a rocket, a flared cylinder with fins and a single engine. It landed unsteadily on three spindly legs. An automatic ramp extended and an utterly absurd robot glided down. It had a perfectly square head and square body and its legs were shiny metal tentacles. It undulated back and forth in front of the cave shouting out a single phrase in a grating voice:

"Take me to your leader! Take me to your leader!"

"What a time to be visited by extra terrestrials!" moaned Jules. He raised his hands in abject surrender.

The robot ignored him and continued screeching its demand. Celia eyed the slowly unwinding clockwork key protruding from its back. "I can guess what's happened. This spacecraft was originally the product of a very advanced alien species. But as it passed through the atmosphere of our planet it encountered all the accumulated clouds of rogue style. Thus it has regressed with its occupants to a time that I judge to be the early 1940s."

"Shall we take him to the President?" asked Jules.

"You can do what you like," sniffed Celia. "I'm not doing anything at all. Apart from resigning."

Big Boss Barium opened his mouth to speak again but Celia suddenly frowned and added, "You know something, I think I am feeling a twinge of nostalgia after all. Nostalgia for a time when the worst I had to deal with were storm eyes and terrorists!"

"That changes everything!" Big Boss Barium cried.

"Will we become unstuck, *mon cheri*?"

"Take me to your leader! Take me to your leader!"

Celia felt herself choking and reached up a hand. She was wearing a ruff and a complicated dress. Jules was covered in lace and sequins and his long hair fell in ringlets over his shoulders. Big Boss Barium wore vast yellow trousers and a shirt with slashed sleeves. Mr and Mrs Diode were less elaborately attired, sporting black clothes and tall hats that symbolised a strict form of purity.

Dogs and rats capered in the narrow streets. The houses were wooden and squat with overhanging eaves and signs that swung in the malodorous breeze. A window above opened and a pan of something foul was hurled on them, apparently without malice.

"Well, we're not back to our original age," croaked Big Boss Barium, "but you've done a fine job of piling on the centuries. Does anyone else feel nostalgia for anything?"

There was a general silence. He gazed at Celia.

"It's up to you again."

She shook her head. "I'm still resigning," she said.

(2006)

Castle Cesare

Possibly I am the only man alive with two different ages. I am both 28 and 9,731,065 years old. My skeleton, flesh and thoughts are defined by the first figure and thus I am no more special than any other youthful baron in this century of ours, inheritor of a venerable estate, sole occupier of the glowering castle which presently encloses me, less like a tomb than a universe, for my destiny has been peculiar. But my eyes have witnessed seasons that total in the millions and I have slept through almost as many. I refuse to accept this as normal.

How may these numbers be reconciled? First allow me to introduce myself with more dignity. I am the last scion of a remarkable family settled in these lands long before the Lombards invaded from the north. My ancestors maintained control of their estates through a combination of bribery and unobtrusiveness. Rarely did they resort to horror. As the centuries passed, they grew more isolated and introverted, withdrawing from political life and concentrating on unlocking the mysteries of the cosmos, encouraging each subsequent generation to dip ever deeper into the bottomless pot of academic truth.

Thus I enjoyed a rigorous and somewhat abstract childhood, knowing little of simple pastimes but learning much in the way of philosophy, mathematics and logic. Yet it was in the realms of the empirical sciences that we ventured furthest, astronomy and mechanics being the disciplines in which we took the greatest pleasure and pride. From the balconies of our highest turrets the entire firmament was accessible to our curiosity and in the extensive cellars winding deep into the rock of the crag that held aloft our brooding residence existed facilities for the manufacture of those magnifying lenses which guaranteed the superiority of our researches over our unknown rivals.

Dimly I recall the inscrutable visitor who knocked on our gates one late afternoon to offer his services. He was a wandering maker of clocks who wanted to know if we had any timepieces in need of repair. We had none but there was other work for him. He was an inhabitant of the country of the Bulgars and gave his name as Sneakios, which even to my immature ears sounded implausible. My father commissioned him to design a machine known as an *orrery*, a model of the solar system with moving planets powered by clockwork, a task the fellow accepted with relish.

He remained with us for many months. The sounds of construction next to my bedroom kept me awake during the long nights and my health suffered. Not once did I directly converse with Sneakios. One morning his assigned project was finished and he left us. I was taken to view his creation in the immense hall at the centre of the castle. The *orrery* filled the room entire, each world a different colour and size but made of the same strange material, a highly adhesive resin which one of our ancestors had invented in a previous century. I was particularly astonished by the representation of the Earth, viewed as if from outer space.

Not only were all the continents and mountain ranges carved on its surface with superb attention to detail but the miniature oceans between the landmasses consisted of liquid water. For an *orrery* this was unprecedented and thrilled me even more than the sheer scale of the device. Why these oceans simply did not pour off the sphere onto the floor below was a riddle never explained to me, nor have I yet solved it, but they remained in place, defying the laws of gravity as surely as my upbringing had contravened the rules of innocence. I wondered at the skill of Sneakios and perhaps also trembled a little.

The machine was not in motion, for first the giant spring that gave it energy had to be fully wound, a process apparently requiring years. A donkey was ushered in from one of our fields and harnessed to a windlass and the laborious task of turning the heavy key a sufficient number of times was commenced. I often visited the hall to view the motionless orbs. At night my smoky torch filled the role of a passing star as I circled the apparatus, casting the distorted shadows of many frozen moons onto the surfaces of planets, cursing them with plagues of bad omens, for I have heard that eclipses are unlucky.

My nocturnal explorations of the machine were eventually curtailed by the growing responsibilities of manhood. Although essentially reclusive, the Cesare family could not afford to wholly ignore the political demands of the time. Every son was required to leave the castle and fight in a distant war. He was also expected to return with a bride. Accordingly, on my eighteenth birthday I rode out into the Puglian dawn, olives in my saddlebag, arquebus over my shoulder, to lend my services to the Prince of Táranto in one of his murky struggles. I was loath to leave my home and the shelter of the forest, but I understood my duties and took them seriously enough. I was ready to be hated and loved.

As events transpired, I found combat but no suitable wife, and after half a year I returned to my castle with a fractured skull and the gloomy prospect of having to conquer our traditional horror of inbreeding and marry one of my cousins. A sword cut had given me a fever and I became more delirious as I crossed into the promontory of the Gargano, the region of Puglia we have made our own, and headed northward into the thick woods and high citrus groves so unique in atmosphere to the Cesare estates. At last I approached the castle itself but discovered I was too weak to call out a greeting.

The heavy iron door was open and there seemed to be great activity within as I dismounted and stumbled over the threshold, but I glimpsed no figures and only heard the familiar voices issuing from adjacent chambers. An irresistible fatigue overwhelmed me and I felt unable to present myself with any dignity, so I painfully climbed the stairs to my bedroom and fell down on the soft mattress, still clutching my arquebus and praying that the anvils of sleep that fell upon the lids of my eyes would not prove to be stepping stones to death. Beneath me as I lost consciousness the sounds of bustle continued.

How long I lay there, I know not, but it was clearly more than one night, perhaps longer than a week or even two, for when my fever broke and I regained my senses I found the castle completely deserted. I was ravenous but not thirsty and abominable tongue tracks on the damp walls revealed how in my delirium I had obtained moisture. The taste of condensation was unpleasant in my mouth as I wandered the passages and halls shouting out the names of family members and our retainers. In the kitchens I found stale bread and old cheese and made a sorry meal in the gloomy light that reluctantly penetrated the narrow windows.

The castle had been deliberately evacuated, that much was certain, for the valuables in all the secret places were gone but there were no signs of wanton destruction and I did not believe that a raid had been made on our estates. It occurred to me that an outbreak of the plague might reasonably explain the situation and I imagined that my parents and servants had fled to Naples or some other suitably distant city until it was deemed safe to return. When night fell I lit candles and brooded among dancing shadows.

I grew agitated and desired activity and eventually I rose from the stool in the kitchen, brushed the crumbs from my clothes, and set forth in search of a telescope. On our highest roof I might perch and scan the horizon for lights in the dark, evidence that our neighbours in their own castles were still in residence. If I perceived no twinkle in my lens the indication would be that the Cesare predicament was not unique and thus my plague theory would become more plausible.

I selected a telescope almost as long as my arquebus and climbed the spiral stairs of the oldest tower, reaching a narrow fissure at the very top, a gap in the crumbling stone walls through which I had often squeezed as a boy, delighting to run over the slippery tiles. It was no longer an easy matter to pass between the edges of jagged granite and I was lacerated and bruised by the time I emerged in the cool night on the other side. So too was I less sure of foot than in the years of my childhood and I picked my way with unmanly caution to my former vantage point at the very edge of the roof. Far below and all around lay a darkness that was more purple than black, the wild forests of the Gargano, dense and peaceful.

As I lifted the telescope to my right eye a moment of vertigo threatened to topple me but I breathed deeply and widened my stance. The stars glimmered faintly on the leaves of the tallest trees but no other traces of illumination could be discerned. I scanned slowly, lingering for many minutes whenever I reached a point where I believed a neighbouring castle stood. My task was disturbed by an ominous sound from behind. Gently I tucked the telescope into my belt, unslung the arquebus from my shoulder and lit the fuse. Then I turned to confront whatever was stalking me. There was nothing there, but the threatening growl was repeated.

Frowning, I stepped over the roof, my finger on the trigger, my eyes straining to catch sight of the hostile presence. Suddenly the surface under my feet gave way and I fell into the vast space of the immense hall at the centre of the castle. As I plunged through dusty air I realised I was the victim of a simple irony: the noise I had interpreted as a growl was no more than the slow breaking of rotten beams under my weight. The black floor of the hall seemed absurdly far away. Obeying my instincts but devoid of rational hope, I braced myself for an impact that came sooner than expected and did not destroy me.

I lay sprawled on a soft surface at an elevation half that of the roof. What had happened? Then I remembered the gigantic *orrery*. By an amazing stroke of luck I had landed on one of the model worlds. A single static moon overhead informed me that I was on the miniature planet Earth. I laughed in relief as I sat up, smelling the tropical forest that had broken my fall, cool sap staining my clothes, tiny branches pricking my legs, but my joy was premature. As I tried to stand, I lost my balance again and the finger that was still on the trigger of the arquebus discharged the weapon in a random but extremely unfortunate direction.

In the flash that preceded the roar and belch of smoke I beheld the skeleton of a donkey far beyond the rim of the world. The bullet smashed the gleaming skull, rebounded and struck the key that wound the *orrery*. Somewhere a spring began uncoiling, a spring tightened over a period of many years, and I was abruptly in motion. The walls of the hall became a blur, the other planets turned in their own courses and the sun at the centre of the machine burst into flame. Light and heat washed over me. The shifting angles of the solar system, its natural laws, became the transformational geometry of my sickness and suffering.

After many hours of groaning and retching I acclimatised to the dread velocity of my new home and it now appeared the castle was awhirl and not I. Like some colossus from fable I lurched to the horizon, my feet straining to free themselves from the sticky surface, pausing after only ten laborious paces for a rest. I made camp and pondered how to escape my predicament. Even were it possible, leaping into space would be suicide, for my own momentum would dash me against a wall of the great chamber, turning me into a sunburst of gore on the naked stones. It might be better simply to wait for the spring to wind down and the device to stop.

Such a wait, however, might outlast my lifespan, for the sheer size of the coil indicated that the mechanism had been designed to run unattended for decades. I preferred to search for the axle that connected the planet to the central gears: by inching my way along it towards the sun I would reduce my speed until it became safe to drop onto the floor. In preparation for this venture I dipped my cloak into the ocean, protection against the heat that would increase as I approached the hub of the solar system, and set off to find the point where the axle met the globe. I counted my steps as I walked.

My journey proved to be frustrating. I had landed in the middle of Africa, a continent the size of a large carpet, and now I made my way across the Sinai Peninsula into Asia. I quenched my thirst in the Caspian Sea, climbed the Himalayas for a better view, saw no connecting rod in evidence, continued striding to the edge of Siberia and jumped the Bering Strait into the Americas. Days and nights passed in rapid succession, for the world was turning on its own axis, and the moon sailed across the sky, casting its gibbous shadow on the spinning walls of the hall. It seemed to be a free body in orbit, unconnected to the greater machine.

This could not be, and I raised my telescope and focussed it on the rim of the yellow satellite but no evidence of shaft or wires could I detect. I struggled to recall that time when I first beheld the *orrery*. Surely I had noticed struts supporting the planets? Perhaps in the gloom of the vast chamber I had merely assumed they were present. I considered alternative methods of keeping spheres suspended in air. Had Sneakios inflated them with phlogiston or a similar gas? But this answer raised another question, namely how free floating objects could interact with the central gears.

There had to be a transmission system of some kind. The phenomenon of magnetism now suggested itself as an explanation and I deemed it probable that the inside of my world was lined with lodestones. Stooping, I began to hack at the ground with the blade of my pocket knife, determined to unearth those objects as proof of my hypothesis, but my efforts at penetrating the crust produced only a spurt of lava that charred the tips of my fingers and persuaded me to retreat into the Atlantic Ocean. Risking damage to my arquebus I swam back to Africa and returned to my camp.

I dried the gunpowder in my flask by pouring it out along the equator. My first circumnavigation of the Earth had given me a good appreciation of the surface area of my prison. The difficulty of walking made small distances seem far. I was hungry and wondered where to find food. Cupping my hands together and plunging them into the sea, then allowing the water to drain through my fingers, I caught infinitesimal fish by the thousands, also squid and whales, and crammed them into my mouth. This meal was uncouth but nourishing and I knew starvation would not be a danger.

In the days, weeks, months that followed I improved my living conditions as best I might, but the psychological burden of my situation remained heavy. I broke off the peaks of mountains for use as stone tools, trawled the oceans with my cloak for food, warmed my hands over active volcanoes on chilly nights. Once I lost my temper with the moon and used it as a target, shattering it into a thousand fragments with my arquebus. The debris tumbled towards the sun in ever decreasing circles and was finally consumed in the heart of that awful furnace. The absence of the moon did nothing to calm the tides of my blood.

My astronomical knowledge served me to a minimal extent. I lay on my back and stared into space. The walls of the universe rotated so rapidly they were perceptible only as a sort of a visual scream, more featureless than a fine mist, and the same held true for the ceiling where it met the walls. The point directly above the sun was the only fixed spot in this bizarre sky. The hole through which I had plunged revolved at a speed proportional to the distance of the Earth from the sun and served me as a marker to count the passing of the artificial years, though this exercise seemed pointless to my demoralised inner self.

I struggled to assume a more optimistic attitude. Surely my family would return one day and halt the machine? I forced myself to calculate the orbital periods of all the planets, using an entire desert as my blackboard and my finger as a stick of chalk, to keep my intellect fresh. My equations were possibly faulty: I foresaw nothing useful coming out of this chore. I lived in a condition of monotonous fear, fishing the oceans for protein, inventing new curses to express my opinion of Sneakios, opening my bowels, dreaming of escape: such became my stagnant routine.

The matter of disposing of my bodily wastes, though unpleasant a topic, must be dealt with in some detail because it has a significant bearing on my ultimate fate. At first I decided to select a clearly defined area of the globe as my privy. I refused to pollute the sea. A small country in the far west of Europe, a land I believe is called Wales, became my dung heap. A random choice but one that instinctively felt appropriate. However, after many months, the stench became too powerful even in Africa, my base continent, and so I began hurling my dung into space towards the sun and more often than not it was burned up in the flames.

I was a fully grown man, a not inexperienced soldier, and I had long since outgrown the excitement of birthdays, but now they came so thick and fast as my little world rushed around its sun that I ceased to even acknowledge them. However in the evening of one such name day I received an unexpected gift: a moving point of light far beyond the orbit of the most distant planet. The hours passed, the object came closer, resolved itself into the semblance of a comet. I watched as it approached the sun, trailing behind it a tail of silver ribbons, and a reckless idea took full possession of my brain.

It was clear that after this comet swung around the sun and began its return journey into the void, it would approach Earth closely. I made a noose from my belt and waited on the summit of Kilimanjaro, balanced precariously on one leg, to snare it as it grazed the phoney ionosphere. My cast was successful: I held on tightly and allowed the celestial wanderer to drag me off my world. Muscles straining, I climbed the length of the belt, pulled myself onto an orb no wider than a cushion and howled my joy. Astride a comet I was leaving the solar system for a region of the castle where I might dismount without injury.

Or so I imagined. In actuality, hope made me careless and I turned to wave farewell to the receding blue globe. I had already passed Mars and was entering the Asteroid Belt. A sudden blow on the skull dazed me and almost knocked me from my perch. I had collided with that dwarf planet known as Ceres. Only half conscious I struggled to maintain my grip and found it impossible to do more than act as a passive observer as the comet passed through an open door in one of the walls and continued along a dim passage. The clicking of an unseen ratchet slowly roused me to a more sensible condition but I remained dizzy with pain.

The comet trundled down a stairway into the network of cellars that become natural caverns illuminated by phosphorescent slime. It was cold. Far beyond the solar system, space was not as empty as I had imagined: here was a storeroom for comets, hundreds of them, a convocation of frosty bodies, tails hanging limp and bedraggled. The sharp stalagmites on the cavern floor made any abrupt descent a lethal prospect. What could I do? I merely clung on until my comet turned and began its journey back towards the sun, my teeth chattering in the subterranean chill. Here was the frost of the interstellar underground!

My extra weight had altered the comet's orbital period, reducing it by many years if not centuries, and in my delusion I imagined that the other comets were frowning at us in disapproval, condemning our impetuosity. When we re-entered the hall I was unable to see the planets: they were spinning too rapidly. But as the comet synchronised itself to the movements of the other parts of the *orrery* it accelerated in a wide sweep and gradually the sticky worlds loomed out of the background blur. Then I wished I was back in the icy cavern because I realised that if I remained on my perch I would be toasted alive. The path of the comet meant that it would skim the sun before swinging around on its next outbound journey.

At this moment the calculations I had worked out in the desert with my finger proved their worth, for I was comfortably familiar with the orbits of all the planets. I knew that the comet would pass above Saturn and that my only chance of survival lay in leaping down onto its rings. I landed on the thickest of these and rolled towards the edge, stopping myself just in time and standing to survey my new environment. Suddenly much lighter, the comet accelerated with an alarming wobble in its motion, emitting a horrible screech, but I was more concerned with the barrenness around me, the featureless loops of polished steel.

With the blade of my dagger I sawed at the rings, cutting them through and prising them apart until they formed a long and extremely narrow walkway jutting in the direction of the sun. Then I waited for the right moment. When it came I ran at full tilt along this ludicrous gangplank and used the very end as a springboard to launch myself high. Jupiter grew large before me. I landed with a terrific jolt on Ganymede, largest of the Jovian moons, thankfully without breaking any bones. Had I fallen onto Jupiter itself I doubt I would ever have escaped its powerful adhesion, but the stickiness of Ganymede was relatively weak.

My dagger was blunted but it served well enough to dig a deep hole in the surface of the satellite. No lava spurted to burn away my ambitions: this world was geologically dead. I inserted my arquebus into the hole until only the tip of the barrel showed above the surface. Then I poured all my remaining gunpowder into it, waited again for the right moment and showered sparks into the barrel. The detonation was more deafening than a stereotypical thunderclap. Ganymede was blasted off its orbit and into the Asteroid Belt, knocking those foolish lumps aside like cosmic skittles, and sailing casually past blushing Mars.

The arquebus was wrecked but such was the price I was willing to pay for survival. The callow satellite, an awkward nomad, came close to the Earth and I made my final leap. Any thoughts I had that Ganymede might find a new orbit here and replace the old broken moon were frustrated, for it continued to drift towards the sun and was ultimately incinerated, a fate identical to that of the unsteady comet and many of the scattered asteroids. I had managed to cause a great deal of damage in the solar system, no mean feat for an ordinary mortal. It is true that humans are the most destructive species!

I noticed a change in the sun after this incident, an

increasing brightness and agitation of its flames, but soon I was confronted with more immediate distractions. One morning I was assailed by a curious buzzing sound. A peculiar vehicle no larger than a table hovered over my head. It descended a few paces distant and a hatch opened to permit the emergence of two diminutive figures, both completely hairless and no less mechanical than their craft. I frowned at their grey skins and slanting black eyes. Visitors from an extraterrestrial civilisation? I opened my arms in a gesture of peace but one of the figures raised a small weapon.

A wooden bolt of lightning, painted bright yellow, shot out on a spring and jabbed my chest. I bellowed in fury and stalked forward in a vengeful manner. The figures retreated and the vehicle rose back into the sky. I had no arquebus but my blunted dagger would serve as a deadly enough projectile. I threw it with the skill of a conjurer and my aim was true. The alien craft veered sideways and careened into the sun, exciting the flames even more. Thereafter boredom returned to my life. And heat. I sweltered and basted in my own juices and even swimming the night side oceans cooled me insufficiently. The Earth was becoming inhospitable.

"Baron! Can you hear me?"

The voice was not inside my head. I was not yet mad. In as nonchalant a manner as possible I replied, "Yes indeed. What do you want?"

"I am Sneakios, the creator of the machine."

I peered in all directions but saw no man: he was part of the blur of the revolving walls. I pulled my ears. "Will you join me for supper?"

"By no means. I am standing in a doorway of the hall and dare not approach more closely. The *orrery* is about to detonate. I am using a special device to communicate with you, an amplifier that modulates sound waves relative to your velocity. Another one of my astounding inventions! All solar systems have finite lifespans and this one is no exception. Your sun will die in an extremely violent fashion."

"What became of my family, you rascally Bulgar?"

"The religious authorities decided to formally denounce modern astronomy and declared that all adherents of a sun-centred system were potential heretics. The *orrery* was too bulky to dismantle and its existence here became a fatal liability, so it was prudent for the inhabitants of this castle to depart. As for myself, the edict almost ruined me: I have returned to my former profession of repairing clocks."

"Why did you arrange for the machine to explode?"

"That was not my doing. I merely programmed the sun to swell and then collapse into a cool white star, but somehow the central furnace has acquired extra mass, enough to ensure that it will destroy itself in a supernova, a word I recently coined."

"Bah!" I snorted, but I could not shrug off my guilt. The debris from my plunge through the roof, the shattered moon, the comet, the asteroids, Ganymede, the spacecraft, my dung: all had contributed to changing the destiny of the sun. The fault was entirely mine. As if aware of my thoughts, the sun began to groan.

"Farewell Baron!" called Sneakios. "I wanted to pay

my respects to all my wonderful toys. Now I must depart, but if you wish to save yourself you should visit Italy and peer down over Puglia, where you will observe a tiny dot. That dot is your own castle and inside its largest hall is a second *orrery*, a microscopic version of this one. It controls everything. Squash the castle with your thumb and you will stop time and shut off the sun. I wish you luck!"

Cursing myself for a dullard, I strode to the coast of North Africa, splashed through the Mediterranean Sea, hauled myself up spluttering on Sicily. Why had it not occurred to me to take this course of action before? I hurried onwards, stood high above Puglia and leaned forward to search the landscape. At this point the sun exploded. I felt myself flung high and closed my eyes, certain I would be dashed against the sides of the hall. But the walls no longer existed. I was soaring away from a ruin, over the forest, the sun sinking in a sky that was bounded by no walls. I was outside again, in the real world. I was free!

I saw that I was approaching the castle of our nearest neighbour. No lights shone on the battlements: the place appeared to be deserted. An open window gaped wider before me. With a howl of dismay I shot through it into a vast chamber. Spheres rotated around a central furnace. I landed with the birth of many bruises on a planet larger than the Earth. Several moons rose on its horizon. I recognised the furnace: a representation of the star Alpha Centauri. There are planetary systems everywhere in the universe, or so I now believe. Indeed they are almost as common and unremarkable as unlucky men.

(2006)

The Mirror in the Looking Glass

Mad inventors are plentiful in this world of ours but only one sits on a genuine throne and rules his own city like an ancient king. Frabjal Troose of Moonville has many dubious talents, including the ability to flap his ears; they squeak. But his cybernetics expertise is considerable and his contributions to the design and manufacture of artificial nervous systems are almost unparalleled. Only his perversity prevents him from becoming the saviour of the human race.

Perhaps I am overstating the case, but his monumental achievements are singularly unhelpful to his own subjects and the citizens of every other realm. What amuses Frabjal Troose is to install human intelligence in inanimate objects. With the aid of extremely small but excessively clever devices, part electronic and part mechanical, he can bestow the gift of consciousness with all its attendant emotions on chairs, crockery, table lamps, shoes, clocks, flutes.

He can and he does. Frequently.

His other hobby is to worship the moon…

One morning Frabjal Troose awoke with the urge to give thoughts and feelings to a mirror. He foresaw all manner of comic and tragic potential in the reality of a self-aware looking glass. To make the joke even more piquant he decided to equip his victim with prosthetic legs and allow it to roam freely around the city. He left his enormous bed and went to the bathroom and there he saw an appropriate mirror hanging on the wall above the moon-shaped sink.

The operation took several days. Frabjal Troose is a perfectionist and he wanted the circuits and cogs to be tastefully integrated into the frame of the mirror. In the end the workings ran over the surface of the wooden frame like complex ornamentation. By this time, the mirror could already think for itself and was slowly coming to terms with its sudden awareness and the need to develop an identity. It was no longer a mere object but a precious sentient being.

It even had a name. Guildo Glimmer.

Guildo learned to walk within his first hour. Wandering the palace of Frabjal Troose, little more than a large house stuffed with components for new gadgets, he came into contact with the occasional servant. At each encounter the same thing happened: the servant bent down and made a face at Guildo. Sometimes the servant picked him up and held him at arm's length while plucking a nose hair or squeezing a pimple. What did this mean? Guildo was bewildered.

He continued his explorations and discovered that the front door of the palace was open and unguarded. Through it he hurried, into the lunar themed spaces of the city. Moon buggies rolled past on the roads and the public squares were craters filled with people dressed in silver and yellow clothes. I know that Frabjal Troose once issued an edict forbidding any grins that were not perfect crescents. He also forbade any cakes that were not perfect croissants.

Guildo proceeded down the street. He desperately

needed time for reflection, but citizens just would not leave him in peace and they treated him in precisely the same way as the palace servants had, making blatant faces at him, grimacing and yawning and even frowning in disgust. Guildo began to experience the state of mind known as 'paranoia'. What was wrong with his appearance? What was it about him that provoked such reactions in strangers?

He must be ugly, a horrible freak, a grotesque mutant: there was no other explanation. He was overwhelmed with a desire to view his own face, to confront his visage, to learn the foul truth for himself. But he could think of no way to accomplish this. Are you stupid, Guildo Glimmer? he asked himself. There must be a method of seeing one's own face, but what? Because he was so new to the conventions of society, he always spoke his thoughts aloud.

"I know a reliable way," declared a passerby.

This passerby was a droll fellow, a practical joker. He told Guildo that when men and women wanted to look at their own faces they made use of a 'reflection'. What was one of those? Well, reflections existed in a variety of natural settings, in quiet lakes and slow rivers and the lids of clean saucepans, but only in the depths of mirrors did they realise their full potential. That is where the highest quality reflections dwelled, untroubled by ripples or cooking stains.

"You must look into a mirror!" he announced.

Guildo was astonished but grateful and he decided to follow this advice. The passerby chuckled and passed on. He was later arrested for not chuckling in the shape of a crescent, but that is another story. No, it is this story!

No matter, I will ignore it in favour of what happened to poor Guildo. His little metallic legs carried him to the market, a bustling place where anything one desired might be bought, provided one's desires were modest or at least plausible.

Guildo's were. He approached a stall selling mirrors.

The man who owned the stall was talking to another customer and so Guildo was free to hop onto a table and examine the mirrors on display. He chose a circular mirror that was nearly the same circumference as his own head and he stepped in front of it. What he saw was totally unexpected and utterly profound. He saw an immensely long tunnel, a tunnel that stretched perhaps as far as the moon or infinity.

It must be pointed out once again that Guildo Glimmer was a living mirror. A mirror is simply unable to view its own reflection. The moment a mirror gazes into another mirror, its image will be endlessly bounced back and forth between the two reflecting surfaces. Hence the illusion of a tunnel. This is a law of geometry and a rule of physics, but Guildo knew nothing of such disciplines. His education had not covered the sciences.

As far as he was concerned, the illusory tunnel was an accurate representation of his form. This meant that he really was a tunnel! Now he understood why people kept frowning at him and why he was so dissatisfied. It was because he was not fulfilling his correct role. He was a tunnel and ought to do what tunnels do, act like tunnels act, think what tunnels think. He rushed out of the market to embrace his true destiny.

Later that afternoon, the splinters of a smashed mirror were picked up from the tracks of the main railway line leading into Moonville. When pieced together they could be identified as the remains of Guildo Glimmer. There was no way of resurrecting him. Frabjal Troose came to pay his hypocritical respects but he quickly lost interest and returned to his palace in a land-boat powered by moonbeams. By this time the sun had gone down and the moon was up.

People said that Guildo committed suicide, that he was too full of despair to continue his existence. Why else would he stand in the path of a moving train? But as I watched the billowing sails of the receding land-boat, I realised that I knew better. Guildo was simply serving a mistaken function. Tunnels are there for trains to pass through, after all. I was the driver of that train: in fact I am the train itself, an earlier example of the unnatural quest to give intelligence to inanimate objects.

(2007)

Oh Ho!

Because people like ghost stories, and refuse to stop telling them, ghosts exist. Because people want ghosts to be malevolent, that is how they are.

But Sidney Fudge believed that rage, frustration and pain were the main ingredients necessary to turn a normal human being into an evil phantom after death. In this he was mistaken.

Such emotions, indeed emotions of any kind, can only be experienced and authentically expressed by a corporeal body, never by a disembodied spirit, for the reason that lack of a nervous system renders impossible the biological changes vital for the generation, development and cessation of a *feeling*. Hatred and a thirst for revenge do not merely increase heart rate and raise blood pressure but are intimately connected with those physical processes in a positive feedback loop.

With no blood pressure to raise, no glands to secrete hormones, no lungs to quicken breath, no pulse to throb to bursting in the veins, ghosts must be curiously emotionless beings. This is not the same as saying they are serene, gentle or forgiving. No.

The dead feel a cold, distant, purely cerebral, almost indifferent anger, for no other kind is available to them.

In time Sidney Fudge discovered this fact for himself.

He was a sickly child, the sort of boy who is easy prey

for bullies and seems to attract them almost against their will. Despite his eagerness to capitulate immediately to any aggression, to submit to every humiliation, the aforementioned bullies were unable to resist beating him savagely as a regular fixture of school life.

Black eyes and bloody noses became Sidney's trademark. In addition he had the rare talent of encouraging casual bystanders, who otherwise might have interfered with the punishment he received, to unconsciously adopt a policy of neutrality. Even mature adults watched his ordeals with blank faces, unaffected, bored.

Sometimes the adults quietly assisted the bullying. When a group of pupils resolved to push Sidney down the disused school well, the elderly janitor loaned his chisels and a crowbar to the conspirators to help them break the seal on the hole, to no avail as it happened, for the ancient well refused to open just for that antic.

It never occurred to Sidney to fight back, nor even to protect the most vulnerable parts of his anatomy in a manner wholly instinctive in other boys, nor would resistance have availed him, for already he had caught the attention of Pincher Gottlieb, the worst bully in his town and possibly the entire district. Mental torment was now added to physical, for Pincher was a specialist and fanatic and regarded bullying not only as a dignified artform but also as a sacred duty.

Sidney became the quivering shrine at which Pincher worshipped the Gods of Bullying, perfecting his techniques until he attained a level close to sainthood in the terms of his personal religion. Destined for greatness, at least in the estimation of his tutors, Pincher was openly admired for his extreme ferocity and inventiveness.

On one memorable occasion he cornered Sidney in the lavatory and managed to improve the notorious but generally overrated Water Torture by the simple but ingenious expedient of de-purifying the medium of its operating principle. Screams!

On another occasion he stripped Sidney, jabbed his pink flabby body full of rosebush thorns, then set fire to them one at a time with astounding dexterity until they were all ablaze and Sidney was persuaded to dance in an unconvincing fashion. Shrieks!

A third incident to be mentioned in passing was the forcing of Sidney to climb a ladder to the roof of the school, leaving him stranded when the ladder was removed. Not so innovative a prank, one might suppose, but Pincher had paid careful attention to the weather forecast. Furthermore he had clad Sidney in pots and pans and the violent clattering of this homely armour when the hailstorm broke so disturbed the afternoon lessons that Sidney was brutally and excessively whipped by the teachers when they managed to get him down. Wails!

And so it went on, day after day. For years.

The only evasive action that Sidney ever implemented was a sequence of pathetic attempts to avoid Pincher by taking complicated routes home. Instead of leaving school by the main gate, or even one of the side exits, he would climb the boundary wall and drop into the garden of a private house, making his way over several other walls and through a series of adjacent gardens until he found himself climbing the last crumbling wall and dropping down in the woods.

He attempted this ruse half a dozen times.

In the woods he felt marginally safer, but he always took to his heels immediately, weaving between the rotting trunks of ancient trees, putting as much distance between himself and school as possible, his unfit body straining with exertion to such a degree that it might even be argued that he bullied himself as he ran.

Deeper into the misty realm of rumoured bears and wolves he lurched, never heading in the direction of home, where an alcoholic mother and syphilitic father and crippled siblings rarely noticed his existence anyway, but always in random patterns, not caring where he ended up provided it was where Pincher Gottlieb was not.

But Pincher always appeared at the last instant, with a look of hideous delight on his face, popping up from behind a rock or bush when Sidney Fudge finally had to stop running, his lungs burning, legs trembling, heart exploding, and the bully always pointed a casual index finger and uttered the same exclamation, "Oh ho!"

Those two words became the essence of vocalised evil for Sidney, the victory shout of the personification of misery. How Pincher managed to work out where his victim would run to, when even Sidney did not know that, and how he was able to arrive first at the destination, were mysteries only compounding the horror.

"Oh ho! What do we have here then?"

When Sidney was in the embrace of his nemesis anything unpleasant might happen, and usually it did. The woods provided fertile ground for all kinds of potentially fatal pranks. Pincher once fed Sidney a banquet of toadstools and Sidney was left to crawl with excruciating cramps to the nearest hospital, where his stomach was thoroughly pumped and he was berated for his ignorance of fungi.

Also must not be forgotten the day when a tramp discovered a body hanging from a branch on a noose. He climbed the tree, severed the rope with his knife and lowered the corpse to the ground, then plundered its pockets for loose change. The corpse gasped, for it was still alive, so the tramp ran off and alerted the police, who came with medics to revive and retrieve Sidney. His recovery was marred by a universal lack of pity for his ordeal and when he returned to school he was treated to a lecture on the immorality of suicide by the headmaster, who publicly flogged him in the refractory to emphasise his point.

The next morning Pincher Gottlieb chased Sidney into the cloakroom and dangled him by his collar from one of the hooks generally reserved for coats. "Oh ho!" he boomed.

Sidney hung there for six hours and was later caned by all the teachers whose classes he missed. It would be unfair to give the impression that his pleas for assistance were utterly ignored. At one point an anonymous member of staff emerged from his office to investigate the disturbance and subsequently stuffed his handkerchief into Sidney's mouth to stifle the sounds before returning to work.

Waking life was an unremitting hell for the boy.

But not even the deeps of sleep were a refuge, because all his dreams were nightmares and involved Pincher springing up from unexpected and impossible hiding places to bellow "Oh ho!" before commencing some grotesque outrage on his person. If Sidney screamed or even whimpered in his sleep his alcoholic mother would be sure to enter his room and beat him mercilessly until he awoke.

Sidney developed an obsession that his mother somehow *was* Pincher, that if he reached out and tore off her rubber mask, the horrid face of the bully would loom there instead.

He even imagined the utterance she would make:

"Oh ho! Fruit of my loins are you now? Is that what you are? My own son, runt of the litter. Oh ho!"

And one night, unable to sleep, Sidney thought he could hear Pincher's voice coming from downstairs. Slipping out of bed, he listened with his ear to the floor but the words that rumbled below were incomprehensible, so he crept gently down the stairs. The lights were out but the voice still muttered and Sidney gained the bottom step. Then he lost his nerve and turned to go back up but missed his footing and sprawled awkwardly with a sprained ankle. The lights came on. Pincher and his mother stood there together and his theory was disproved.

"Oh ho! Have a drink on the house, dear chap!"

An empty gin bottle rebounded off his skull and he lost consciousness. His scalp remained hairless and discoloured at the point of impact for the rest of his life, but this incident was only the opening of a new chapter in the annals of his suffering.

Pincher called round every day for almost a year. He had convinced Sidney's parents that he was Sidney's best friend and he often told them lies about their son calculated to induce cyclones of rage in their strange minds. The slander about what experiments Sidney had been conducting with his own disabled sisters had momentous consequences for the boy and his development. Details are scarce but garden shears and a talent for singing soprano were factors.

The missing anatomical segments were kept by Pincher in a little cloth bag which he frequently opened for Sidney's appalled inspection with the ejaculation "Oh ho!" until they went too ripe and had to be discarded. The use of the word 'ejaculation' in the preceding sentence is correct but rather tasteless in context. Ah well.

To add stinging insult to hideous injury, Sidney's parents allowed the bully to 'borrow' every treasured possession Sidney ever owned. The few items that had given the boy some small measure of comfort, his toys and books and photographs, vanished forever. Sidney was left with nothing at all save the deepest despair.

"Oh ho! Set them all on fire, I did!"

The passing years became a decade and Sidney left school and ended up working in a factory. Unlike many bullied children he did not manage to escape his tormentor by entering the world of adult work, for Pincher applied for a job at the same factory and secured a position as a manager directly above Sidney. He would materialise behind Sidney and scream at the top of his voice, "Oh ho!"

So entertaining did his colleagues find Sidney's reaction to this mantra that they adopted it for themselves and utilised it as a reliable method of decreasing the ambient monotony of their environment. Scarcely an hour passed without an "Oh ho!" triggering a series of convulsions in Sidney's undeveloped frame. But Pincher was too conscientious a bully to delegate tyranny to underlings and never ceased to involve himself personally in Sidney's systematic degradation.

"You will avoid my attentions," he mockingly explained, "not for the full span of your existence. Seventy years are our allotted time on earth, a figure determined by the religion and healthcare of our society. So that's the length of your hell. Oh ho!"

The incessant shock ruined the nerves of Sidney Fudge, turning him into a quivering wreck of a man who dribbled uncontrollably and made so many mistakes on the production line that his wages were cut to the bare minimum as a punitive measure.

One afternoon he decided to run away.

He requested permission to empty a bladder, presumably his own, then abandoned his position at the conveyor belt and hastened in the direction of the communal bathrooms.

His absence was noted half an hour later and the manager sent for, but Pincher was also found to be absent. There was no ambiguity about what this meant. The bully had anticipated the escape bid of his victim and had gone to intercept him. The workers grinned to themselves and shook their heads and puffed their cheeks in admiration of Pincher's prescience. Truly he was the perfect oppressor!

Sidney recalled his school predilection for climbing boundary walls, scaled the factory fence and hurried over a dark wasteland littered with a decadent civilisation's premature fossils. Discarded bedsteads and broken washing machines impeded his progress, used nappies and condoms vied for dominance of tar pits, the blackened chassis of a stolen car smoked in the drizzle and our unfortunate hero used the oily vapours as cover for his flight, gibbering as he ran.

Genuinely he believed he was heading into freedom, and his mind was unable to confront the inevitable fact that his fate was his own at no point but belonged to Pincher Gottlieb.

He reached the lip of an embankment that sloped down to a motorway and frowned as he regarded this impassable river of moving steel, a visual scream that deafened his eyes, blinded his ears, did other mixed up things to his other bewildered senses.

He would have to turn back and find some other route. At that instant he felt damp sardonic breath on the nape of his neck and time froze into jagged blocks of chronic ice that scraped their way through his organism one by one. Pincher was right behind him, had been behind every step of the way. He realised that now.

A mouth fixed itself to his ear and a clawed whisper more awful than any shout plucked his nerves so utterly they would have vibrated forever had they been given the chance.

"Oh ho! Fancy meeting *you* here. Oh ho!"

Sidney did not turn but slid and rolled down the embankment. The oncoming vehicles were part of the bullying, or so it seemed, in league with Pincher, a stream of giant bullets aimed at his entire existence. He would never make it alive to the other side. Then he noticed a speeding ambulance and a desperate hope seized him.

If he had to be run down by a vehicle, an ambulance was a fine choice. An ambulance would contain people who knew how to save his life, if any spark of it remained, and it would also be in a position to hurry him to hospital for further treatment. He might as well throw himself in front of it before it went past. Yes. So he did.

The screech of brakes, the sickening thud, the slick of blood, the grin of Pincher far away, the voices, the rough manhandling into the back of the vehicle, all these elements and more became clues in a riddle that he attempted to solve as he lay on the stretcher and stared at the equipment and medicines around him.

At last the answer came. He was still alive.

That was the solution to the riddle! He was alive! In fact his injuries were minor, a few bruises and cuts, a tender spot on the side of his skull, blurred vision in one eye. His desperate stratagem had worked and he had outwitted Pincher in grand style.

A figure loomed above him, clearly a medic.

"How far to the hospital?" Sidney inquired. "And may I have a room all to myself, with a television?"

"Such matters aren't my concern," came the reply.

"Indeed? And why is that?"

"Because I'm not a member of the ambulance crew."

"Then who are you, pray?"

"The ghost of the last person to die in this vehicle."

"Your answer isn't one that pleases me to any extent. I assumed I was finally in a location of safety."

The ghost chuckled darkly and said:

"Did you not stop to wonder, before they lifted you inside, how many people have died in this small space, right here, on the way to hospital? The same holds true for every ambulance, of course, but this one has an especially poor track record."

"What do you intend to do with me?" asked Sidney.

"Scare you to death, I'm afraid."

"But why? I have done nothing to you. My injuries are mild and not life threatening. The nastiness of your avowed intent is thus gratuitous and I must ask you to reconsider."

"Your request is denied. But let me tell you something about myself to help you understand my bitterness."

"Thanks. I would welcome that," said Sidney.

"Well, I too had only minor injuries when I was lifted into the back of this vehicle. Then the ghost of my predecessor appeared and frightened me so badly I died. Turned out he had gone through the same thing years before, and his predecessor too, and *his*, and so on all the way back to the first person to die inside this ambulance, who was actually the only one of us to expire from natural causes."

"What an ironic causal chain of spooky anger venting!"

"Certainly is. Now I thirst for vengeance and intend to slake it on you. Wouldn't be fair for you to escape what I had to endure, would it? But my fury and hatred are purely cerebral because I have no nervous system to embody them. Does that help?"

"To a degree so miniscule I must shake my head."

The ghost sighed. "Sidney Fudge, your time on earth is done. You will reach the hospital as a cadaver. The process of scaring men to death takes between five and ten minutes."

"Will I lose control of my bowels?"

"You already have…"

It is perhaps better to skip the details of the concentrated haunting that followed. The ghost was a professional and even if Sidney had wanted to defend himself he would have found it futile to do so. Then suddenly the fear was gone and he felt calm, collected, but still unhappy. He inspected the prone form below, realised it was his own corpse, but felt no shock or nausea at the sight, just detached curiosity. The older ghost had vanished, having satisfied its pallid craving for getting its own back on this unfair world. Sidney was therefore the new ambulance phantom and presumably it was now his obligation to take his own revenge on the next patient with minor injuries who came inside.

But Sidney made a resolution to break the chain and end the process of misdirected spectral retribution. Instead of avenging himself at a tangent by discharging his trauma and misery onto an innocent victim, he would focus his attention exclusively on Pincher, harrying only the one who had harried him. "The bullying buck stops here!" he declared, a statement that might have occasioned sarcastic mirth among the young aggressive male deer in the vicinity, had there been any with exceptional hearing abilities who understood his language.

Some stags did live in the woods, and the woods bordered the hospital, but Sidney decided to vacate the ambulance while it was still moving on the motorway. He recapped the essentials of his resolution. Do not carry on bullying in an endless chain. Oppress only the one who oppressed him. Haunt Pincher. That was his agenda and it necessitated his floating over the landscape until he found his target.

Pincher Gottlieb was returning to the factory and had just skirted the final tar pit when Sidney caught up with him. For an atheist like Pincher, the appearance of icy invisible fingers around his throat accompanied by mouthless laughter was a deeply unpleasant spiritual jolt. He wriggled out of the choking embrace and ran for the safety of the factory, but Sidney appeared ahead of him, herding him away from the boundary fence and back over the foul wasteland.

For many hours Pincher dodged and twisted and sought to escape but found it impossible to elude his pursuer, who more often than not waited at the precise spot where Pincher hoped to find refuge, inside the chassis of a wrecked car, for example, or in the depths of a mutant pram designed to hold four or more underclass brats. The only reason Sidney eventually desisted and allowed Pincher to escape was to extend his sport to the next day. He wanted the game to last many moons, for his list of grievances was a document of considerable length.

As for Pincher, he concluded he must be unwell and went home to bed and shivered under extra blankets all night. In the morning his confidence returned, strapping fellow that he was, and he dismissed his ordeal as an unusual consequence of food poisoning. He simply did not realise that his own purgatory had just begun.

He rose, stretched himself, yawned, took a quick shower, but preferred not to dress himself just yet, wrapping his waist in a towel before going in search of coffee and croissants.

Sidney was waiting for him in the kitchen.

After Pincher was made dramatically aware of this fact, he ran out of the house with a squeal, but the ghost was unavoidable and Pincher had to endure a full day's haunting on an empty stomach. Wherever the bully went to seek sanctuary, Sidney lurked already. Then the towel fell off and Pincher became an object of shocked amusement to the pedestrians of the town centre, which is where Sidney herded him, up and down the busiest streets. A policeman was alerted and Pincher was chased and caught in a more conventional fashion.

At this point Sidney decided to leave off and resume the fun when the bully was alone once more. An hour later, Pincher was released from the police station with a caution and a spiritually refreshed Sidney pounced and fixed his extinct lips like a cold leech to his enemy's neck and sucked out the last vestiges of Pincher's reason and calmness. The bully threw up his arms and emitted a sound so inhuman that even Sidney was startled. Then Pincher leaped sideways, ran full tilt into a lamppost, got up again and accelerated down an alley.

Sidney floated high and calmly observed the progress of the terrified bully through the labyrinth of backstreets that led nowhere in particular. Able to descend at will to any point, the phantom appeared around every corner that Pincher turned, a harrowing game that continued through the afternoon and into the evening. The setting sun turned to blood the sweat on Pincher's brow and the rising moon spread evil butter on his pale skin until he resembled an especially unpleasing open sandwich. A snack of panic. A midnight feast of fear.

The following day passed in a similar manner, and the one after it, and the one after *that*, and these days slowly turned into weeks, until Pincher had ingested so many drops of his own medicine that he was cured of any semblance of courage or sanity.

One night Sidney chased him into the school.

How it happened they ended up here, in a place resonating so strongly with Sidney's pain and indignity, is not presently within the grasp of easy understanding. Maybe it was an accident. Sidney certainly did not want to return to this particular locale, for the memories it evoked were too grim and upsetting even for use as an automatic goad for vengeance. But into the school they went nonetheless.

In the middle of a courtyard was the disused well. For some reason the seal was broken and the hole gaped wide. Perhaps workmen were in the act of filling the shaft with cement and had managed to complete only the first stage of the project, the pit's exposure, and no other. So the mouth of darkness yawned large and horrible.

One moment Pincher was stumbling on the cobbles with Sidney's icy fingers tickling him under the ribs, the next he had vanished. There was a faint plop but no piercing scream.

Sidney frowned. What had happened? He studied the ground. When he realised the truth, he permitted himself a shallow smile. A shame his revenge had been cut short just as he was beginning to become an expert at cold vindictiveness! No matter. He could finally relax and spend the remainder of his afterlife in easy retirement. So he turned to drift gently away in the direction of the moon.

A voice hissed at his back and the sluggish ectoplasm in his spectral veins turned solid and glacial, but his anguish still lacked real emotion and remained an awkward travesty.

The voice repeated itself. Sidney quivered and gasped.

A third time it came: "Oh ho!"

And now Sidney turned to watch his nemesis float out of the well and approach with fluttering eyelids.

The ghost of a victim may be more than a match for a bully, but when the bully also becomes a ghost the old relationship will return to exactly the same state as when both lived.

"Oh ho! What do we have here? Oh ho!"

A man can be bullied for the entire span of his life, seventy years on average. In the same manner, a ghost can be bullied for the entire span of its afterlife, a period of time rarely less than five hundred years and often as long as two thousand. All spectres do fade eventually, but not quickly enough for Sidney Fudge. He flees through every level of the astral plane, the nastiest ghost imaginable cold on his heels. His existence is no longer a living hell but far worse than that.

(2008)

Loneliness

I turn the key in my door and enter my flat. Two small rooms connected by a corridor in such a manner they almost bear no relation to each other. The layout is certainly odd. The bathroom is part of my bedroom and the kitchen occupies half the living room, everything is unbearably cramped, and yet that connecting corridor is very long and high, an immense length of wasted space that represents nothing domestic. It is like a segment of an unhappy journey brought indoors, or part of a sculpture of a lonely walk without a walker, which naturally makes it more lonely, more itself. I have no affection for that corridor. Once I tried keeping a bicycle in it but that only made matters worse, for it gave the impression the bicycle had been abandoned in a place nobody ever went and consequently I felt guilty mounting it, like a thief. So the corridor is empty again and I have no plans to fill it with anything else.

After firmly closing and bolting my door I stroll along that corridor to my living room as rapidly as possible, the same as always, a voyage on foot that never feels heroic, though perhaps it should, passing the door of my bedroom near the start of the journey but refusing to acknowledge it with a nod or glance, because those actions always seem to slow matters, though really I am sure they do not.

When I finally reach my destination and leave the

corridor somewhere behind, set the kettle to boil, struggle out of my coat and collapse into my easy chair, I am suddenly overwhelmed with a feeling of loneliness. Too difficult to put into words the sheer power of the sensation, the wrenching deep inside my gut, the apparent unwrapping of that bone bandage called a skull to expose my mind to the vast disinterest of the cosmos. I know at once I am the loneliest man alive.

To be lonely is nothing new for me. I am shy of my own reflection in mirror, spoon and shiny shoe, have no family or friends, and no talent for conversing with strangers, yet I regard myself as perfectly normal and unworthy of pity or special regard, for each of us has felt extreme mental and spiritual isolation at one time or another. All varieties of loneliness have enough aches and pangs in common to bind a victim closely to his fellow sufferers, so in shared loneliness we are one, together, united. This curious truth resembles an escape clause in an insurance contract but is more palatable to those who sell no insurance, for on this occasion we are the beneficiaries of the perversity.

So much for ordinary loneliness, but the loneliness I now experience is different, far more intense, so excruciating I am forced to twist, shrug and blink furiously in my chair as the bleakness envelops me. Immediately I fail to understand how emptiness can be a tangible force, how an absence can be a presence, how a negative can be so positively damaging that my deepest desire is to have enemies, anybody at all to keep me company, to protect me from the utter void.

Yes, my solitude is total, and a conventional lack of

friends and family is certainly not enough to account for the magnitude of my despair. There must be more to it than that, something unbelievable, unhinged, dramatic but subtle. And soon enough, without even needing to jump up and ruffle my hair, I shockingly realise the truth. My apartment is *not* haunted. That is the wild fact of the weird matter. Not haunted, nor has it ever been. No ghost has drifted along that improbable corridor since the dawn of death, not one. I share my living space with no malignancy. Unwatched, I dwell in the exact middle of seclusion.

This peculiar situation is possibly unique in the present century. As the world slowly grows older, ghosts thicken on the continents, crammed into houses and spilling onto streets, shifting, ebbing, heaving like exasperated sighs on currents powered by jostling insubstantial elbows. The cities and spaces between cities are overcrowded with spectres, young, old, bad and good, shapeless, elaborate, thin and obese. On each step of every staircase they crouch or sit, under every table.

The cure for my loneliness becomes apparent. To encourage a ghost to move in with me. To be haunted.

I understand why no spectre has taken residence in my apartment. Not just a question of anyone failing to die between my walls. Perhaps whole families were murdered here. No, the plan of the place, the layout itself, is the problem. When a ghost drifts down a simple passage in an ordinary building, the quiet understanding is that something worth floating for can be found at one end or the other. But not where I live. My corridor is too abnormal for that, more important than the rooms it leads to, a destination in its own right. It can go nowhere because it already *is* somewhere. The rooms are less than afterthoughts.

And what ghost would choose to patronise such an absurd situation? They are not without pride, I hear.

I must spend my evenings praying for a ghost to come from outside, to occupy my hideous hollowness, take the place of my old bicycle, disturb my sleep, rattle cups, make me less lonely, to drift with gaping mouth up and down that horrid passage. In return I will do anything to increase its standing in the supernatural realm, to enhance its reputation as a force to be reckoned with, sleep with it, paint it, suckle it on whatever shadows it prefers, anything at all, shameless.

But my prayers remain unanswered, the homemade spells ineffective, ritual webs wasted, because the phantoms outside already know about my corridor, have heard the truth from the spirits of those slain families who voluntarily chose to depart this place, despite its cubic freedom, and join the highly compressed mob in the street. I cannot trick the dead so easily and now must find an alternative method of forcing a companion into my space and keeping it here, more faithful than any bicycle. A little surplus thought and I have the solution.

I reverse the direction of my desire, promptly, abruptly, and pray in a loud voice for my apartment to become even lonelier, for my loneliness to increase rather than decrease. Is such a thing possible in a place where there are no ghosts? Hardly. Yet this is how I do it: with total integrity I vow that if I should die here, or in my bedroom, or in the corridor, I too will depart the premises in spirit form and never return. And to make this threat realistic I take a clean kitchen knife from the sink without having to rise from my chair, simply by leaning over with my long arms and pulling it toward me, cold and dripping.

Then I dry it on a trouser leg, just above my knee, the flat of the blade swept twice against the fabric, and lift the implement to my throat. This is no game and I prepare to cut.

A gust of impossible wind swirls in the corners. A voice both resonant and desiccated says: "I am the Spirit of Loneliness. I am here because this is the loneliest spot on earth."

"I am not prepared for visitors," I answer modestly.

"You called me from the coldest ice cap, the deepest cave, the highest cloud, and I came at once, for I feel at home only where nobody else ever goes. I dream of an age when only one mind existed in the universe. Next time that mind will be mine."

"I am glad you have come," I reply.

"You cannot be glad, for there can be nobody lonelier than you. Even your future ghost has deserted this spot. There are still many places in the world where there are no ghosts, but this is the only place I know where there never *will* be a ghost."

"A shame. But now I have you," I smile.

"I do not understand."

"Then listen carefully with your lonely ears. I could not pray for less loneliness, so I prayed for more, so much more that *you* hurried here, the actual personification of loneliness."

"Truly that is what I am. No friend of yours."

"I admit that a human companion, alive or dead, would suit me better, but that option seems not to exist, and you are better than nothing, even though you represent nothingness. In your presence I am utterly alone, even more lonely than before, because you *are* nothing, but I also feel less lonely because you are here."

He points at me with a bony finger because it is a gesture required of all ghosts. I realise that his eyes have no faraway look but really do exist elsewhere, that his sockets drink light with an insatiable thirst. "I have no patience at all with paradoxes."

"This one is not unpleasing."

He does not agree, the Spirit of Loneliness, and admits that he finds my duplicity quite exasperating, but it is too late for him. He is truly here, where I am, and together we are bound to each other. It is better to feel lonely in company than lonely alone, even when you are lonely because of that company. Is it not? On the floor of my living room my discarded coat tangles the legs of his intangible spirit like a deflated apartment with two hungry corridors for sleeves.

(2008)

Hell Toupée

"You want a magical wig, have wanted one a long time, and finally think you've come to the right place to buy one. And you're not wrong. So step this way and I'll show you the wig of your dreams, just down this narrow passage, mind your head on the stalactites. That's right. Not much further. Let me tell you what to expect. Made from real yeti hair it is, genuine and certified. That's what I said, bona fide abominable snowman was tracked across snowy wastes for days, eventually got tired of running, turned for a fight, threw black boulders for an hour, used an icicle as a lance. Yeti in a tight spot's the meanest critter in creation, but finally got a blowpipe dart in his neck and his cryptozoological dozen tons tumbled down a slope to demolish a village at the bottom.

"That dart was a tranquilliser, not a poison, a massive dose of what the eggheads mix up in their laboratories when decent folk are in bed and call *carfentanil* or something like that. Doesn't do permanent damage. A yeti's too rare to kill for its fur. The trackers clip the scalp with shears when it's snoring louder than a communist tractor and then they wait for the hair to grow back. Maybe hunt the same beast five years later. A difficult job, so yeti wigs don't come cheap, but they're special. When you put one on, the hairs grow down, into your own scalp, and the wig becomes an integrated part of your head. That's not a wig, it's a transplant with a different name! Tunnel gets narrower round the next bend, by the way, and we have to go down on hands and knees. Sorry.

"Did you know that yetis generally walk about on stilts to put trackers off the trail? Or wear snowshoes like big tennis rackets. I'm friendly with a fellow north of here who illegally exports snowshoes to Tibet and Nepal for the yetis. That's the real racket! Has even been known for a yeti to fix snowshoes on the ends of his stilts to make it trickier for the hunters. And maybe that's fair enough. Time to light the wick of my lantern now and I suggest you stay close behind me. Real labyrinth down here, a tangle of subterranean tunnels regularly used by the Underground Hiking Society, some members of which may still be wandering lost from the last outing. Happens every time. But another half hour of crawling and we'll be in the storeroom with the quality stuff.

"What's that? You don't need a wig. Why come here in that case with your baldness reflecting the glow of the phosphorescent walls in a wholly unpleasant manner. You want a non-sequitur instead? You walked in here to buy a non-sequitur? Sorry buddy, you got the wrong shop. This shop is a wig emporium. Sells wigs and related scalp products. Nothing else. The non-sequitur store's next door. Easy mistake to make, is made all the time in fact, no skin off my nose. The nose of a yeti's no use in the making of wigs, incidentally. Well now. Don't return the same way but climb up this escape ladder instead. It'll take you to the rear of the emporium at ground level and you can let yourself out the back door. I'm sure the non-sequitur store has a rear entrance too, ok?"

And so I climbed the rusty old ladder in unseemly haste, getting away as rapidly as possible from that hideous underground lair. I dislike confined spaces, always have, and my love for weird proprietors isn't much higher. Some of the rungs were missing.

I finally emerged into a purer kind of light, the slanting ruby beams of a setting sun filtering through thick unwashed glass. I was in a junkroom and the windows were small and circular. Dust motes and forgotten boxes were everywhere. I had a sneezing fit.

At the back there was a door that would have opened onto a garden if it wasn't locked. I rattled it a few times in despair but the wood was rotten and splintered easily. So I was able to kick my way onto a shattered patio and deeply breathe my lungs clean.

"I'll linger just for a few minutes and then jump over the wall into the garden of the non-sequitur store."

That's what I said to myself and I nodded in reply.

Jumping over garden walls has been a hobby of mine most of my life, ever since I was a mischievous child. It can be stated with only minimal exaggeration that I prefer sneaking secretly through sequences of private gardens to walking down the street.

But first I wanted to enjoy the ambience.

It was clear that nobody had been in this garden for a long time. Years or even decades. Everything was untended, even the spades and forks that had been stabbed into the soft earth of flowerbeds and left to turn to seed. But garden tools don't really do that.

I took a step forward. Nature had reclaimed the place utterly, set up a new organic regime. I saw a snail riding on the back of a tortoise for the sake of greater speed. Life in the fast lane. Bit of a daredevil that mollusc, but we're all young once, aren't we?

The moment I entered the undergrowth I knew this route wasn't going to be the shortcut I'd hoped for. Couldn't see the boundary wall. Must be somewhere behind the sunflowers. Thorns snagged my elbows as I went onward, attracting my attention, but they had little to say. Like children, briars. Finally I lost patience.

"What is it? What do you want this time?"

To my surprise the wall wasn't behind the sunflowers after all. I kept going and broke off a flexible branch to use as a cutting whip. Almost as effective as a machete if wielded properly. Blossoms flew loose about me and berries were juiced in midair.

Then I stumbled on a vegetable plot long forsaken and crouched amid the weeds and uprooted wild versions of potatoes, parsnips and carrots. I stuffed those in my jacket, slipped an artichoke heart into my shirt pocket. Pure instinct. I'm a survivor.

But I began to grow worried. What if darkness fell before I got inside the non-sequitur store? Might be better to turn around and work my way through the wig emporium like a meal in reverse, emerging back onto the street. Then I could stroll next door and enter the non-sequitur shop from the front. Sensible, civilised.

But the sun was already going down. And from which

direction had I come? My efforts to retrace my steps were really rather laughable. I was lost in a suburban jungle, orchids underfoot, big ants too, moths, bats and fireflies failing to guide me anywhere useful. I wandered in circles, ovals and spirals. A geometric joke.

"Get a grip, Mr Heckoid. It's not so awful really. There seems to be the remains of a path over there."

"So let's investigate," I answered myself.

The path could faintly be discerned in the twilight, an overgrown and eroded line of paving stones that twisted and dipped through arbours and around ferns and brambles. Slightly easier work than stumbling blind into the mass of roots and tendrils that existed elsewhere. I even hummed as I walked, an improvised tune.

My eyes gradually adjusted to the dictates of dusk and the old broken slabs under my feet glimmered sufficiently in the starlight to prevent any wandering off course. Then my ears detected a crackling. A glow in the distance aroused my curiosity.

I came to a sudden clearing in the monstrous growth and was forced into a frenzy of chin stroking when I realised what sat on the chipped rim of a choked marble fountain. Her back was to me but her luxuriant tresses convinced me at once of her delectability. She had hair down to her heels and it was a dark golden colour.

"Señorita! Young damsel! Slip of a thing!"

She turned slowly at my shout. Has a man ever been so disappointed and terrified in consequence of a gallant greeting? It was not a lady after all, but a yeti. From behind in poor light the mistake brings no shame on the person who makes it, I say.

It held up a massive paw, warning me not to run or possibly reassuring me of its kindly intentions. To flee from a yeti is a difficult process and I considered myself badly qualified for the attempt. I shudderingly decided to stay where I was and grin.

"Will you share my fire?" it asked quietly.

"Are you sure you want to associate with a human, bearing in mind the callous way we treat your kind?"

"I never pre-judge an individual," it answered.

"That's very noble of you, so I'll accept your offer gladly. Do you plan to camp here the whole night?"

"Seems the best place in the vicinity, unless you've seen better on your travels. But I take it you haven't or you wouldn't be wandering in the dark with just a stick for protection."

"Is it dangerous in these parts?" I wondered.

The yeti whistled slowly through its fangs, nodded its head, then did something with the embers on the edge of the fire. It was roasting nuts, I realised, fresh from the nearby almond and chestnut trees. Squirrels gazed down in envious admiration.

"Share my food. It's nearly ready."

I sat on the ground at the opposite side of the fire, my front half soon roasting, my back freezing, a most typical scenario of bivouacs like that. The yeti introduced himself without offering his paw to shake. Has never been the monster way. I didn't tell him about the fresh vegetables hidden about my person. I'm selfish.

"My name's MeMeMeMeMe U," he said.

"Pleased to make your acquaintance. And I'm Albert Guppy Heckoid. I got confused looking for a non-sequitur store. Entered a wig emporium by mistake. Now I'm out here."

"Rather odd," he mused, as he pinched nuts from the flames, juggled them to coolness, four at a time, handed an equal share to me, "for I had the exact reciprocal experience."

"Looking for the wig emporium?" I prompted.

"Yep, but went into the non-sequitur store instead. Came out the back, planned to take a shortcut through the gardens, found it to be something beyond possibility. There's a kink in the spacetime continuum or a similar contrived explanatory mechanism hereabouts and we've fallen out of our cosmos into a new dimension."

I was shocked. "Have we really?"

He shrugged. "Dunno. That was just a guess."

"What does the non-sequitur store look like? If I knew that, I might be able to keep an eye out for it."

He nodded and chewed the flesh of nuts. "Sleep here tonight and we'll travel together tomorrow. I've had enough of this climate, just want to get back home or anywhere else snowy. I've heard rumours about places even snowier than Tibet. Are those rumours true? Is there a genuine country by the name of Snowva Scotia where it snows forever, even when it's sunny, even when it's *not* snowing?"

"No there isn't. Sorry," I said.

"Shame. Why am I always so gullible?"

"Caution is a keyword. So is prudence. Caution and prudence. Never believe everything you're told."

"It looks like a pyramid, by the way," he added.

"The non-sequitur store?"

"Among other things, yes."

I swallowed a nut. "Just looks like one?"

"Is one," he corrected.

"That's useful. I'm grateful," I said.

He nodded. "I'm going to ask you a serious question and I want you to give me your best answer. Tree hugging. Comforting or traumatic for the tree? I mean, hippies often quote hugging a tree as an ultimate example of spreading love and peaceful energy. But I wonder. For the tree it might be a nasty experience, making it think it's being strangled by a parasite like a fig. Choke other trees, figs do."

"I don't know, I just don't know," I said.

"Fair enough. I respect your honesty. Tomorrow I'll abandon my own quest and escort you on yours. My original plan was to give the owner of the wig emporium a savage beating for the trouble he causes my kind but I no longer have the heart for it."

"Just as well if you can't find the place."

"Life's too short anyway. In the language of my country I'm not called *yeti* but *metoh-kangmi*. Not that it matters. I also suspect that trees hate to be embraced. They aren't bears."

I noticed two long poles in the shadows. "What are those things there? Are they stilts? Are they yours?"

"That's right. My stilts. Used them to get here, to stride over boundary walls, of which there are dozens or hundreds in every direction. Walking over difficult terrain is easier with stilts, Mr Heckoid, and is good fun too. Considerable skill is required to attain speeds faster than a tiger or stoat, and stilt running is a major yeti accomplishment, but it's not confined to our species. The human peasants of La forêt des Landes in Gascony have the ability too, so I'm informed."

"Can you juggle?" I pressed.

"Never cared to learn that. Nor the swallowing of swords. Finish your nuts and get some sleep, you'll need energy for tomorrow. There are wild dogs on the loose, the descendants of domesticated breeds whose kennels fell apart generations ago. The fire will discourage them, but if you need to get up in the middle of the night and relieve yourself, don't wander too far into the bushes. They're hungry."

"The bushes or the dogs?" I shivered.

He laughed at that, the great friendly brute, and the brief remainder of my conscious evening passed in making myself as snug as possible while the echoes of his mirth fanned the flames with diminishing impetus. Nuts in belly, dry leaves for bedding, clump of grass for a pillow, I quickly fell asleep despite the early hour. The stars shone without twinkling, probably because the twigs were crackling on the fire, and twinkling *and* crackling is an overseasoning of backdrop.

Worms moved in the world under my body while I slept. Humans drill the soil for what it conceals, worms for what it is. Who's the fool, who the brains, in that set up? I dreamed vivid dreams all night. First I dreamed I was sliding down the side of a pyramid, sacred crocodiles snapping in the river, desert sands drifting into dunes on the horizon, while animal-faced gods played musical instruments.

Then I dreamed I fell down a fissure and landed inside the pyramid. It was pitch black and I was bruised and nervous. I wanted to shout for help, but before I could make any noise, a voice cried, "No more non-sequiturs in stock! Come back some other soup!" Suddenly I felt more disappointed than ever before. A big furry hand shook me gently. This didn't belong to the dream. I opened moist eyes.

"Dawn already," said the yeti with a smile.

"Rosy fingered. Thumbs up."

"Did you sleep like a log?" he asked.

"Like a transitional passage," I corrected. "Are you boiling peppermint leaves for breakfast tea, Mr U?"

"Please don't be so formal. Call me MeMeMeMeMe. You're my guest and my responsibility. Now then. There's no way you'll keep up on your own legs when we set off, so I'll carry you. My upraised arms will serve as *your* stilts. Hope you have a good head for heights. Especially as we'll be mounting some lofty walls."

We sipped the tea, which turned out to be an infusion of betel leaves rather than peppermint, then embarked on our journey. The yeti's strong hands grasped my ankles and held me aloft while he slipped his hairy feet into the straps of his own stilts and hopped upright with incredible agility. We set off at alarming speed.

"What's the weather like up there?" he joked.

"I can see for miles. I'm drunk with freedom and wind

and smeared in the glow of the rising sun, blowing kisses at the fading stars, an emperor of a backdoor rainforest surveying his emerald realm from the vantage of stilted stilts. That's how I am."

"Yes, but what's it like?" he pressed.

I couldn't answer, for I was too exhilarated, too invigorated, too dizzy, and only with the most extreme effort could I recall that my duty was to watch for the non-sequitur store. It wasn't in evidence. No sign of the wig emporium either. Just gardens.

We bounded over one decaying wall into a rockery where cacti in their sappy sentience daydreamed about spiking ears or getting students drunk and disgusted in cahoots with maguey worms. Probably. The vicious dogs that MeMeMeMeMe had warned me about were plentiful here but with their rabid drools safely below.

Another wall, another garden. An endless patchwork of gardens with a wall between each one. Some walls were higher than others. One was so high it could only be reached by using a leaning elm as a ramp. We strode along the top, searching for a way down the other side. At that moment I was the most elevated thing in the circumference of my vision. Or was I? A shadow smothered my pride.

"What the heck?" cried MeMeMeMeMe.

"Hot air balloon," I replied.

"It's very low. Ask directions from it."

I took his advice. The basket swung next to my head, its occupant so close to my mouth that I was easily understood when I asked, "Is there a non-sequitur store hereabouts?"

Lower drifted the globe until I could see that the basket

was stuffed to the brim with antique junk and curious artistic objects, tools, lamps, coils of rope, robes, machines, bottles, kettles, books and similar random items and the balloonist was almost lost among them. Doffing his hat to expose another hat, he responded:

"Haven't seen one, but I can sell you a non-sequitur myself if you're so keen on acquiring them. I have a single pristine example left. I'm a sort of aerial bric-a-brac merchant."

"May I inspect the product on offer?"

"No time for that. Due to my dependency on the wind, which is fickle at the best of times, my business has to be conducted rapidly, without the standard niceties of examination and haggling. You'll have to purchase it on the strength of my recommendation alone. But it's in perfect condition and won't ever let you down."

And he quoted a surprising sum at me.

I wanted to ignore the temptation and turn away, but either my hand or wallet suddenly developed a mind of its own, for I found myself passing a fistful of new banknotes over.

"Remember prudence," MeMeMeMeMe hissed.

"Don't worry," I said, "for if the non-sequitur turns out to be deficient, I'll simply reach out with my stick and thrash this conman to an excessive degree. That's my insurance."

"I can tell I'm dealing with a shrewd customer," smirked the balloonist approvingly. Then he rummaged among the miscellaneous objects at his feet and picked up a box, small but very heavy, made of iridium or some other awfully dense metal.

"Catch!" he shrieked as he threw it at me.

That box nearly knocked me off my perch, but a yeti's grip is mythical as well as legendary, so I fully absorbed the impact without plummeting to my destruction. Free of its expensive ballast, the balloon rose into the sky with fantastic velocity and I realised this was the balloonist's normal method of escaping retribution.

I craned my neck up at a steep angle and cupped my hands around my mouth. "Who exactly are you?"

"Tommy Tindertub," he called back faintly, and I was satisfied when I heard that, because it gave me a definite name to curse if it turned out I'd been swindled by a charlatan.

Then I opened his box and looked inside.

The streets of Huknibonk-on-Stench are narrow and cobbled and often in the festive season flooded with cheap wine that pours into the low plazas from the high taverns that crowd about the citadel hill. A man who climbs up at those times ought to wear rubber boots, unless the drying of socks is a special hobby of his, and the same applies to women. Discrimination of gender counts for naught in that place when it comes to drunken glee and immodest revels. They are all ravers. The smoking of crystallised cocaine is also popular but less common.

The city smells rotten not just because of the human waste tipped from open windows out of traditional chamber pots decorated with scenes from the writings of the Bad Ochre Poets but chiefly due to its location above a stinking marsh. The hidden quicksands still gurgle and gulp and buildings sink another inch every month. Some authorities even attest that wills-o'-the-wisp seep up in thin spirals through cracks in the pavements to dance without music on the longest night, but these 'authorities' are inspectors of tax and trusted by nobody at all.

The worst of the Bad Ochre Poets was probably Cassius Befuddle. His complete works can only be borrowed from public libraries with a special permit, rarely issued, and nobody ever talks about him, despite the pots in every bedroom that feature illustrations from his sonnets. But this present tale isn't concerned with his existence, so no secrets will have to be prised from sealed lips, no confidences broken. Prudence Mooncup is the main character instead, a dreamy student at a decaying university that is nearly always closed for another holiday.

Prudence had chosen aeronautics as her subject, for she greatly craved a career in the sky, but the professors who only occasionally turned up to deliver lectures already knew less about that science than did she. Full of liquid and vaporous stimulants, those gowned dunces drew simple wings, engines and propellers on the blackboard with chalk and made derogatory remarks about landing gear and ailerons. Then they would yawn, abandon the lesson with a shrug of malnourished shoulders and devote themselves to the consumption of more wine.

Our heroine remained dissatisfied with this style of teaching, but there was no place for her to lodge complaints. The chancellor of the university was a drunkard bigger than the rest, an old soak with literal gin tears who hoped to lighten the duties of the professors in his charge still further and reduce his own working hours to zero. His goal was for the university to open half a day every year and no more. His ears were deafer than lemon slices to Prudence's protests, his contemptuous spittle like old tonic water. She could expect no aid from him.

And so she progressed painfully slowly with her studies. Most of what she learned came from observation and experiment. She watched the few birds brave enough to fly over Huknibonk-on-Stench and made accurate notes from which she was able to design and construct model ornithopters that flapped over filthy roofs like severed applause. But always her flying machines rapidly ran out of power and crashed. One midnight a drunken tax inspector was felled by her analogue of an owl and remained prostrate until the end of the financial year.

Something had to be done. An answer must be found. But how, where, when? She often roamed the streets, wading in wine, ignoring the hisses and whispers from shadowy doorways, never with a fixed destination in mind, until she found herself back at the stairway that spiralled tightly to her lonely attic. But on one occasion she strayed further than usual, ended up on the steepest slope of the citadel hill, sat on a boulder and wept over the wasted opportunities below. Snatches of inebriated song reached her, the fumes of champagne and crack.

"All I want is a solution to the riddle of excessive power consumption in heavier-than-air flying devices based on the flapping wing technique of nocturnal birds of prey!" she wailed.

"Is that really so much to ask for?" she added.

Then she frowned deeply. "Wait a moment! I don't believe it was me who made that second remark. It came from above, from a male throat, and I'm down below and female!"

She gazed up. A hot air balloon was descending slowly and it finally halted very close to her head, hovering there with its burner reduced to a minimal flame. The occupant of the wicker basket wore two simultaneous hats at least and introduced himself with a courtesy restricted by the mass of bizarre junk around him. He resembled a peg inserted into an eccentric uncle's pocket, you know the kind I mean. Prudence was less shocked and intrigued by his arrival than might be expected, for now she was a jaded woman, beyond simple reactions.

"You're in luck," announced Tommy Tindertub.

"Why's that?" she sighed.

"Because I have just the thing you're after. But it'll cost you dear, for I desire the object myself. Yet I'm a trader through and through, so I'll give you a chance to purchase it first."

He quoted a price at her and she gasped.

"I thought I was beyond amazement, but clearly I'm not, for that figure truly made me quiver," she said.

"It can easily be doubled," declared Tommy.

"No thanks. I'll settle for the first price if I decide to buy. But are you sure you're offering me the secret of *heavier* than air flight? I don't count balloons as authentic aviation."

"You won't be disappointed, young lady."

"Here's the bulk of my savings. I shouldn't do this but either my hand or purse has evolved a mind of its own and wants you to take this fistful of banknotes. Where's the secret?"

"Catch!" roared Tommy as he shot up.

Prudence snatched the object that came spinning at her. "A bottle! One lousy bottle of non-sequiturs! I detest fresh non-sequiturs but the pickled variety are even worse. It's not even full, but empty! I've been conned by a hoodwinker with extra headgear. But it's an old bottle and the cork pops out with a giggle. What's this?"

Up rose a genie with expanding turban and benevolence. "Any wish at all is yours. If it's logical I'll do my best. Don't wish for extra wishes. That loophole was closed ages ago."

Prudence fumed. "Of all the fabulous things that come from the East, a genie is one I can do without."

"Sorry to hear that," said the genie.

"I'd rather have a magic carpet. They can fly but don't need wings. All the lift is generated by the shape of the rug itself. As for propulsion, they don't require engines or fuel."

"Like frisbees," ventured the genie.

"Not quite. You should be teaching at the local university if that's the way your intellect operates."

And so it appeared. A magic carpet. Woven by the slaves of perverted monks in icy Tibetan sweatshops from yeti hair, which naturally levitates, hence the necessity for it to grow downwards into scalps to stop it flying off. Prudence Mooncup mounted it and carefully sat in the exact middle with crossed legs and fingers. The fibres itched her upper thighs, exposed legs being her one concession to bohemianism. Smooth, creamy. And she flew away. Soon enough, Huknibonk-on-Stench was no more than a stain on a world tablecloth far below.

Remember Prudence, for Prudence is wise.

Like caution. And owls.

＊

I let the iridium box slip through my fingers and it grazed the yeti's left elbow as it went down, then bounced with a hollow boom off the lip of the wall, clattered into a thicket.

"Disappointed?" asked MeMeMeMeMe.

"Yes," I admitted sourly, "for it wasn't even a proper non-sequitur. At first it seemed not to follow from anything that had gone before, then the balloonist turned up and the illusion was exposed. I don't suppose I'll ever get a refund. What an idiot!"

"No you're not. You're mildly clever."

"I was referring to Tommy Tindertub. He's the cretin! He'll never win an award for good business ethics if he keeps behaving like that. I parted with cash for plain recursion."

"Maybe it's not nearly as bad as that."

"Meaning what, Mr U?"

"Told you before not to call me that. Anyway. Perhaps it really was a genuine non-sequitur. Maybe Tommy's intrusion into it was just a sort of copyright notice or trademark symbol. It's *his* non-sequitur, after all, and we must protect our memes."

"Our *what*?" I spluttered angrily.

"Memes, Mr Heckoid. Mental genes. Ideas passed from mind to mind like buttons among the coatless."

"Oh those. I thought you said 'mimes'."

"I assure you I didn't. I don't believe in protecting *mimes*. Not at all. I dislike street theatre intensely. I even advocate smiting those pavement thespians with bunched fists!"

And so I was reassured. Almost. Not quite.

I said, "Consider the pun on the word 'prudence'. That also relates the tale to what occurred earlier."

"Could be coincidence. Give it the benefit of the doubt."

"Expected to grant another benefit of the doubt, am I? Enough doubts on benefit already. We need to break their dependence on benefit, smash the benefit culture!" I roared.

"Here, here!" he replied with a nod.

"You concur?" I squinted.

"No, I was merely indicating that *here* is a good place for us to climb down from the wall safely."

And it was. So we did. Slowly, awkwardly. At the bottom a wild dog locked hungry and unreasoning jaws onto the base of MeMeMeMeMe's right stilt but was kicked off instantly. I watched it soar in a high arc and lap sunshine with its tongue.

"Do yeti hairs really levitate?" I asked.

"They contain natural hydrogen peroxide, which is why they're so pale blond in colour. In the distant past the peroxide ran out. Now each hair is a sealed tube filled with gas."

"What's your favourite musical instrument?"

"The honest lyre," he said.

Hell Toupée

"Have you ever stolen a cheese through an open window of a house by spearing it on the end of a stilt?"

He nodded without shame. "Yes I have."

"What flavour of cheese?"

"Stilton. After the impalement…"

"If a canoe takes twelve times as long as a book to float down a river of ink, how much longer than a worried frown does it take a broad smile to float down a river of tears?"

"I really don't care, Mr Heckoid."

"The reason I ask these questions is because I want to get to know you much better. It's possible that a sincere friendship might evolve from our unhygienic physical proximity."

"I doubt it. Will you be quiet please?"

A lesser man would have smarted at such a rebuke but I merely sagged into a bottomless depression. Yet I didn't drop my gaze. Then I caught the glint of something remarkable in the distance. I shielded my eyes with my hands and blinked. Yes, it was there, without a doubt, a pyramid! It had to be the non-sequitur store. I glimpsed it for a moment between the waving branches of a willow and though it was lost to sight again, at least I had a definite direction to aim for. MeMeMeMeMe was too far beneath to have spotted it, so I said casually:

"Turn about ten degrees to the south west."

"For any particular reason?"

"You'll learn soon enough. There are roses and a patch of convolvulus to get through, then a forest of mutant daises and buttercups. Then you'll have to pass a *dandy lion*, a lion dressed in antique clothes. I bet Tommy Tindertub sold them to it!"

"He's quite the vertical entrepreneur!"

"Politely put. Indeed."

We waded into a tangle of rose bushes, scattering petals in our wake, filling the air with intoxicating perfume. I felt drunk. Then I realised that MeMeMeMeMe had accidentally trodden on a whisky still, forgotten and illegal, from way back. That's why the scent was so heady. Nothing to do with overrated roses, but everything to do with alcohol. I caught a second glimpse of the pyramid, bigger now, before we reached the convolvulus. We were on the brink of cheating a nightmare, an achievement that's only a daydream for most people.

The other obstacles in our path turned out to be minor annoyances and no match for an adult yeti. We suddenly broke out into a clearing. Across a smooth plain stood the pyramid. It was surrounded by smaller buildings and seemed part of a lost city.

MeMeMeMeMe needed no spare urging to accelerate toward it and he allowed the wind to comb his hair into the style of a comet as he hastened over the level ground with great galumphing strides that struck xylophone notes from the parched earth.

But something wasn't quite right.

Having said that, nothing's ever quite right, so the fact that something wasn't quite right now was normal enough. Then I relaxed. But maybe I relaxed too much. Bad omen.

In yeti culture, bad omens are lucky.

But I was Albert Guppy Heckoid, a kind of man. Not a yeti, not yet or ever. Not even a kind man.

Which made the situation trickier.

By this time we had reached the base of the gigantic pyramid and were bounding up the steps eight at a time. Then I knew what the problem was. Steps. Do pyramids have steps? The Egyptian sort certainly don't, but the Mexican type do. We were ascending the wrong sacred edifice! The non-sequitur store must be elsewhere. This was Mayan or Aztec territory and consequently I was utterly afraid. Irreversible sacrifice of newcomers was too significant a component of the worldview of those chaps for my taste and I wanted to be elsewhere.

But MeMeMeMeMe was already at the top.

And I was there with him!

He lowered me to the ground against my will and I shivered anxiously while he regained his monstrous breath. He soon had it back. We looked around and listened. A faint rasping came from behind the altar. Peering over it, the yeti beckoned me to look. Gingerly I complied and saw a low feathered couch with a nude figure lying on it, a priest racked with fevers and slick with sweats. He looked familiar, mostly because he was, partly because he was holding in his weak grip a mirror angled towards me with my own pale face framed in it.

"He's dying but obsessed with studying his complexion in that looking glass. How vain can you get?"

The yeti stroked his Himalayan chin. "That's incorrect. He's checking to see if his breath makes mist on the reflective surface. A reliable way of knowing if he's alive or not."

"Now it's sliding out of his fingers…"

There was a dull thud rather than a tinkling crash. This mirror wasn't a glass model but a circle of polished obsidian. MeMeMeMeMe walked to the couch and kneeled next to the sick priest, feeling his wrist to take his pulse and clucking his tongue.

Now I had an opportunity to slip quietly away, but I dithered too long while I tried to work out *why* the doomed priest was familiar to me. Then he turned his dim gaze in my direction and wheezed a greeting. Abruptly I knew exactly who he was.

"The owner of the wig emporium!"

He displayed long black teeth, not rotten but stained with psychotropic juice from some divine plant.

"Yep, it's me, right enough. Toupée Amaru is my name. Bet you want to know how I got here before you? The Underground Hiking Society are responsible for that, having mapped the entire network of tunnels that run under the gargantuan expanse of grotesque gardens. I was never in danger of getting lost. There's a passage that directly connects my shop with this pyramid and it's fairly easy to traverse, with none of the hazards of upper world travel, no dogs, walls or thorns. Truth is, I've always been an Aztec priest, the wigs are just a front for my real concerns, all of which involve the worship of Huehuecoyotl, god of mischief and trickery, a shapeshifter whose hobbies include creating strife between living mortals. I adore him and do bad stuff in his name."

"That sounds lovely and constructive," I lied.

"Let me declare," he continued, "my hatred of non-sequiturs. I simply can't stand them. I like things to

Hell Toupée

directly follow from other things. Cause and effect. Logical progression's the only responsible kind! That's why I located my wig shop next to the non-sequitur store. Gave me a chance to sabotage the despicable business, to misdirect potential clients away from their portals, reduce the number of non-sequiturs in circulation. A bitter struggle for me, but I had a secret weapon. Wigs. What mightier tool can one imagine against the tyranny of randomness? So many meanings, so many separate branches of progression! For example, *wig* is an old word for 'holy'. And the whigs were strong political fellows. Another meaning of WIG relates to aviation."

"A round of applause for that!" I cried.

"No really, it does. Stands for Wing In Ground, which is a specialised effect that allows suitably designed vehicles to ride over a cushion of air between two short wings and the surface. Aircraft that utilise this system are still at the experimental stage but an influential cartel of engineers has invested faith and money in their ultimate success, not least because of the vastly increased fuel efficiency. So much for that! Every day I pray to Huehuecoyotl for fresh hairpiece-themed notions to thwart those pesky non-sequiturs! My existence has been directed to that single purpose, but I'm dying now and don't have a successor. The other Aztecs who dwelled here emigrated to find jobs in catering, retail and surveying. They forsook the gods and abandoned me."

"That's all very nice but really we must be getting along now. We only popped up here for the view."

"In that case I'm sorry for wasting…"

At this point the yeti interrupted. "Don't listen to Mr

235

Heckoid, he's not really in a rush and neither am I. On the contrary, if we can aid you in any capacity before you expire, let us know. Having said that, I'm unclear on one detail. The name Toupée Amaru sounds more Inca to me than Aztec. You're not a fake, are you?"

"I'll check. One moment. No, I'm not."

"Good. That's settled then. My offer's sincere and stands for as long as breath remains in your body."

"As a matter of fact," gasped Toupée Amaru, "there *is* one small thing you can do. I need an heir."

"Well you're a major wig merchant…"

"I didn't say *hair*, I said 'heir'. A successor. Will you become the next high priest of Huehuecoyotl for my sake? I can initiate you with just one word. The duties aren't onerous, apart from the sacrificing. There's lots of *that*, of course, which is further evidence that I am who I claim to be, for the Incas don't sacrifice as many victims as the Aztecs do. It's a question of quality versus quantity."

The yeti shrugged. "Fair enough. I accept."

"Thanks. Nice scalp you've got on you, by the way. Now I can die in peace, or if not in peace then at least in a slightly more bearable state of horrendous agony. Before I forget, here's the word of initiation. Ready? I'll say it only once. Pate."

"Pâté?" echoed the yeti with a frown.

"No, that's a kind of spread," corrected the priest. "I said *pate*, which is another name for a bald head."

"You ended up saying it twice," I pointed out.

"Does that stop it being right?" he challenged.

"No, but it's a feeble word!"

"But prudent," he sniffed, "and prudence is wise."

"Already know that, the yeti and me. MeMeMeMeMe U and I, I mean, to be grammatically correct."

I was smugly pleased with that wordplay.

But Toupée Amaru was dead…

He went like a tortilla. Bubbled and blackened.

I was aghast at this development and had to linger in the most extreme trepidation to learn what the yeti would do now. Not a good place to wait, but I wasn't there very long.

"Better sacrifice you, I suppose," he sighed.

"Are you sure?" I gulped.

"Yes I am. Why, aren't you? Come on!" And he snatched me up by the scruff and forced me down on the altar on my back, keeping me in place with one paw on my chest while he groped with the other for the obsidian knife resting on the floor nearby.

I was too compressed to protest. Up went the blade, flashing in the sun like a rotten cruel smile. I didn't shut my eyes though I barked an internal order for them to do so immediately. My lids were probably too scared to obey my terror. Can't blame them.

Down came the knife. Did blood spurt like a clotting salsa? No. I still don't know what saved me from death, whether it was MeMeMeMeMe's ignorance of correct Aztec sacrificial procedure or his natural dislike of butchery. Yetis are vegetarians.

At any rate, the tip of the knife penetrated my shirt but left untouched the skin below. Threads parted like model sinews. Then the yeti plunged his fist into my shredded top pocket and plucked out the artichoke heart secreted there the previous day.

It was still unbeating as he lifted it to the sun!

Because vegetables don't beat!

Then he threw the pale green object onto a smouldering brazier next to the altar where it hissed and broiled like a nice supper. I wondered for an instant if he planned to establish a new dynasty of Vegetarian Aztecs that might one day conquer Spain, but I didn't dare ask him. I pretended to be dead instead. He should have flung my body down the pyramid steps but he forgot that part of his job.

I remained unmoving and safe.

But what becomes of the broken shirted?

The sun sank into the suburban jungles of the west, staining the few intact greenhouses a crimson that clashed with the feral tomatoes that ballooned within. Even from this elevation there was no sign of a non-sequitur store anywhere in the panorama. But I could see a rusty communist tractor on its side with an oak growing out of it, and in the topmost branches of that tree a dozen frisbees were stuck. Lower down sagged a washing line once used to dry wine-soaked socks.

Everything was contriving to be relevant to what had occurred before. How pathetic! I even heard the yeti murmuring a Cassius Befuddle poem before he went to sleep on the couch. He could relax in comfort now, for the body of Toupée Amaru had gone. One hour after the priest died, owls unexpectedly descended to snag talons in his rotting flesh and carry him off. I watched them flap to the horizon and drop him over that imaginary line with a thud. What a hoot!

Is that where all dead people go? Are uncountable corpses piled up on the far side of the horizon? It would mean that when we stumble across a massacre it's because we're standing just beyond someone else's horizon. I'd like to find that someone and teach them a lesson! Probably geography with some statistical analysis. But I'm not a real teacher and when the sun sets it must burn all the cadavers in its path. Very economical that, except on foggy days without horizons.

My captor was snoring loudly, but yetis have sensitive hearing and if I tried to sneak down the pyramid steps to freedom he would awake and reprimand me with another sacrifice, perhaps a more effective one. I had to find an alternative escape route. Somehow one of the stilts had become lodged under the yeti's sleeping form and the far end of the pole extended into thin air over the edge of the pyramid. I licked my sore lips and came to a sudden reckless decision.

I ran as fast as I could along that narrow beam of wood and at the very end I jumped high, using the stilt like a springboard. There was a mighty twang! I heard the yeti wake up behind me, but I was already soaring into the sky. Stars high above, but no moon, just an oblong of black where the moon should be, a flying shadow. What did that mean? The yeti ordered me to come back. I shrugged my shoulders in response. Then I was above the shadow and falling onto it.

Now I was creamed in full moonlight and saw that

I was about to land on a magic carpet piloted by a girl with bare thighs. Prudence Mooncup! That's precisely the sort of coincidence I can't bring myself to write letters of complaint to newspapers about. Ah well! She welcomed me with open arms despite her astonishment. Maybe her aerial rug utilised the Wing in Ground Effect to stay aloft. Didn't know then and I still don't. The science of aeronautics is over my head.

I emptied my pockets. She was dismissive of my potatoes, but hugely impressed with my parsnips and carrots. An affair was inevitable. Before we started canoodling there was a conversation to be had. So she asked me what I was looking for and I described my adventures with very few embellishments. She chuckled.

"You'll never find the non-sequitur store in these gardens. It can't exist inside any coherent narrative! No, it's located out there, in the real world, in the cosmos of the reader, beyond the last paragraph of this story where what happens next certainly won't follow what has taken place here! You looked in the wrong direction!"

I digested this by covering my fingers with regurgitated stomach acids and poking them into my ears.

Not really. I'd never do something like that.

I used my thumbs instead.

"You mean to tell me," I gasped, "that when this story comes to an end the reader will probably do something that has absolutely no relevance to our fictional lives, that takes no account of the weird plot that has allowed us to reach this point? Does that somehow make the reader the *proprietor* of the non-sequitur store?"

"Maybe it does, maybe it doesn't. We'll find out soon enough. That's right, we're nearly there!"

"I'll see you on the other side, won't I?"

She tilted her head and laughed. It was a wild laugh and didn't fill me with confidence. At the same time she urged the carpet to greater speed, so that these sentences flashed by like an audible rant and I was knocked flat by the acceleration. Prudence and caution must be different keywords after all! And now I'm here.

Before I shoot off the edge of this paragraph, I achingly wonder what the reader will do when it's all over. Go for a walk, brew coffee, dance? No way for me to know. But for you, there's no way of *not* knowing. Out there, confined by the invisible and intangible walls of your non-sequitur store, you are logically condemned to know. By the way, are you going bald yet? Because if you are…

(2009)

Inside the Outline

She was an actress and she worked for the most highly respected shadow theatre in the city of Eclipseville.

Prudence Clearwater was her name and nobody in the history of that rather shady kind of drama has ever performed the classic tragedies with half the exuberance of her umbra.

It was the toast of the town, her shadow; a burned piece of toast to be sure, if you like foolish wordplay.

An artform respected in many cultures, shadow theatre has attained an outstanding elegance in a few of them. In Java and Burma, Morocco and Malta, we may easily discover this.

But in Eclipseville long ago it became much more than an amusement or an intense aesthetic indulgence. It evolved into a pseudo-religion with a fundamentally fanatical fanbase.

On one side the Literalists considered every performed gesture, every undulation, to be the unsullied truth. On the other, the Symbolists argued that nothing was quite what it seemed, that each play was a metaphor for something else, a hidden wisdom.

And Prudence was trapped in the middle.

But she remained undaunted by her predicament and continued to act with a verisimilitude so exact that even her portrayals of indifference and apathy were totally convincing.

Her shadow was clearly fated to be fêted.

The streets of Eclipseville are chock with gliding profiles and to stand out from the anonymous spludge of moving outlines, especially when one considers the unremitting flatness of shadows, is no mean feat, nor a kind one, but the professional silhouette of Prudence Clearwater managed on a daily basis to do precisely that.

Everybody recognised her shadow in public.

Even on cloudy days. Even when the diffusion of light made it faint or blurred into smokiness its edges.

For Prudence honed her abilities to the degree where she could convey one emotion with her umbra and a second emotion, perhaps even opposed to the first, with her penumbra.

She did this not only in the theatre but also while walking down streets in her own private hours, an act of generosity to her followers that had no precedence among shadow actors.

At this point, I deem it acceptable to point out that the word 'spludge' didn't exist until the chief guardian of the city, Sacerdotal Bagge, lurking in his private box, coined it after an early memorable performance by her youthful outline. He desired a term to describe the shadows of her rivals, so smitten was he by her talent.

Neither Literalist nor Symbolist, the venerable Bagge was a synthesis of both, a Symbliterite, the only one in the world, with no notion of what he advocated or objected to.

Consequently he was much feared.

But not by Prudence…

She had entered the theatre after failing every exam at a school where her fellow pupils and even her teachers had consistently ignored her; and with a determination to be finally noticed by a world that seemed to want her to shrink to a singularity.

The theatre promised revenge and love.

But despite the fame that now surrounded her profile, she could never be truly happy in Eclipseville. The problem was that her corporeal form, her flesh and blood self, continued to be ignored. People were interested only in her shadow, not in her.

Nobody knew what her face looked like.

The actual woman might have been a shop window mannequin; or one of those huge clockwork puppets that distress the city of Chaud-Mellé, far from here, for all anyone cared.

They were interested only in her shadow.

Whenever she left her house to stroll in public places, her most ardent admirers soon clustered around her outline but they never looked directly at her, as if they regarded the source of the shadow as irrelevant. Roughly pushing past her to reach the side of the famed umbra, they acted as if her existence hadn't been proven.

A state of affairs that finally became intolerable!

She had to remedy the situation…

The shadow theatres of Eclipseville are grander than those in realistic lands and each one resembles a giant seashell with a screen of pure silk stretched over its mouth. Rows of seats face this smooth square and for the wealthy patrons there are a small number of wooden boxes balanced on poles thrust into the earth.

Carefully ground lenses and powerful lamps that are very reliable but cooler to the touch than glow-worms project the shadows of the actors. The variable clarity and size of an outline is used to convey astonishingly subtle degrees of sincerity, ambition, vivacity, charm and turpitude. Lute music accompanies the action.

The special language of shadow theatre in that city is complex indeed and books have been written on the subject so large and dense that coral atolls are frequently easier to store on a shelf, an exaggeration brought to you courtesy of Hyperbole Inc.

But Prudence had mastered every nuance.

She has never been bettered…

If you ever journey to Eclipseville for cultural purposes I'm afraid you will learn that to your cost. But it's a low cost. The price of a single ticket for admission is just a few froats.

There was no such word as 'froat' until Sacerdotal Bagge misspelled the word *groat*. From such accidents neologisms are stillborn, smacked back into unnatural life by evil doctors, set free to wander the banter of simple filk, his misspelling of folk…

The most popular writers for the shadow theatre are still those ancient geniuses, Omar Sixual, Virgil Rydikolos, Nitrogen Parsley and Vibration Javelin, but more modern authors aren't neglected. Cassius Befuddle and Jimjam Spreadwinkle have recently penned mighty epics that look likely to become classics of the future.

Sacerdotal Bagge unluckily also regards himself as

a playwright and it won't be long before he forces the performance of one of his works on the inhabitants of his metropolis…

But when Prudence was at the apotheosis of her popularity, an upstart by the name of Groopinfoorth Crikey was the most commonly performed author. Many young playwrights live in attics but Groopinfoorth dwelled, or rather *pulsated*, in a pantry.

His plays were half comedy, half tragedy, half impossible fraction, and his favourite subject matter concerned the tribulations of revivalists, those eccentric people in every epoch who work so hard to revive the styles of older epochs, including epochs containing people who want to revive the styles of even older epochs…

And so on forever, or at least for a long time.

For a season Groopinfoorth's vision held sway. He was responsible for the brief revival of revivalism.

The premiere of his new and long awaited masterpiece was scheduled for the night of the next new moon. In Eclipseville the moon is one of the most celebrated celestial bodies and its phases are carefully anticipated by all and sundry, even by sundry's servants, and those servants' slaves, and those slaves' pets, for many very important festivals are timed to coincide with a particular shape of moon.

During nights of a gibbous moon the inhabitants of Eclipseville like to monkey around. I speak no lie.

A crescent moon has become a symbol of Frabjal Troose, the ancient tyrant who founded half the metropolis, nobody knows which half, and a gala of grins is held in his honour.

When the moon is full, Sacerdotal Bagge blows on an oboe tinted pink and leads people outside the city for an orgy where any unloved soul may have his frustrations vented...

But shadow theatre has a more practical need for data about the phases of that buttery orb, because its waxing and waning light can affect how an actor's shadow appears on a screen.

Complete darkness is best for a decent show.

Hence the new moon rule...

Prudence decided to use the premiere of Groopinfoorth's latest play to protest against her treatment in public, about the bias given to her shadow over her real body. She had no intention of enduring the humiliation more than a few extra weeks at most.

The title of Groopinfoorth's work was *The Stars were Jars* and it was a sequel to *The Planets are Pots*, and like the earlier play it called for a cast of healthy, buxom shadows.

But Prudence stopped eating. She planned to starve herself and famish her shadow into the bargain...

Yes, she wanted to punish her umbra, to castigate a silhouette that had the temerity and contrast to be more worshipped than her own erect form, that had created a situation where a solid living woman was jealous of her own two-dimensional profile!

She also deprived herself of sleep...

Reasoning that if her mind lost focus, so would her outline, she pushed herself to weird extremes, for instance using her bed as a trampoline and juggling uneaten buns until the springs and her fingers no longer worked, or laughing continuously for an entire day at the realisation that a spider's knees are higher than its head.

Once she hypnotised herself into believing she was not a woman but a regular polyhedron, I'm not sure which one, maybe just a cube, by staring at the pendulum of an antique clock on her mantelpiece for twenty hours. The effect wore off the following day, but not before she had tried to use herself as a cutlery storage box.

The minor wounds inflicted by the forks and knives festered and grew ugly, swelling into pustules, further distorting her facial contours, but the pain of the infection meant nothing to her. She intended to put so much stress on her form, to subject it to so many odd outrages that it must begin to warp and transform itself.

In the three weeks remaining before the premiere, she abused her body to such a degree that it truly did twist and shrink; but at these changes she merely smirked. A contorted body casts a contorted shadow. It can't help but follow the laws of geometry.

Now her shadow wouldn't be so appealing, and even its most ardent admirers would be shocked into an understanding that beyond the profile stood an unhappy human being.

And if those admirers desired a beautiful shadow to undulate for their entertainment, they would have to pay more attention to the solid woman who cast it. Prudence wanted them to make up for lost time, to fawn over every pinch of her meat and bones.

She was confident they would…

The big moonless night eventually arrived.

Sacerdotal Bagge brought his own ladder to mount a private box that was actually a modified vegetable crate perched on a pair of ships' masts lashed together. Groopinfoorth Crikey also had a private box, the second highest in the audience, half the height of the chief guardian's. The third highest box was occupied by rich merchant Rimsky Mooncup, a man who kept the city supplied with chives.

The ordinary public shifted impatiently on their stools, waiting for the lutists to tune up and for the projectionist to finish wiping the lens of his projector with a crimson cloth.

Then the silk screen was lowered into place and tightened until it had the acoustic properties of a drum membrane. A deep hush settled over the audience; a lute string twanged.

The Theatre of Tangible Absences was easily the most imposing and magnificent in the city. Not only everyone who was anyone attended its premieres, but all nobodies also.

With a soft hum the projector turned the screen into a glowing square of magic. Then more lute chords came. A shadow moved on a corner of the taut silk. Groopinfoorth grunted muffled delight, sighs were expelled, eyes bulged, mouths watered.

The play had commenced!

But what was this? The shadow slid closer to the middle of the screen and waited there, but it wasn't the coolly curvaceous shadow of Prudence Clearwater. How could it be?

Yet it had a certain familiarity about it. Maybe it *was* her shadow, but horribly attenuated, a shadow of its former self, in other words a shadow of a shadow, which as everyone knows is less endearing than the echo of an echo. There was a unanimous gasp of disapproval and even Sacerdotal Bagge muttered disparagingly.

Then the sympathies turned…

An audience member cried, "The shadow must be ill!"

"Yes, that's right," called another voice, "it has a disease of some kind. Poor shadow! It needs to rest!"

"Not so!" countered a third opinion. "Antibiotics are the answer! Can I inject a profile, do you think?"

"What a bizarre suggestion! Who are you?"

"An evil doctor, as it happens."

"I thought as much. An evil doctor *would* suggest what you just did. A needle full of awful medicine… But this outline doesn't want your drugs. Fattening is a better solution."

"Really! How exactly does one feed a shadow?"

"Toast and jackfruit jam…"

"You're guessing, aren't you? What a fake!"

"Citizens!" boomed Sacerdotal Bagge. "Cease bickering at once! It is most unseemly. Clearly a specialist in shady ailments must be consulted and I pledge to secure the services of the right fellow within a week. The show will resume, I promise!"

"Hurrah for the chief guardian!" shouted Groopinfoorth Crikey.

"Hip hip!" added Rimsky Mooncup.

"Pelvis, sternum, kneecap!" roared an anonymous wit.

There's always one joker in a theatre crowd.

The play was halted at this point and the projector turned off, much to the fury of Prudence, who wanted to display her lamentable condition for the entire duration of the performance. For the first time in her career, she left the stage without the thunder of applause to accompany her departure. But worse was to come. Sacerdotal Bagge went backstage in person with more than a dozen attendants and fussed over her shadow in her dressing room; but still they ignored her.

An identical outcome awaited her in the street the following day. The empathies of the other pedestrians were directed exclusively at that point where her shadow glided over cobbles and walls, and nobody had even a cursory glance for the real woman. This behaviour was repeated on each subsequent occasion and the deflated actress was forced to admit that her self-chastisement had been in vain. Yet she didn't abandon the behaviour that had distorted her physique.

Her shadow alone was the star; and she was merely the black vacuum of interstellar space that surrounded this point of light and permitted it to shine so gloriously. Ironic that a living woman should be a nobody while her own shadow was a substantial presence, but that's how things were in Eclipseville at that time. Prudence was a malnourished void. Before she had a chance to die of starvation, she was visited one morning by a group of men who burst into her house.

They broke open her front door with hammers and rushed up her stairs before she could jump out of bed and defend herself. Hired by Sacerdotal Bagge, they included a specialist in shadows from a distant town where it is still legal to experiment on silhouettes. His assistants held her in a tight embrace while the specialist went to work. First he fitted stiff cardboard margins to her body with straps. Then he ordered a sheet to be pulled off her bed and suspended in the air.

Two men stretched the cloth between them and held it steady without a crease, while the specialist utilised his powerful portable lamp to direct Prudence's shadow against it. The cardboard margins didn't fail. Her new outline was the same as her old…

They left her alone then, without even an apology, and when Prudence stumbled to a window and looked out, she saw the chief guardian himself standing in the street and waving, but not really at her; no, his wave went beyond the glass to her false shadow on the wall. Doubtless he expected it to return to acting immediately.

The entire city wanted a Prudence Clearwater revival, and there might have been one, but suddenly a bad moon rose in her head. In Eclipseville a bad moon is any moon deemed unsuitable for a festival of any kind. As every possible moon shape is good enough for a gala of some description it can be seen that bad moons are rare or even impossible. It simply meant that she couldn't take any more…

This happens to actors all over the world.

Prudence decided to clear out for good, leaving in her wake the fates of everyone connected with her career in any way. And so she did. And this is how some of them fared:

Groopinfoorth Crikey's meteoric rise fizzled out before the end of the summer. During the opening night of his third epic, *The Quasars shall be Spoons*, he was forced to run from a disgruntled audience that turned into a crazy mob. Seats were ripped up and hurled at the screen and expensive projectors tinkled into oblivion.

He never wrote another play and his obscurity was so profound that he later became famous for just that.

Sacerdotal Bagge, on the other hand, managed to persuade one of the less salubrious theatres to stage a work of his own, but he gave the actors no script to rehearse with. The premiere has been postponed until after his probable death at the hands of an assassin, maybe next year. Until then he refines his role as chief guardian of the metropolis and the shadows of his ears and jowls are everywhere.

Meanwhile, the Literalists begin to question the significance of their given name and whether it has any hidden meanings; and the Symbolists realise that if symbolism represents adherence to a truism that something might not represent itself, they can't continue to exist until the meaning of symbolism becomes less literal.

That's the standard of inner struggle among intellectuals over there. I hope you're not like that yourself?

Even if you are, you'll be interested to know about one theatre fanatic who doesn't care about such matters. The anonymous wit in the audience was killed when the office tower of Hyperbole Inc collapsed on him, all twenty thousand floors of it, in a hurricane featuring winds stronger than any recorded before by anyone.

As for Prudence, she married chive merchant Rimsky Mooncup and took his surname. Much safer that way. The couple left Eclipseville on a steam-driven tandem bicycle and settled in Huknibonk-on-Stench, a city with its own special disasters.

But the marriage didn't last very long and Rimsky ran off with the six sultry shadows he discovered in the highest room of their new house, and Prudence didn't get the chance to tell him they were his own outlines, cast by lamps positioned in alcoves.

It didn't matter. She enrolled in the local university, where she decided to study aeronautics, because that science has no obvious connection with acting or shadows, but she didn't graduate. She ended up flying away on a magic carpet instead. Curious.

(2009)

Discrepancy

It must surely have come to the attention of certain scholars that increasing numbers of people are appearing in more than one place at the same time. Individual scientists, travellers, pirates, geniuses, fools, musicians, and all other kinds of characters have been recorded living multiple lives in sundry locations; and some of them have even been observed dying several deaths instead of the usual single death that is our proper allowance. These inconsistencies of time and space must be explained and this brief account will attempt to do that.

High in the Alps at a point almost midway between Vaduz and Chur may be found the quaint city-state of Chaud-Mellé. It occupies an entire valley where also glitters a mysterious lake that tastes like wine. But this tale is not concerned with bodies of water; it wishes instead to focus on the body, and mind, and doings, of the lovely Coppelia de Retz, a maker of toys by trade who specialises in the design and construction of cunningly wrought automata. Coppelia is skilled at creating life-size puppets that are perfect working replicas of real men and women.

For many years Coppelia accepted commissions from rich aristocrats to duplicate them in order that they might send the clockwork puppets to boring soirées while they stayed at home; but some of her customers clearly also received a thrill at the idea of using their own doppelgängers as butlers or more lowly kinds of domestic servant. These commissions made Coppelia a wealthy woman but they failed to fully satisfy her hunger for mischief. She began making puppet doubles of unwary citizens at random and turning them loose in the world to comic effect.

Her method was as follows… She found an obscure alleyway near one of the city gates and she converted it into an optical trap by renting a house at a point halfway along the crooked street. Most newcomers to Chaud-Mellé proceeded down the main thoroughfare after passing under the gate; a curious or reckless minority close to explore the alley instead. Up the steep gully they puffed, resting for breath at the sharp bend that led to an even steeper stretch of cobbled gloom, and this inevitable pause was exactly what Coppelia required.

Her house was positioned on the bend itself and she had transformed it into a workshop full of remarkable devices relevant to her work. Lenses studded on the outside wall captured the image of her latest victim; while a hidden metal plate under his feet measured his weight as he stood immobile; the quality of his wheezing was also recorded by an artificial ear in order to gauge his probable manner of speaking. The lenses and ear were concealed by the natural darkness of the alley and not once did a passing traveller suspect any theft of vision or sound.

With this information Coppelia was enabled to create a perfect clockwork replica of her subject. At first she laboured at this task with her own hands but she soon realised the expediency of automating the process. In the centre of her workshop stood a machine resembling an iron octopus that possessed a rudimentary mechanical brain and was easily able to process the data collected by the lenses, ear and metal plate. The riveted tentacles moved unerringly, building each puppet double in less than an hour and delivering it to the world through a hatch.

The octopus selected suitable materials from the boxes full of springs, cogs, camshafts, levers, wheels, crystals and relays that stood around it in profusion. Coppelia's instinct for domestic neatness was defective: the workshop was so cluttered with spare parts that her living space was cramped in the extreme; but in fact she only visited this house to monitor the octopus and make occasional repairs. She estimated that it produced ten puppets every week, which demonstrated the unpopularity of the alley as a public way and was a safely modest quantity.

One afternoon, while she was engaged in tightening a loose screw on the tip of one of the tentacles, a traveller happened to arrive in Chaud-Mellé. He passed through the gate and instantly rejected the broad avenue that stretched before him, preferring the picturesque ascent of the alley. Up he went, pausing for breath on the bend as they all did. His weight, voice and angles were captured by the monitoring devices, and in the very instant that Coppelia finished her adjustment, the octopus sprang into action, constructing his perfect double, while Coppelia watched with a frown.

Fifty minutes elapsed before the puppet was ready and functional. During this time Coppelia's frown deepened; there was something about the clockwork being in progress that unnerved her; but she considered it an act of moral weakness to halt the process on the basis of nothing more substantial than an uneasy feeling. As a consequence the octopus continued working until it was done. Then it wound up tight the mannequin and released it through the hatch. Coppelia relaxed her frown but the corners of her mouth sagged with accuracy in the direction of the antipodes.

Her gloominess had suddenly increased because now she thought she recognised the face of the puppet. She needed to be certain. Examining a bookshelf in the darkest corner of the room, she finally selected a thick volume entitled THE LUNATIC INVENTORS OF EUROPE. She turned the pages rapidly, scanning each one. Long before reaching her own entry she found the page that confirmed her worst fears. The traveller was none other than Karl Mondaugen, originally from Munich, a fellow who was no stranger at all to the art of making deceptively realistic clockwork puppets.

Coppelia slammed the book shut with a growl. Creating spare copies of ordinary citizens, with or without their assent, was a pleasurable hobby for her; but she had absolutely no intention of increasing the number of her competitors and rivals. She had unwittingly ensured that the book of mad inventors would require an extra page in its next edition, unless the single entry on Mondaugen could also be said to represent his double, for they were identical in form, character and ability. But it was still Coppelia's duty to rectify her mistake, with the aid of a blunderbuss.

There was one hanging by its trigger-guard from a nail

in the wall. She had anticipated the necessity of destroying the occasional rogue puppet, but not for this particular reason. She took it down and loaded it with calcified teeth and fossilised bone fragments: a blunderbuss full of cogs and brass nuts might suffice to kill an organic being but the arbitrary insertion of such components into a machine could conceivably *improve* its function. At any rate, the symmetry was satisfying. Thus armed, she operated the hatch and hurried off in search of her prey.

But Chaud-Mellé is a labyrinth of a city. The false Mondaugen had vanished in the tangle. She ran one way, then another, lost count of the corners she turned and soon became lost herself. Several times she glimpsed the puppet at the end of a street, passing behind a row of columns or entering a tiny square with a broken fountain; he seemed to be taunting her. Once she spotted him crossing a narrow bridge above her and she raised the blunderbuss to take aim, but it occurred to her that this might be the man, not the replica, and she hesitated.

The opportunity was thus wasted. She wandered aimlessly until night fell, then she paused for a rest in a quiet alley, sitting with crossed legs on the ground and reviewing her options. For a long time she sat there and finally she decided that having an extra Mondaugen loose in the world was not an utter disaster. She rose to her feet and a chill of horror paralysed her limbs as she realised where she was. It was the bend in the crooked alley next to her workshop! The octopus must certainly have copied her while she lingered there…

She hastened to the hatch, shaking off the sensation

of fear as she ran, fully prepared to blast her own double into oblivion. But she was too late: the octopus had already liberated the second Coppelia. So now there was yet another puppet maker at large in the city! And the new Coppelia was able to build another octopus and another trap somewhere else, capturing yet more puppet makers and perhaps the real Coppelia again, and so on, accelerating the duplication process to the point where every human on the planet would own at least one replica.

Overwhelmed with melancholy, Coppelia trudged home under the dim amber and smoky green lanterns of the midnight city. Her husband, the Maréchal Lore de Retz, was sitting on his favourite rattan chair, reading a newspaper, *The Chaud-Mellé Chronicle*. She poured herself a glass of absinthe and told him everything. He advised her to destroy the octopus as soon as possible and offered to help her in this task. She nodded wearily and they retired to bed. The Maréchal snored so rhythmically that Coppelia began to wonder if he was a clockwork puppet too.

The following morning they set off together for the narrow alley and the workshop, the Maréchal carrying a sledgehammer over one shoulder that he had purchased especially for the occasion. When they reached their destination they opened the hatch and clambered through into gloom and dust. The octopus was silent, unmoving, squatting among its boxes of spare parts like a naughty toolboy; the Maréchal walked around it, found the most vulnerable spot of its exposed mechanical brain and swung the heavy hammer upward with a mighty grimace.

But destiny had other ideas and the blow was never

completed. For a new traveller had just reached the bend in the alley and paused there, though not to catch his breath. His name was Wilson the Clockwork Man and he was already a puppet, but a puppet that duplicated no one; he was an original. The name of the inventor that constructed him is not known and it is not beyond the bounds of feasibility that Wilson made himself. Whatever the truth of the matter, he had entered Chaud-Mellé and planned to explore the city.

His artificial eyes immediately detected the lenses and ear on the outer wall of Coppelia's workshop; he stopped to examine them. The information they gathered was relayed to the octopus inside, which followed its programming and commenced the task of building a replica. But a gross irony was the result. Flesh and blood humans are duplicated with steel and crystal parts; according to the logic of the octopus, a man who is already clockwork must be fabricated from bone, skin and gristle. It was a perfectly sensible assumption.

The metal arms reached out and pulled the Maréchal to pieces. His hammer dropped harmlessly to the floor. Before Coppelia could retrieve it, the octopus also seized her and began work. Wilson had a large frame and his duplication required plenty of raw materials; nonetheless there was some left over, indescribable globules quivering and cooling in little mounds. The finished article was thrust through the hatch in an absurd parody of a birth. And Wilson the Organised Man, who would never be aware of his name, drooled happily as he crawled off into the urban chaos.

(2010)

Afterword

ROMANTI-CYNICISM

"Toad in a trombone!"

I coined that exclamation of surprise more than a decade ago; despite my best efforts, it never caught on. Yet I persist in maintaining it has an elegant resonance and conjures up a nice image, comparable to that of a fox piloting a biplane. Perhaps my brain works in a quite different way to the neural networks of everyone else.

Back in 1995 or 1996, flushed by the appearance of my first book and also by my own blood in my own cheeks, I made the mistake that young, bombastic, daft authors often do: I decided to invent a literary movement. I didn't attempt this *just* for the sake of it, but because I wanted to define more clearly the essential effect I was striving for in my fiction. In other words I planned to label myself before anyone else got the chance. As it happened I was far too slow off the mark, for I had already been branded as a writer of humorous dark fantasy!

A reviewer of distinction had read many of my early stories and come to the irreversible conclusion that my work aspired to juxtapose the vision of Thomas Ligotti with that of Woody Allen. This approach was felt to be rather unwise because "horror and comedy always cancel each other out." But my intention wasn't that at all.

Horror-comedy is one thing, perhaps a worthy thing in its own way, but it's not *my* thing. I wasn't hoping for any kind of contrasting or portmanteau effect; I was striving for a synthesis so complete that no join might be noticed.

To explain this more fully I like to fall back on a dubious analogy. It is fortunate for me that dubious analogies are almost sacred in my proposed literary movement. Ready? Here we go!

It's possible to describe water as hydrogen-oxygen but this term is less useful than the one already in common parlance. Water is different from both hydrogen and oxygen, and no objective analysis of the properties of hydrogen and those of oxygen *before combination* can predict what the properties of water may be. There simply is no physical clue in the atoms of either element as to precisely what will happen when they are joined; we only know the result from experience. The properties of water are *not* predetermined by those of hydrogen and oxygen. The sum is different to, if not greater than, the parts, and has unique abilities. See the works of the philosopher David Hume for more details.

I wondered if what was true for physical elements might not also turn out to be true for genres. I have already admitted that an analogy between elements and genres is dubious, so go easy on me! Now then… If we take a pair of unrelated genres, for instance horror and comedy, and mix them correctly, the outcome shouldn't be a chessboard of alternating squares or a salad-dressing of incompatible oil and vinegar, but a molecule, a brand new substance with properties of its own that the original elements don't have.

Afterword

Horror frightens; humour tickles; a perfect blend of these elements should result in a substance that doesn't scare or amuse, or at least doesn't merely do these things, but is capable of effects beyond the reach of those two atomic genres. What those effects *will* be is something that can only be discovered from the procedure itself.

I call this THE MOLECULAR THEORY OF FICTION and it's central to my aforementioned literary movement. Shame therefore that the name of the movement is a portmanteau word consisting of two elements stuck (rather than blended) together. No matter! I'm still happy with it; and in the past I found it even more pleasing than I do now. Indeed, not long after coining the term 'romanti-cynical' I created a manifesto, as daydreaming founders are prone to do, that set out the broad aims of the movement. I kept them less dogmatic than I might have done, for the dogmas of today often turn into the caterwauls of tomorrow, and futuristic mockery is hard to join in when you are still living in the present.

So yes, I wrote a "Romanti-Cynical Manifesto".

The problem is that I have lost it…

I don't have a copy anywhere, even though I've hunted high, low and in-between for one, in boxes, on discs, under beds and elsewhere. I have attempted to trawl my memory to recover the general sense, but that's no substitute for the real thing. Might it still exist somewhere? I think I sent copies to various people: Des Lewis, Mark Samuels, the musician David Tibet (who covered the strange Comus song 'Diana' with his Current 93 project) and Ray Russell too, of course; but it's unlikely they preserved them. Why should they? If someone sent me such a manifesto I'd regard it as a useful way of starting a driftwood fire on the beach, although paper aeroplanes are also an attractive option.

But can I remember any of its contents at all?

Well, I'm sure it made the claim that the 'absurd' was a truer reflection of our universe than the 'real'; that the convulsions of laughter are spasms of clandestine despair; that nothing is certain, not even this statement; that the type of fiction I most desperately yearn to write and read is one that simultaneously takes itself very seriously and mocks itself, with one foot in sober existential horror, one in ironic satire, one in progressive science fiction, one in nostalgic utopian fancies, one in magic, one in naivety, one in cunning, one in fable, one in rationality… with the crucial point being that the total number of these feet must always be *startlingly* greater than feasible. Even a millipede couldn't manage so many! I also recall ending my manifesto with a singular injunction:

"Link arms with toads!"

Why the devil not? The camaraderie of the image is as pleasing as that of a fox in pilot's goggles banking a Sopwith Camel into a roll, or that of a stoat in the reinforced suit of a deep-sea diver surfacing from the wreck of an old Spanish treasure galleon. This urge of mine to absurdify animals is scarcely understandable in psychological terms, but as literary symbols they make perfect sense. To me at least.

Is that all? Anything else?

Indeed. As spiritual and aesthetic godparents and icons of romanti-cynicism, I seem to recall citing Lucian, Apuleius, Rabelais, *Orlando Furioso*, Voltaire's *Candide*,

Afterword

Hoffman, *The Castle of Otranto*, Beckford's *Vathek*, Jan Potocki's *Manuscript Found in Saragossa*, the arabesques of Poe (rather than his grotesques), Anatole France, Max Beerbohm, Saki, Akutagawa, Blaise Cendrars, Flann O'Brien, Raymond Queneau, Boris Vian, the wry fantasies of James Branch Cabell, Italo Calvino and Karel Čapek, the irony-saturated stories of Donald Barthelme, and the work of the more original and outré science-fiction writers of the 1960s, such as Samuel Delany, Roger Zelazny, Brian Aldiss, Tom Disch, John Sladek and Josef Nesvadba. Into this last category I most certainly would have inserted Cordwainer Smith if I had known about him at the time, but not R.A. Lafferty, for even though he is the writer I am most often compared to, I still haven't read any of his books.

I doubt this helps. And yet…

Onwards, forever onwards! Link Arms with Toads!

Publishing History

The Troubadours of Perception -- *Whispers of Wickedness*, Autumn 2003
Number 13 and a Half -- *Ghosts & Scholars #23*
The Taste of the Moon -- *Roadworks #6*, 1999
Lunarhampton -- *The Third Alternative #12*, 1997
The Expanding Woman -- previously unpublished
All Shapes Are Cretans -- previously unpublished
The Innumerable Chambers of the Heart -- *The Skeleton of Contention* (chapbook), 2004
Pity the Pendulum -- previously unpublished
333 and a Third -- previously unpublished
The Candid Slyness of Scurrility Forepaws -- *Whispers of Wickedness #11*, 2005
Ye Olde Resignation -- previously unpublished
Castle Cesare -- *Bust Down the Door and Eat All the Chickens #8*
The Mirror in the Looking Glass -- previously unpublished
Oh Ho! -- previously unpublished
Loneliness -- previously unpublished
Hell Toupée -- previously unpublished
Inside the Outline -- previously unpublished
Discrepancy -- previously unpublished

Acknowledgements

This collection is a highly representative showcase of what I do, and what I have been doing for the past sixteen or more years. I would therefore like to thank those important people who made it possible. Firstly, myself. Secondly, various lovers, friends and rivals. Thirdly, you, for buying this book. I am much obliged!

My website is at: http://rhyshughes.blogspot.com

About the author:

Rhys Hughes was born in 1966 in Cardiff but grew up in the seaside town of Porthcawl. He began writing at an early age but his first publications were chess problems and mathematical puzzles for newspapers. He sold his first short story in 1992 and his first book, *Worming the Harpy*, was published in 1995. Since then he has embarked on a mammoth project of writing exactly 1000 linked 'items' of fiction, including novels, to form a gigantic story cycle. Many of these 'items' have appeared in journals and anthologies around the world, and his books have been translated into Spanish, French, Greek, Portuguese, Russian and Serbian. His work has attracted attention for its originality of ideas, ingenuity of plotting and rich playfulness of his language.

The author says, "Because I have experimented with so many different genres, styles and moods, not one of my individual books to date really provides a full overview of what I actually do. *Link Arms With Toads!* is different because it's a fully representative sampler of my entire body of work and has been designed as a showcase of the new genre I recklessly tried to invent when I was younger. This book is certainly the best entry point to my body of fiction and if you don't like *Toads!* you can be confident you won't like my other books, so it's also the financially wisest choice for any new reader."

When not in the process of working, sleeping or

scheming, Mr Hughes amuses himself with one of his many hobbies. He enjoys the world in general. He likes to travel around it, listening to its music, eating its food and conversing with its people. He is a keen amateur astronomer and a dismal piano player. He is enthralled with the twin ideas of designing and flying his own airship and setting up an inexpensive but acclaimed vegetarian restaurant inside an extinct volcano. He is resigned to the fact he will probably never convey guests to that restaurant in that airship. Not in his lifetime. Maybe he will do something else equally satisfactory and strange instead.

Other Books by the Same Author (as opposed to similar books by other authors):

* Worming the Harpy
* Eyelidiad
* Rawhead & Bloody Bones
* The Smell of Telescopes
* Stories from a Lost Anthology
* Nowhere Near Milk Wood
* Journeys Beyond Advice
* The Percolated Stars
* A New Universal History of Infamy
* At the Molehills of Madness
* Sereia de Curitiba
* The Crystal Cosmos
* The Less Lonely Planet
* The Postmodern Mariner
* Engelbrecht Again!
* Mister Gum
* Twisthorn Bellow
* The Coandă Effect

Also from Chômu Press:

Looking for something else to read? Want a book that will wake you up, not put you to sleep?

"Remember You're a One-Ball!"
By Quentin S. Crisp

I Wonder What Human Flesh Tastes Like
By Justin Isis

Revenants
By Daniel Mills

The Life of Polycrates and Other Stories for Antiquated Children
By Brendan Connell

Nemonymous Night
By D.F. Lewis

For more information about these books and others, please visit: http://chomupress.com/

Subscribe to our mailing list for updates and exclusive rarities.